GOING
OUT IN
STYLE

• CHLOE GREEN •

GOING OUT IN STYLE

KENSINGTON BOOKS
http://www.kensingtonbooks.com

KENSINGTON BOOKS are published by

Kensington Publishing Corp.
850 Third Avenue
New York, NY 10022

Library of Congress Card Catalogue Number: 99-068824
ISBN 1-57566-574-3

First Printing: July, 2000
10 9 8 7 6 5 4 3 2 1

CHAPTER ONE

I'd gone to sleep in the comfort of 420-thread-count sheets, enveloped in the scent of Opium, and sprinkled with starlight. I awoke to the smell of wet flannel, in blackness.

"Don't move," the man said. "I'm sorry about the gun, but you gotta go."

I was frozen; movement was impossible. My bare breasts pressed against the matelassé duvet cover, and my heart pounded in my throat.

"C'mon, I know you are awake," he said. "Turn over."

I didn't move. The sheets felt slick against my sweaty hands, and all I could think was how horrified my grandmama would be, that I died in the nude.

"Dallas O'Connor, I said turn over."

Slowly, I looked over my shoulder. A man stood blocking

my skylight. Stocky, with a baseball cap. How did he know who I was?

"I'm sorry about the twenty I took," he said, "but you know, I needed the cash. You should be more careful about where you leave your purse."

Something was familiar about his voice, the shape of his body.

"Wh-what do you want?" I managed to rasp out.

He sniffed the air like an animal. "Is that Chanel Number 5?" he asked. "Man, that's good. Hey, I hear Marilyn Monroe slept in it, and nothing else, you know what I mean? You think that's true?"

"Uh, yes. But it's Opium," I answered automatically.

"Man, it's awesome, you know," he said conversationally. "It makes me think of those Chinese houses with the roofs that curve up. You know, like Buddha had."

The distance from my bed to the head of the stairs was about twelve feet. If I pushed him hard—and he didn't use the gun—then I could make it down the five steps to the landing. Then it was just another five steps and three locks on my front door to freedom.

"This looks real pretty from here," he said. "The shadows, the shape of your back. Very sexy."

Five steps to the bathroom, but it didn't have a door lock. Or a telephone.

"Well, it's been nice to know you," he said. Then I noticed—no, recalled—his voice. I'd heard it as that psycho had chased me through the photo studio today. A knife-wielding Spanish psycho. Who was now here. In my home.

A maniac, a missing friend, and now my own murder. This was my reward for being a conscientious employee.

*   *   *

"No, darling Dallas, you don't understand," Gary said, as though he were speaking to a recalcitrant child. "I want them hanging. Preferably by the neck, though that may be too . . ."

"Graphic?" I suggested, as I negotiated the curve off I-30, and tried not to spill the coffee I held between my knees, or drop my cell phone onto the floor. Or have a wreck. My truck's headlights barely illuminated the rainy predawn darkness of Deep Ellum.

AT&T transmitted Gary's sigh down the phone line. It was eloquent, subtle, and highly manipulative. Then again, as the art director of *Metamorphosis*, The Store's quarterly catalog, Gary was not only exquisitely talented, he was a master at maneuvering.

Unfortunately, what he wanted changed daily, sometimes hourly. He'd just seen some movie about prerevolutionary Argentina, which featured a lot of tango dancing, and it had inspired him to modify the last shoot. We were three days from finishing, and he wanted to rethink the concept.

If I didn't love him so much, I would kill him.

"Yes, the girls hanging in the background," he said. "I think the Dolce & Gabbana would be perfect against—remind me, what color are those walls?"

Monday they had been Minoan Russet. Yesterday he wanted them Bali-Sand. I tried to describe the most current color as appealingly as possible, since I would be responsible for changing it if he suddenly decided he liked Apricot Parfait or Celestine Aqua better.

Why do paint companies have such ludicrous names for their products? I wonder who gets to make them up and how

much money she makes. It has to be more than I'm making—
and I bet she is still asleep.

There was another sigh, followed by a long pause. "Really
Dallas," he said. "Bali-Sand? With the Dolce & Gabbana? I'd
almost prefer that aqua shade. A blue background would just
make those colors pop."

This issue of *Metamorphosis* was jointly mine and Gary's.
Though normally I worked as a stylist for The Store, for this
book I was production manager. He did the creative thinking
as the art director, I made it happen. Consequently, it was my
responsibility to make his vision concrete—or Bali-Sand, or
Celestine Aqua, or a 1920's Spanish plaza.

Fool the people, I thought. That is my motto. I just wish
I was doing it for more money and had some time left over to
have a life. Freelancing was looking like a better option every
day. I just needed a new vehicle—and the nerve to get started.

As Gary discussed shades and tints of blue, and different
merchandise options, I pulled into the empty parking lot of
the studio. Rain was falling harder, which was par for the
course, since I had a ton of props to haul inside. Surprisingly,
I was early. The clock on the dashboard read 5:45 A.M. A great
time to be in downtown Dallas. If you wanted to be a victim,
that is.

The studio, Mere Illusion, was one of the largest in the
city, boasting more than fifty thousand square feet, all of which
The Store was using. Some was for the fashion shoot, of which
I was a part, and the rest was home furnishings, linens, and
additional soft merchandise. At least seventy people came in
and out of here daily, filling this enormous parking lot. They
would start arriving in forty-five minutes, ready for coffee,
breakfast, and clear direction.

None of which I had ready.

"I'll call you when I have the Polaroids," I told Gary, attempting a not-so-obvious compromise. "We'll upload them, and you can print them on your end, see what you think." Of course, that would probably be a disaster because the color wouldn't be true.

But I wanted to make this as easy for Gary as possible, since he was taking care of his cancer-ridden mother this week. His sister, who had been doing the nursing, had decided she needed a vacation and just left, leaving Gary to shoulder the burden. Stressed and overworked, he still considered family his top priority, so he took off for Georgia to clean, cook, and coddle. If he wanted the talent hanging, I'd hang them. Gary needed some ease in his life. You had to admire a man who honored his commitments.

I also wanted to get him off the phone before he started asking the complicated questions.

"Thank you, my darling Dallas," he said.

"You are so welcome, my dearest Gary," I replied. "Take care of yourself."

I had almost pushed the END key on my lime green Nokia when he said, "Dallas—"

It was a tone of voice I'd come to know well. So much for avoiding complications. "Yes?" I turned off the engine, watching the rain on the windshield.

"How is the talent?"

The talent was what we called models.

"Specifically," he said, his voice growing harder, "has anyone heard from that flighty child?"

That flighty child was Ileana Karagonis, a nineteen-year-old single mother, who had the most versatile face in the business. My friend Leo Pastriani had "discovered" her when she was sitting on Santa's lap at Northpark Mall in 1992. He became her agent on the spot.

Since then, we had all watched her go through drugs, an unplanned pregnancy, and emerge still beautiful. To her benefit, the hard knocks had given her face, her expressions, a maturity and depth without actually aging her. There is no accounting for genetics.

However, Ileana was MIA. She'd booked herself out, which means she had called in to take time off, two weeks ago, but was supposed to have arrived yesterday for today's shoot. In fact, she had leased the other half of my duplex for the next few days. But I hadn't heard from her.

"Is she back on heroin?"

Heroin *was* a great way to stay thin, and Ileana had used that method briefly. "I'm sure she's not," I said. "She has Kalista now, she's taking everything very seriously. You know she did last season's shows and they had nothing but good to say about her."

Gary sighed. "Call me the second she shows her lovely Calypso face." He was silent for a moment. "I thought she was doing so well. It's disappointing to think she may not be."

Gary had been the one to check her into rehab the time it had finally worked.

"I'll talk to you then," he said. "Bye, my darling. Don't forget the mannequins." He sighed again—Gary spoke through his sighs. "Especially if Ileana doesn't show."

"Will do," I said, clicking the phone off.

The rain had abated somewhat and I unlocked the doors,

preparing to dash into the studio. It had been only three hours since I'd left, racing home for a short nap, a shorter shower, and another pair of shoes. Concrete studio floors were my nemesis.

It's almost over, I reminded myself. Just hang the manne-quins like Gary wants, then shoot the merch, and it will be done. Done is good. Turning up the collar of my raincoat, I grabbed my bag and my keys, and made a mad dash through the rain. Then I was under the awning, staring at the keypad, trying to recall the entry code. I'd only been using it every day for a month. Just goes to show how brain-dead I am, I thought. I punched it in, heard the interior buzzer, and pushed the door open.

Refrigerated air enveloped me. In Texas, air-conditioning is a way of life, sometimes even in March, despite its status as the coldest month. Goose bumps broke out underneath my coat as I fumbled for the light switch in the foyer.

The foyer was set apart from the rest of the studio, which was currently chopped into small bedroom and dining and kitchen sets, each with its own lighting and theme. By day's end this room would be filled with miscellaneous bags, back-packs, and totes. I left mine as the first.

Before I did anything else, I walked down the hallway to the kitchen and flipped on the coffeemaker, grateful I'd set it up before I went home this morning. I walked to the CD changer, but decided against turning it on. The silence was nice. Silence that would only last until six, since I'd resched-uled the Cuban artist who'd done the backdrops to come by then to collect his check.

A Latin male. I'd never met him before, but his voice

was gorgeous on the phone, and with my predisposition for Latin males, I figured I was doomed. He was a brilliant artist; it was a shame he was painting backdrops. At least it was work, though.

I needed to get breakfast ordered and my gear inside before he arrived. If I got my order in before six, I had a waiter at Café Brazil who would actually deliver it to me.

I glanced at my Movado for the time. And froze. Had I heard a sound? Don't be silly, I chided myself. The building is locked. The parking lot is empty. Probably just something settling. After all, the studio was packed with merch. I walked back toward the foyer, my feet familiar with this dark path. Another noise. Like a rustle, or a slip.

A slip. A mannequin. A mannequin slipping from its moorings. A fragile five-thousand-dollar mannequin, that I was responsible for, might smash on the concrete floor at any second. I took off running, dodging my way through the bedroom vignettes and dining-room sets, to the back of the studio where the fashion set was, almost silent in my three-inch foam-soled shoes.

I'd spent all last evening arranging the mannequins to look like they were crawling the walls, just exactly the way that Gary had wanted.

The look that he wanted yesterday. Oh God, I couldn't believe I might have to redo it. We'd been working ten-hour days for four weeks. The crew was nearly wiped, and I was a zombie.

If Ileana was late and I had to wait for her replacement, which would delay us further, I might have a disaster on my hands. We had thirteen more shots to get. The crew was booked for other jobs after Friday, so I had only three days to finish. Which was very reasonable if everyone showed up and did their jobs. On time.

I told myself that even if I were freelancing, this part wouldn't be that different. Except I could go to Acapulco for a week afterward. Instead I still have to show up at the office bright and early Monday morning.

Once at the back set, I stepped over cords and ducked beneath photographers' paraphernalia: softboxes, hotlights, and umbrellas, until I found the keylight I'd used last night. In the darkness I heard an odd plinking noise—like a leaky faucet. Suddenly I was aware of holding my breath, listening. I felt strangely alone. I'd even beat Kevin, the photo assistant, to work.

The plinking sound was regular, rhythmic.

I clicked on the light, blinking at the white glare. A man stood on the set, transfixed beneath the mannequins. He looked straight at me. His eyes were brilliant green against Bali-Sand-colored skin. We stood staring at each other for a moment. He seemed as surprised to see me as I was to see him.

In that moment of complete and total focus, the small, persistent sound seemed amplified. Plink. Plink. Plink. My gaze was drawn past the man and up the wall. Six mannequins in Dolce & Gabbana crawled the walls, three on each side of a Spanish archway. They were uniform in their size six and luxurious-wigged perfection.

Then there was the seventh.

Nude, front forward, a mannequin hung by her neck, her lacquered toenails and burgundy hair stark against the Bali-Sand background. I saw the drops of red, too bright to be

Minoan Russet, plinking into a pool on the floor. A chill went through me.

She had the body of a mannequin, long and angular, but she was human. Alive. Or had been, I thought as I looked back at the man, his wide staring eyes.

Then, and only then, did I notice the knife in his hand.

CHAPTER TWO

The green-eyed man's gaze followed mine to the weapon. I watched his hand open wider, the blade lying across his palm. Adrenaline zagged through my tired brain. Dallas! Dead model. Man with knife. Hello?

He stepped forward, "Man, it's—"

But I was gone, fleeing through the studio. I heard his steps behind me. We were running blind. It was darker in this section of the building, but I had the advantage since it had been part of my job to acquire most of the props. I knew that a rake, coordinated ottomans, and a nine-foot-tall giraffe were somewhere in my path.

"Hold on, man! I can explain!" he called out.

Maybe I could lead this green-eyed maniac past something dangerous, make him trip and fall. I ducked under a rectangular softbox, waiting for a moment. I heard his hard heels on the floor, so I knew he couldn't sneak up on me. I'd hide behind something, let him think he was chasing me, then I'd backtrack to the front, and get to my truck.

The sound of footsteps ceased. I was holding my breath, waiting for a noise to indicate where he was.

"Man, it's not what you're thinking," he shouted in heavily accented English. It sounded as though he was standing in the cyclorama, the edgeless corner of the studio—his voice just kept bouncing around. My eyes had adjusted. I was in the children's fashion set, a world of giant toys.

I took one step. I heard nothing. Then I heard his breathing. Closer. Had he taken off his boots? I charged forward, accidentally knocking over some giant Crayola crayons. He was behind me in moments. "Just listen!"

There was no point in hiding, I thought, just run. I spilled flowers in my wake, but it didn't slow him. I pulled a rolling tea tray, complete with a Limoges service for four and small faux tea cakes, into his path. Seconds later he crashed into it, but just kept coming. Around this corner, I thought—then screeched to a halt.

A wall that hadn't been there yesterday suddenly blocked my escape. I heard my cell phone ring in the foyer.

Please be help, I thought.

The knife man barreled into me, cursing in Spanish as he grasped for my upper arms with both his hands. No knife, Dallas. He might have been explaining, but I didn't hear anything above the pounding of my heart. I ducked beneath his reach, and bolted for the other end of the studio.

I sprinted around a summertime bed set that looked as though it were in a field of violets, dodged a formal dining room that could have graced a Newburyport estate, and raced through an artificial beach, complete with palm trees.

"I won't hurt you, c'mon" he shouted behind me. Yeah, right, I thought. I bet that model believed you, too. Spotlights and tripods stood like sentinels between me and the side door. And even in my state of fear I realized I better not knock any of them over—so I changed lanes, leaping over a cane-backed sofa and losing my balance just where the hardwood floor met an accent rug.

I staggered up and ran smack into a clothes steamer, and spilled water all over the floor in the process. "You gotta believe me. I was just going to cut her—" the psycho said. As I tried to catch my balance, my legs got tangled in the cord, and I tripped again. He was on my tail. I scrabbled forward on my knees and touched the door.

In a rush I remembered the cargo doors were chained and padlocked. Hopeless, stretched out on the floor, I just stopped moving.

The psycho tripped over me, smashing headfirst into the metal door. Falling on me. He weighed a ton, solid muscle that had my left shoulder pinned to the ground. Everything was suddenly tomb silent. Had he knocked himself out. I squirmed from underneath him and ran for the dressing rooms. I'd lock myself in and wait for someone to arrive. But would the psycho get whoever came first? Or was the knifeman just after . . . women?

I stumbled through the darkness and into a small room, deadbolting the door behind me. Then I pushed furniture in front of that, to barricade myself until help arrived. I looked at my watch; it was 6:01.

"Dallas?"

I was saved.

"Dallas?" someone called.

"Watch out!" I shouted, my voice frail in my ears.

The sound of footsteps—squeaks of tennis shoes on the floor—grew louder as the person moved farther into the studio. I couldn't figure out the voice. "Are you in the bathroom?" Kevin, the photo assistant, shouted.

"Man, just give me a chance, you know? I can prove my innocent!" the Spanish-speaker whispered to me from the other side of the door. He'd found me. "I have film." Terrified, I held my breath. "It proves everything." After he said that, I heard nothing other than the approach of sneakers.

"Watch out!" I shouted to whoever was there.

"What on earth?" I heard Kevin say, then the sounds of furniture moving. I pressed my ear against the door, listening for the knifeman. Was he going to attack Kevin? A whine of metal on metal tore through the building. The cargo doors! The killer was getting away.

I shoved the furniture aside and fumbled frantically with the dead bolt. We couldn't let this guy run free. I opened the door just in time to hear Kevin shout, "Who's there" and then his tennis shoes squelched on the floor, moving toward the front.

I looked around me, dazed and disoriented in this studio I knew so well. Adrenaline shook my hands and I felt light-headed. To my left, rain trickled beneath the open cargo door. The Spanish psycho had either slipped out through an eight-inch gap, or he'd faked us out. How had he opened the padlocks? I took another step, wary. Was he really gone?

I heard Kevin's muffled curse. He had found the body. The body. It wasn't a suicide. Oh God, a murder? What else could it be? And a man with a knife? Who had just chased me? I sat down in an ultramodern steel-and-pine kitchen. My knees were too unsteady to walk farther.

"Dallas, are you here?" Kevin shouted. "Dallas!"

"I'm okay," I said, almost too weak to hear myself. I wiped perspiration off my face, listening as Kevin dialed the phone. I got up and took a few more steps, then plopped on to a bale of hay. I felt my lower lip trembling. Who was hanging in the other room.

"Nine-one-one? I need to report, uh, something," Kevin said. "Yes, an ambulance, I think so anyway. Yeah, and cops. A break-in. Someone has been—" his voice became too soft to hear. I staggered back through the studio, forcing myself onto the set.

She was still there. Frail. Ashen. Her face was half-hidden by her dark red hair. Her head sagged to the side, as if she was tired. The angular perfection of her body—shoulders like a clothes hanger, coral-tipped breasts, jutting hipbones, and long, shapely legs—was static, waiting to move.

I couldn't look at her face.

The pool of blood beneath the body was small, drying in the air-conditioning. A sickly-sweet smell was starting to emanate from the body: decomposition. I swallowed down bile and took a step closer. The knife was lying on the ground, the edge dried red.

"Dallas, don't go in there," Kevin called.

I took a step closer, looking at the woman's hands. They were solid, spatulate, and she had a French manicure. Familiar.

"You shouldn't be in here," he said from behind me.

I jumped, then turned around. It was Kevin. "Are they coming?" I asked.

"Who?" He looked over my head at the body. "Holy hell, what is this?"

"Didn't you just call the police?" I asked.

He couldn't take his eyes away from her. "Yeah, they'll be here in a minute."

I turned back to the corpse, noticing that it wasn't hanging straight anymore. The monofilament was starting to saw through the flesh. But I also knew we couldn't cut her down, even if it were the most human approach.

"You're early today," he said. "Why are you so early?"

Unable to help myself, I looked up, into her face, cataloging her features. Aquiline nose, high cheekbones, squared chin. Suddenly, I started shaking. Her exquisite, mobile face was now unemotional and frozen. Forever.

"Do you know who it is?" Kevin asked.

The front door slammed shut.

CHAPTER THREE

"Your name?"

"Dallas O'Connor."

"Address?"

"Twenty-two twenty Madrid Street, Dallas, 75206."

"Telephone?"

"It's (214)555-2661."

The cop, Officer Williams, looked at me, his brown gaze inscrutable. "You found the body?"

"Uh, yes."

"It was hanging, you say?"

"Yes."

"Why were you here this morning?"

"I'm the production manager for this." Then it dawned on me what he probably saw. My J. Crew jeans were tattered, and my turtleneck sweater, though cashmere, was old. My blond hair was tangled, matted from the rain, and I'd only bothered with moisturizer today. I certainly didn't look like a person in charge. What was it Grandmama always said? Go out looking like heck, and you will run into everyone you've ever known.

With the circles under my brown eyes from late nights, a fading bottled tan, and my terrified shaking, he probably thought I was a well-fed junkie. "It's a photo shoot," I said.

"What do you do?" he asked.

"I have two roles," I said. "As a stylist, my job is to prepare the set," I explained my unexplainable job. "I make sure it has the right look for the art director. I arrange the props, prep the merch and the talent, so that the photographer and the other artists can do their jobs, unimpeded."

Williams didn't look impressed. I'm also responsible for keeping the talent fed, I thought, and making the photographer happy. "As production manager I organize the shoots so they will meet the specific requirements set by The Store."

"What brought you into this room?" he asked, glancing over his shoulder. Cops were swarming the place. Someone from the Medical Examiner's office had been here, cut the monofilament lines that had suspended the corpse, and removed her . . . in a body bag.

The mannequins still clung to the walls. I should have been chilled—but it was all surreal. After all, this was fashion. Fooling the people. Nothing was real. Especially this.

Keep telling yourself that, Dallas.

"It's the set," I said, looking around me. "This is where I work." While I watched, they photographed the blood puddle and cordoned off the area with yellow crime-scene tape. That was real. Another detective was expected any minute, and Kevin and I had been separated so they could get our stories.

It was madness.

I'd called the creative director at The Store. Even this early, he wasn't home, then I remembered why. He was in Houston, with another team, scheduled to arrive this morning. I left a message that there was an emergency and he was needed here immediately.

Then I'd called Gary.

"Dallas. What's up?"

"Gary, uh, we uh, found her."

"Excellent! How is the flighty little thing?"

"Gary." I couldn't find enough moisture in my throat to speak. "Uh, sit down."

"What's wrong?"

"Gary, Gary, she was murdered."

He'd gone ballistic. His plan was to find his sister in Acapulco and get her to come home. Then he would catch the next flight from Atlanta. The next flight after his sister returned, which meant this mess was still on my hands. "You will have to call Leo," he said, his voice strangled. "I just can't do it."

I couldn't think of anything I wanted to do less, but Leo was her agent, and my friend.

"You knew the deceased?" the officer asked.

"Yes."

"How well?"

"She was a model."

"Did you know her personally?"

I licked my lips, striving to appear calm. "We were friends, sort of." At least that was all he needed to know. The rest was history, long-buried.

He raised both brows. "Sort of?"

"She was a great kid. She'd been through a lot, but she was . . . a survivor," I said. The irony was choking.

"Did she live in Dallas?"

I shrugged. Models rarely lived anywhere exclusively, but he wanted solid yeas and nays. "I don't know."

"Where did she stay when she was here?"

"Usually? I don't know."

The studio doors banged open and I heard shouting—voices I recognized. There must be a crowd growing outside. "Ah, Detective Mansfield," the cop who was interviewing me called. He walked over to a dark woman dressed in cargo pants and polo shirt.

"Who are all those people in the parking lot?" a different cop asked me.

I rubbed my eyes. "The crew," I said. Dozens of people reporting for work. It must be near eight o'clock, I thought wearily.

Detective Mansfield came over and introduced herself as Diana. "I understand it was you who found the body?" she asked.

"Yes."

"And you said there was a man, here?" Williams, my original interviewer, asked.

"Yes."

"And he had a weapon?"

"He had a hunting knife, with blood on it," I said.

"How do you know it wasn't just a kitchen knife? A utility knife?" Williams inquired. Diana watched me with brown doe eyes, while the other officer scribbled in his notebook. "Or maybe it was a knife from here?"

"It was a hunting knife," I repeated.

"How do you know that?"

Because I'm from a crazy, standard-issue Texas family, and although I'm a vegetarian, hunting has always been a part of my life, since my sixth birthday. Or do I say that I've worked on outdoor shoots, which is also true. "I've seen them before," I said. "It was a lockback hunting knife, about four inches long, with a serrated blade."

His expression was cold as he looked at me again. "You know a lot about knives."

I shrugged and said nothing.

"And what did this man look like?"

"My height, maybe shorter. Well built, wearing jeans and a flannel shirt, baseball cap and boots. I didn't see much of his face, but his eyes were green."

"What color hair?"

"He had on a cap, I don't know."

"Anything else identifiable about him?"

I shivered, remembering my fear as I ran through the dark. "Not that I recall."

"Had you ever seen him before?" Diana asked.

"No."

"Are you sure?"

"Yes."

"You claim this man chased you through the place?" the interviewer asked. "Why did you go to the back?"

"I knew there were cargo doors, but I realized too late that I wouldn't have enough time to open them before he got there."

"Did he say anything to you?"

"He was shouting that he was innocent."

"While he chased you?"

"Yes."

"And you didn't listen to his explanation?"

I sighed. "The man had a knife. I had just seen a dead woman, and blood. I guess you could say I panicked and didn't ask for details."

His eyes narrowed at my sarcastic tone. "Can we reach you at this number, if we have more questions?"

"Yes."

"Do you have an alternative number we could use?"

Give the police my cell phone number? I don't think so. "If you need to get me, leave a message at that number. I check it all the time."

He turned to Detective Mansfield and they spoke quietly for a moment. "We'll have to ask you not to leave town, Miss Dallas," Williams said.

"It's Ms. O'Connor. And I won't. Am I free to go?" I stood up—suddenly overwhelmed by all I had to do. No one had even gotten breakfast yet. Despite this tragedy, things still had to be taken care of, either rescheduled or postponed, questions answered and people handled. And I had to call Leo.

"Actually," Detective Mansfield said, "if you could wait a few more minutes, I'd like to look over the scene, then ask you some more questions. Can you do that?"

The talent, the artists, and the photographers were all sitting in the parking lot, probably starving to death. Death. We were too flippant with that word. "May I make some phone calls in the interim?" I asked.

"Please don't use any of the phones in here," she said. "They are part of the scene." I nodded in agreement and got my Nokia, first calling Leo, begging him to call me ASAP but trying not to alarm him, then dialing Café Brazil. After arranging for breakfast to be delivered—I didn't care about cost—I started gathering my thoughts. The crew was outside. Waiting.

If I thought about why they weren't working, I would fall into a million pieces. I wanted to get as far away as I could. Just straighten up here, then you can leave, I told myself. That poor girl.

"Ms. O'Connor," Detective Mansfield asked, "would you please repeat what you saw when you arrived?"

I started into my tale: opening the door, the noises, the body, the chase, and finally Kevin's phone call.

"You identified the model almost immediately?"

"It's easy for me to recognize faces," I said. "Hair, and skin, and even eye color can change, but bone structure is easy to recall." It was the first time I'd seen her as anything other than blond, and that had thrown me.

"Was there any reason for her to be here?"

"She was part of today's shoot."

"Why was she the first person here?"

"I don't know."

"Could she have been meeting someone?"

"It's possible, but I don't know. A model would never arrive before the makeup artist. Not at this hour."

"Who is the makeup artist?"

"Coco Wasserstein, but she wasn't supposed to be here until seven-thirty."

"So this model was extremely early."

"Yes."

"Who was here last night, before you discovered the body?"

"Me," I said. "I left at two-thirty, or thereabouts."

"And returned at five-forty-five? That's a very long day for you," she said with a smile.

"We have three days left, and a lot to do. Everyone is really pushing hard, so we're working later than usual." Which meant that didn't leave much of a window of opportunity for someone to kill the model and string her up.

"How are those mannequins suspended?" Diana asked.

"Monofilament."

"Is that spool on these premises?"

Had I left my stuff here? "I don't know," I said. "I could have left it behind."

"So we will find your fingerprints on it?"

"On the spool?" I felt a little sick. "Yes."

"How long did it take you to suspend each of those figures?"

I leaned forward, rubbing my face. "The first one took about two hours, just because I kept changing her position," I said. "By the time I was on the sixth, maybe fifteen minutes. By then I knew how I wanted it to look."

"And how did you do it? That is a big, high wall. How much does one of those dummies weigh?"

"They are about fifteen pounds, apiece," I said. "I tied the wires on the figures, then used the monofilament over the ladder rungs, as a pulley, to maneuver the mannequins into place."

"Where is that ladder?" Diana asked.

"I pushed it into the other set," I said, gesturing around the corner.

She dispatched a cop to check my story. "Are you positive this body is her?" she asked me. "Did you know Ileana Karagonis?"

We were standing by the bar, with a stack of current fashion magazines. I reached for Italian *Vogue* and flipped through, stopping on an ad for sparkling water. It had a millennial twist: Ileana, blond, was nude in a bubble of clear water, like a space suit, floating through outer space.

" 'Venus comes of age,' " Detective Mansfield read the copy.

"She was one of Alliance Artists' top girls," I said quietly. "Everything was going her way."

Diana scrutinized me. "Were you and Ileana friends? Acquaintances? Enemies?"

"We were both in the business. We knew each other."

"So there was some tension between you?"

"No, it was just a professional relationship."

"You only worked together then."

"Yes," I said after a moment too long of hesitation. *Now* we only worked together.

"When you did talk, what was the topic of conversation?"

I sighed. "Normal things, what she was doing, her next job or trip."

"Would you discuss those things while you were here, on this, what did you call it—set?"

"No. We didn't talk on the set. We worked. The photographer would tell her to move, and then I would pin or fit the garment so that it looked its best. If she confided in anyone, it would be the makeup artist."

"Coco," she said.

"Whoever the makeup artist was on that shoot," I clarified. "That's who she would talk to."

"Where was she before arriving in Dallas?"

I shrugged. "I don't know." Leo could answer that question.

"You say the man chasing you went out the cargo doors?"

"I think so."

"The same cargo doors that were supposed to be padlocked?"

"Yeah, I don't know how he did it. Wait a minute, did you say 'supposed' to be?"

She looked at me, her expression inscrutable. "They weren't locked."

"That's weird. They were when I left this morning."

She noted something in her notebook. "The chains and locks were not on them. Are you positive they were when you left?"

Had I checked them before? "Yeah, well, I think so."

Diana half smiled. "That's an iffy positive."

"Yes, they were. Or rather, there was no reason for them not to be."

"What about the knife?"

"I saw the Spanish-speaking guy holding it."

"Did he have it while he chased you?"

"Yes. For a while."

She wrote down something else. "How do you think it got back to the set, which is where we found it."

"I have no idea. Maybe he went through the front, dropped it then?"

"Why would he open the cargo doors?"

To confuse us? You're the cop. "I don't know," I said.

Diana stared at me a moment longer, then took down a list of the crew's names and responsibilities. After a moment, the detective closed the *Vogue*. "I'll be in touch," she said. "Don't leave town."

I swallowed hard. "Am I a witness or suspect or something?"

CHAPTER FOUR

Detective Diana Mansfield turned around, one hand on her hip. "By your own account, you were only gone for three hours. Your fingerprints, again by your own admission, are on the monofilament, and you, the designer of this scene, took two hours getting a fifteen-pound mannequin up there." She paused for a moment. "Or fifteen minutes. Moreover, you knew the victim."

I felt more than sick; I was scared. "What about that man?" I said. "He had the knife, he chased me."

"We haven't found any evidence of this man," she said. "You are the only person who alleges to have seen him."

I opened my mouth to ask if Kevin had said anything, but then I remembered that he had only heard someone, not seen anyone. I was the only one; but there had to be a trace of that Spanish psycho here. They had to believe me.

"Are you accusing me of something?" I asked quietly. Even saying the words seemed bizarre and melodramatic.

"Are you confessing to something?"

"I have nothing to confess," I said. "Why would I kill anyone, especially a model?"

"You would have those answers, if you did it," Detective Mansfield said.

My lips were dry again, but if I licked them again, I might look like a suspect. Nervous. Where was my Lip Smacker when I needed it? My eyes probably looked shifty, too. I could almost hear my brother the attorney telling me to shut the hell up. I chose to listen for a change.

"People kill each other for basic reasons," the detective said. "Jealousy. Anger. Greed. Lust. Do any of those strike a chord with you?"

"Do I need an attorney?" My voice was getting smaller.

"No. Not now. Here's my card if you think of anything else." She handed it to me and walked away. Williams appeared.

"When will your people be finished in here?" I asked, trying to lasso my brain.

"Ms. O'Connor," he said stiffly. "This is the scene of a crime. A woman was murdered here. These premises will be off-limits until at least the end of the week."

"What? This can't be the scene of the murder. There isn't enough . . . blood—" I choked on the last. Great, Dallas, give them more ammo.

"Very good observation, Ms. O'Connor," he said. "You will note I said 'crime.' You said 'murder.' Any idea where she could have been killed?"

"No." I couldn't really be having this conversation. This

was Ileana, beautiful, changeable Ileana, not just some body. Oh God, I couldn't think about this. Not in a personal way.

"This studio will be closed to all non-law-enforcement officials," he said, "in answer to your question."

"My people need to pick up their equipment," I stammered.

"That's impossible," he said.

"At least I need the clothes," I said to the officer. "The ensembles the mannequins are wearing. They can't have anything to do with the investigation and—"

"Of course we will cooperate in any way you see fit, Officer," a smooth, masculine voice said from behind me. I didn't need to turn to see that the voice was matched by riveting good looks. Or that the head was attached to a perfect physique, appropriately attired—regardless of the circumstances.

Fresh off the plane from Houston, it was Damon Whitside, The Store's creative director, which made him Gary's boss and a minor deity compared to my position. Unlike most creative types, Damon was also excellent at business and PR. A triple threat in one slick package, if ever there was one.

We both worked out at the Premier Club.

The cop looked at Damon, and I saw Williams's face go slack. Often, people were struck by the first glance because Damon was so good-looking it almost hurt. Until you realized he was a rat, or you built up a tolerance.

I hated to think how many young women had fallen for that smile. Or young men, for that matter.

"Uh, thank you sir," the cop stammered. "You are?"

I turned around, just to watch the snake charmer in action. I was right; he was perfectly groomed and attired: Polo shirt,

Hilfiger khakis, Cole Haan loafers, gold Cartier tank watch on a brown alligator band, and Perry Ellis baseball cap.

He glanced at me, "Dressed to impress, as always, Dallas?" he murmured.

Did I mention that he kept my employee file filled with critiques about what I wore? Or that he'd actually tried to fire me because of my clothing? I dress for my job instead of his expectations. Of course, today was the day I looked like a gravedigger.

Or, in the minds of the DPD, a murderess.

Ominous thought, Dallas.

"Don't forget the film for *Metamorphosis* is due Monday," he said.

I stared, openmouthed. We were supposed to work today? We'd just found the body of a model we all knew, we—

"The crew is waiting in the parking lot," he said.

"But the studio," I started, slowly computing that he expected us to shoot in the remaining daylight hours.

"Do it someplace else," Damon said, not even looking at me.

"Merch," I said. "They—"

"Get your people and go. Don't forget your deadline." Damon's tone was final.

I ground my teeth in frustration. We couldn't do a shoot with just Scotch tape and a flashlight. We needed duct tape.

We needed the specific clothes, shoes, jewelry—what we were selling. The photographers, Francis and Jacob, would come up with camera gear and solve the other equipment problems. My brain kicked into overdrive.

I needed to reschedule the talent. I needed duplicate

merch. I needed a studio. I needed a new concept. I needed Gary.

"They won't release the merch," I said. "We can't shoot today."

Both men ignored me, and Damon continued to speak to Williams in his silky PR voice. "Is there any way The Store can further cooperate in resolving this tragic event?"

I muttered my good-byes and headed toward the front door. As if I could forget my deadline. I was already dialing Gary. Busy.

Instinctively, I touched my throat, shaking again. If Damon had known what the DPD had asked me, he would have fired me on the spot. Thoughts of work and clothes and selling seemed callous when I considered Mrs. Karagonis didn't have a daughter anymore.

And little Kalista didn't have a mother.

The thought brought me up short. Who was going to tell Ileana's little girl that her mommy was dead? More jobs for Leo. Oh God. I dialed his cell phone. No answer.

"I got another studio, Dallas," Kevin said, touching my shoulder as he walked by. "And a backup. What are we doing about merch?"

I was dialing the agency. "The question of the hour—" I began, but Lindsay picked up on the third ring, sounding crisp, breathless, and extremely British. "Alliance Artists." Great, that meant she was in a bad mood. Her accent got stronger the more irritated she was. I wasn't going to make her day any easier.

"Hey, I need another girl."

"Dallas? For today?"

I already had six. "Yes, she's a"—I winced at the word—"replacement, for uh, Ileana."

Except there was no replacement for Ileana, for the way she moved, how she literally changed her face and became a dozen different women, no replacement for the way clothing clasped her body and light loved her face.

I overheard Kevin on his cell phone with The Store, talking to the merch manager, or calming her, more likely. All around us, cops were taking photographs and conversing in low voices. And we were rescheduling a fashion shoot.

Don't think about it, Dallas.

"Did she not show?" Lindsay asked. "Perhaps she's in traffic. Oh dear, I just checked the time. It's quite late. Certainly, I will send someone. Do you need her immediately?"

I looked at my watch, too. It had been three hours since I'd arrived. How had all this horror happened so fast. "I don't know," I said. "I'll call you, just find me someone. For tomorrow. And Friday, too." At least in a studio we could shoot all day and all night if need be.

"Rough morning, love?" Lindsay said. "Oh God," she whispered. "April Alexander just walked in. I can hear her at the front."

I looked over my shoulder. Francis, one of the photographers, was peeking through the front door's glass inset, gesturing impatiently.

"Pardon?" Lindsay said to someone in the office.

"Come on," I hissed. "I gotta go."

"Pierre-Alain is here, too," she said, naming one of the best hairstylists in the business.

"I thought he was booked today," I said.

"It canceled, from what I can overhear," Lindsay said.

"They both flew in from Houston this morning, now they are at a bit of loose ends."

Dear God, April Alexander.

"Back to the girl, the replacement, and I am so sorry for that. Ileana is usually quite professional. I can't imagine—"

Do I tell my good friend about the murder, or let her find out through the proper channels? "Is Leo around?"

"No, I haven't seen him for days. You know, absentee ownership. He tries to stay out of the city for his deals." I could hear her clicking away on the computer. "Right. Do you want a girl who looks like Ileana? Or do you want a different feel altogether?"

"Just surprise me," I muttered unprofessionally. From here I could read Francis's lips as he shouted his frustration at the door. "I'll call you back with the new location for the talent, and call times," I said, and hung up. As I gathered my stuff, I dodged police officers and redialed Gary, praying for creativity.

"What the hell is going on?" Francis demanded when I stepped outside. His red beard was enflamed by the morning sun. "The police won't say anything, Damon walked right by—"

"We can't shoot here," I said. "Kevin has another studio."

"Damn." His expression softened. "Are you okay, Dallas? Did they steal much?"

"Steal?"

"With all the police and everything, that's what—" He grabbed my arm. "Wait. Was someone hurt? What—"

"Ileana," I whispered. "Ileana was murdered."

Francis's blue eyes widened, and his hand on my arm tightened. "You're kidding."

I stood silently, looking at my indigo-painted toenails. "I wish I were."

"Oh God, I'm sorry," he said. "I didn't mean that the way it sounded. What can I do?"

"I don't know. The cops have the merch, it's evidence or something. We don't have duplicates, and Gary's talking on the phone."

"Damon's decision?"

I sighed. Damon was my last resort. If we could take a "rain day," it would give us time to find the duplicates, get the talent, arrange everything. We could even work through the weekend, and still make Monday's deadline.

My Nokia rang and I saw the Georgia area code on the caller ID. "About Ileana—" Gary started.

I couldn't think about the killing, about the reality. All I could do was focus on *Metamorphosis*. "Actually, I need to talk to you about the job."

"I've been on the phone with Damon," Gary said.

"I'm sorry."

"You have to get it done today, Dallas."

"We're searching for merch."

"What's downtown?" he asked.

Kevin walked by, handed me his notes from talking to the merch manager, and I reeled off the remaining Dolce & Gabbana options. "There's also some D&G," I said, naming their other line. However, I knew that any changes to the merch at this point would have serious repercussions—none of us, even Damon, had the authority to change what we were shooting.

"Any ideas?" Gary asked. "My mind is shot, I can't believe

that about Ileana. Are you sure, Dallas? Are you certain it was her?"

"Yeah." I held the phone, wondering what else to say, trying not to cry. Work, Dallas, work. "Well, if we can find merch," I said.

Kevin tapped me on the shoulder. "Houston is sending four of the seven outfits. On the next flight, arriving at Love Field at," he looked at my watch, "ten-fifty."

"We have merch," I said to Gary. We were going to get this done, and it would be a miracle. "You said you'd like to see them against blue, so why not do that instead of re-creating the last set?" We already had backdrops at The Store, layers of tissue paper in shades of blue, with silver seaweed props.

"What accessories?" he asked.

Damn. Did we have duplicates of those, too? "If we were doing blue," I said, thinking over what the buyers had shown at the last pre-pro meeting, wondering what we had left to shoot. "Versace? That mermaid stuff?"

"It's not scheduled."

"I know, but . . . I really doubt there are duplicates of everything," I said.

"Try to find what you can," Gary said, sighing. "I'll call Damon back."

Kevin had a studio, and the talent was due there in two hours; the other assistant had gear, and I was getting into Francis's SUV to go get the merch, when the door opened and Damon stepped out, smiling, talking on his cell phone. "She's right here," Damon said. "Looking as . . . distinctive, as ever."

He curdled my blood.

"I agree," Damon said, then good-bye, and hung up. "That was Gary."

"We have it covered," I volunteered. "Even a blue studio. You'll have your film by Monday."

"Studio?" Damon repeated. "It's a gorgeous spring day! Who wants to be inside?"

"It was supposed to be a studio," Francis said.

"It was also supposed to be a Spanish plaza," Damon reminded him sharply, then turned back to me. "Do you have merch, Dallas?"

"On my way to get it," I said. I didn't tell him that we were still looking for three more of the outfits. Calls were out to all of The Store branches, seeing what we had.

"Then you have a new concept, too," Damon said. "On location."

My mind fumbled with implications. On location. Outdoor light, wind, sun to melt the makeup, permits for places. And light that would be gone by five, maybe five-thirty if we were really lucky. "It would be much easier—" I said.

"You always look for the easy way out," Damon snapped. "Perhaps this position is too much for you?"

"Take it easy, Damon," Francis soothed. "With Ileana and everything, Dallas has had a rough day."

"Oh my word," Damon said. "I wouldn't want to stress delicate Dallas out. We'll just cancel it. We'll only be a few days behind in getting the film out, which will push back all of production." He shrugged. "But obviously Ms. O'Connor wants to have the singular reputation of being the person who delayed *Metamorphosis*. In the history of its publication that's never happened." The jerk smiled. "You could be the one, Dallas."

"Why not a studio?" I asked quietly. I was doomed; there was no physical way to pull off this shoot. The earliest we could start would be this afternoon, with four hours of light. I knew he hated me, I just never guessed he'd put *Metamorphosis* in jeopardy.

"Location, or I'll find someone else," he said.

Jacob was booked in Maine next week, and Francis was working in Miami. We had two and a half days. I glanced at my watch; the plane would be arriving any minute. Damon crossed his arms and looked at me. How could someone so awful be so beautiful?

Taking a deep breath, I plunged in with my location idea. "How about in front of living, fluid water? Not the lake, nothing flat, but what if we gave the talent a liquid background? It would have great depth and theme."

Damon didn't flicker even one of his long dark lashes. "Confirm with Gary, but I also want some shots with solid background. Film on my desk Monday." He shut the door in my face. I stood for a moment, staring at the painted metal, trying to calm down. Every time he said jump, I asked for specs. What was wrong with me?

"Are you going to be okay? Can you do this?" Francis asked gently, putting his hand on my back, treating me like a spooked horse.

"Just don't be nice to me," I said through gritted teeth. "I can't take it today."

Kevin handed my phone back. "They found the other three outfits," he said. "Miami."

"Great. When are they arriving?"

He winced. "They have a show this afternoon. Could be

here by six, but they have to be on their way to Santa Fe by three tomorrow."

"Great," I said, grabbing Francis's keys. "Get those backdrops from downtown, and I'll just head to the Dallas World Aquarium from Love."

Francis walked me to his car, closed the door behind me, then leaned in the window. "We have to tell the crew about Ileana, Dallas. They have seen the cops here all morning, and they aren't stupid. My question is, are you going to break the news to them, or should I?"

"Jacob should," I said. "Where is he, anyway?"

"He phoned me earlier; he's running late."

I'd never known Jacob to be late in my life. Punctuality was a religion with him. I started the car as I pushed redial for Leo again. Voice mail. "Breakfast will be here any minute," I said. "I'll meet you there."

"Do you think the rumors are—were—true about Ileana going under an exclusive contract with Duchesse?" Francis asked as we leaned up against his Jetta, waiting for the three models to be through with makeup and hair.

My friend Coco was doing both, and seriously stressing out. Staying out of her way was the best way to help. The presser was prepping the clothes—the four outfits I'd picked up.

"Leo hadn't said anything outright," I said, "but if so, I imagine he brokered, or was brokering, the deal. I know he thought Ileana could be the next Cindy Crawford, or April Alexander," I said.

"April's sure done well for herself. Just a small-town Texas girl," Francis said.

April Alexander had been the first supermodel from Dallas. And she never let a soul forget it. Unlike Jerry Hall, she hadn't quit modeling to marry a rock star and have children. Instead she had worked the business from every angle. She had been on every magazine cover, sold every product imaginable, and—we all hoped—was about to retire into doing exercise videos or selling feminine-hygiene products. Whatever aged models did.

Almost fifty, and April was amazing. She did runway, she did print, and she'd branched into some film. She still represented the locally grown, internationally known Duchesse Cosmetics. They had been her first client. The joke was that they would be her last. She'd be buried wearing their makeup.

"What about Lindsay?" Francis asked.

"I didn't tell her. Just told her the plan change," I said.

"It's an insane world when a girl as beautiful as Ileana gets killed," Francis said, putting his arm around me.

It was an insane world when the cops, even for a second, suspected me.

CHAPTER FIVE

Progress was under way, when all hell broke loose in the form of April Alexander. The Diva. We were shooting before a painted wall in downtown Dallas, images of life-size whales and sea life in brilliant blue, lending a perfect backdrop to the D&G.

Francis had just said there were about eighty minutes of light left, then we would go to the next venue. Jacob who had shown up an hour late—but he was a photographer and owed no one an explanation—was with his team, shooting in the aquarium building.

The girls who were working were young, but professional. One from New York, one from LA, one out of Miami, and three local girls. Ileana's replacement hadn't arrived yet.

"Keep shooting," I told Francis as I ran to meet a black limo. As the tinted window went down, I heard the squeal of tires around the corner. Suddenly the news vans for Channels 8, 5, 11, and 4, drove up, equipped with satellite dishes, and they were just as free to park here as we were.

I looked back in the now-open window and stifled a groan.

"I'm here from Lindsay for the shoot," she said. "I was so saddened to hear of the death."

My brain was making the calculations: she was too old, of that there was no doubt; she was a little thicker in the waist than the clothes could handle. Her hair, Texas blond, was the wrong shade for this, and she was notorious for her lack of teamwork. "I'm Dallas, the production manager," I said. "Let me call Lindsay, because I think there has been some confusion."

April was already out of the car, fluffing her hair. Her suit was St. John and her makeup was done. "Oh, Damon had Lindsay book me," she said. "Isn't Damon just the most darling? Anyway, ah, I brought you some help," she said.

I looked away for a second. News crews were setting up lights and cameras. I stepped forward, but April Alexander, Dallas's self-proclaimed goddess of fashion, put a hand on my arm. "Why don't you let me handle this?"

"That—" I started, but she was already slinking up to them. Pierre-Alain, one of the world's best hairdressers, got out of the limo, wearing head-to-toe black, with silver-tipped cowboy boots.

"Ah, Dallas," he said, as we exchanged cheek kisses. "I came with April when I heard." His French accent was heavy and his hazel gaze roamed the set. "Is that Coco I see?"

Oh my gosh, two hairdressers on the same set. Two hairdressers who were on-again, off-again lovers, and I didn't know if it was on or off right now. Like life wasn't impossible already. "Yes," I said, "but—"

"It's okay," he said. "I will work under her; I am just here offering a pair of extra hands. It is a difficult day, no?" He hugged me again, turning me away from April and her growing audience. "Despite rumors," he said with a wink, "I can be tractable."

Only a foreigner uses words like that, I thought. "Dallas!" Francis shouted.

I ran over to him, scanning the Polaroids he'd shot. The clothes looked good, the models looked good. Coco was beaming. I guess the romance was on-again. "Do it," I told Francis. He nodded and traded his Polaroid back for the roll film back that Kevin held.

"What's going on over there?" one of the local models asked, craning to see the parking lot.

"I don't know," Francis said.

"It's April," I said under my breath. "She's replacing Ileana."

Francis continued shooting, with no comment.

Though I didn't know the whole story, I knew that April, the Diva; Leo, my agent and friend; Jacob and Francis, the photographers, went way, way back. But Francis hadn't spoken to April in three years, so I didn't think he would start today.

"Is she in makeup now?" he asked.

I turned around and watched for a moment. "No," I said, "she's on TV."

"We are shooting in broad daylight," Francis said.

"I know, her face is going to look like a road map. I hope Damon knows that this isn't the best way to sell these clothes," I whispered.

"No, I can modify the lighting," Francis said, then heaved a sigh and exchanged camera backs with Kevin. "Just get her in makeup soon," he said, glancing at the sky. "We're running out of daytime."

"No!" one of the models screamed, and I spun around. While I'd been focused on the conversation, the girls had crept closer to where April was spilling the beans about Ileana, in graphic fashion, before the cameras.

How did *she* know? One of the local girls had burst into tears. The cameras swung around to her, then got footage of April photogenically comforting her.

I was going to puke.

"Ms. Alexander," one of the reporters shouted, "did you know Ileana well?"

The Diva drew herself up, making sure they only filmed her left—best—side. "Ileana was my little sister of the spirit," she said. "From the time she was a child, until her untimely death, we were always in touch."

"If being 'in touch' means within clawing distance," Coco whispered in my ear. "She hated Ileana."

"She's paranoid," I said.

"If the rumors were true, she had a reason to be," Coco said. "I can't believe she brought Pierre-Alain."

"I can't believe she's here at all," I said, resignedly. The light was fading, and the crew, making thousands of dollars, stood watching the Diva in action.

Two makeup artists at $650 a day; four models at $1,500 and another one at $5,000. Two photographers, earning $5,000; Kevin the assistant was $150; the on-figure stylist, $600; and an animal handler with Dobermans for $600.

And me, earning considerably less. At least the vans were loaded. As April waxed eloquent about the ups and downs of modeling, the shifting sands of success, yada yada yada, I looked away, studying the face of the five-thousand-dollar-a-day model.

Without makeup she was invisible; away from a camera she was a leggy, frail-looking dragonfly of a girl. But she made a better living than my tenured university-professor father.

That money, in turn, was nothing compared to what the big models, like Cindy or even homespun April, made. That was the path, the fast track, Ileana had been on. Why would someone kill her?

April made some reference to Alliance Artists Agency, and Coco grabbed my arm and turned to me, her almond eyes wide behind her rectangular Armani glasses. "Oh God, Leo. Has anyone told Leo?"

"Can't get hold of him."

"Ms. Alexander!" one of the reporters called. "Did you find the body?"

"You should be answering that," Coco said. "Why don't you stop her?"

"She Alexanderized again."

"She went over your head to Damon?" April had done it so often, and so flawlessly, that any sneakiness on the part of a model was called pulling an Alexander, or Alexanderizing.

"Some people are kleptomaniacs," I said. "They have a disease that makes them take things. April's disease is that she—"

"Is a bitch?"

"Is April Alexander."

*   *   *

At last, April was finished with questions, and ready to get to work. "Okay y'all," I said to the group, "we'll finish this up at Fair Park, at their aquarium."

We drove through downtown and Deep Ellum to the old state fair complex, one of the largest examples of art deco design still standing in the United States. The sister of a former boyfriend now ran the place, and would postdate the shooting permit so we could finish today.

By the time we arrived and set up, most of the models had puffy eyes, and streaked complexions. I sent Kevin for cucumbers and tea bags, while Coco sharpened her white eye pencil and passed out Murine samples. By four-thirty, the lights were up, the girls were dressed, and it looked awful.

Budget was about to go into overtime. We needed a miracle. "Do you have your drop-focus lens?" I asked Jacob.

"It's as close as my studio," he said.

"He can use mine," Francis said.

"What do you have in mind?" Jacob asked. He looked pretty haggard, too.

I raced out to my Chevy and opened my Trukbox. Stylists carry a lot of gear, depending on what kind of styling they do. Working for The Store, I'd been called on to do most anything, so I had a strange assortment of props. I ran my idea past the crew, then scrambled to get it going.

While Coco and Pierre-Alain changed the hair and makeup, I called The Store for different jewelry and toenail polish, and Kevin ran to Northpark Mall for body shimmer. At last, stuck in one of my boxes, I found what I was looking for: twenty yards of silver mesh that looked very much like fishnet.

By six, things were rocking. The models, in D&G bottoms, body shimmer, and carefully placed jewelry instead of tops, had shades of blue on their toes and lips, and were wrapped in the mesh. Their faces were exotically shadowed and shaded, and their hair was adorned with glitter, shells, and whatever else we could find around The Store.

For the next shot, we'd do the opposite: D&G tops and mesh bottoms. I'd scheduled April alone, since I didn't want the comparison of her forty-eight-year-old face to their seventeen-year-old faces.

April stepped in front of the camera, in her D&G top and mesh bottom, and I was reluctantly impressed. She was staggering, incredible. The way she moved, the emotion she communicated in just a glance, a twist of her shoulder. She was what Ileana was—had been—becoming. What a miserable waste. I shook my head as I looked at my watch. Jacob handed me another Polaroid.

I didn't even need to look at it. "Excellent. Shoot it."

CHAPTER SIX

I pulled into the driveway, noticing my porch light was off. But maybe I had just turned it off when I left—I glanced at the dashboard clock—twenty-two hours ago.

Normally, my house was a cheery Tudor-style duplex, nestled under a few of Dallas's tall trees, on the only cul-de-sac in the M Street district. Now it looked forlorn and sad, the porch swing moving gently in the breeze under the crescent moon, stalks of dead irises and daffodils poking up like fence posts beside the walkway.

I was minutes away from being safely asleep. I'd just leave my stuff in the truck; only take my purse in. I wanted Tylenol, San Pellegrino, and a cucumber and chutney sandwich, in that order. Followed by an icy cold Shiner Bock beer. That thought alone prompted me to unlock the truck's doors.

Turning off the headlights, then grabbing my bag, I

stepped out of the truck. Immediately a flash went off, blinding me. "Ms. O'Connor!" I heard.

Oh no, please. Not more media.

"Ms. O'Connor, please!" the female behind the bulb repeated, dazzling me again.

"Put your damn camera down," I said, shielding my eyes. "And it's after two in the morning, so stop shouting."

"Did you know the deceased, Ms. O'Connor?"

Spots lingered in front of my eyes. I felt like crying, I was so tired. "Why do you want to know?" I asked, trying to see the woman's face. "Are you a cop?"

"No, I'm not," she said. "Are you wanted by the cops?"

"Then who are you?" I asked, glaring at her, though she stood in darkness. But I could tell she was petite. I couldn't see anything else—strangely enough, the streetlights around my house were out. Perfect.

"I'm Carla Chou with the *Morning News.*"

"Which department?"

"Uh, I'm, um, a crime reporter."

"Then get my story from the police, I had to tell them at least four times." All I wanted was to shower and sleep—to drink my Shiner. Couldn't I be left alone for just a little while?

"But, Ms. O'Connor," she protested. "You found the body, right?"

I started walking away, glancing at my neighbors' to see if anyone noticed the ruckus outside. The woman across the street was notoriously nosy. Had the curtain moved? "Ms. O'Connor!" the reporter shouted.

Spinning on my oh-so-tired heel, I spoke to her. "The *Morning News* crime reporter was on the scene with the police,"

I said. "Now I don't know who you are, but I'm not talking to you. Get off my front lawn before—" I shut up, just before threatening to call the cops. I didn't want them here. In fact, if I never spoke to another police officer, ever, I'd be happy.

"Please," she said. "You found the body right? They said you are linked to the homicide." I halted. Homicide. Killing a Homo sapien. The word had all new meaning now. Homicide.

"Sources say Ileana Karagonis was killed by a stab wound," the reporter said to my back. "They haven't been able to establish a time of death, because the body had been frozen."

I felt nauseated. That wasn't a crime of passion—that was sick.

"Do you have a deep freeze, Ms. O'Connor?"

I climbed the steps to my front porch, and she walked up behind me. "I apologize for being rude," she said, "but I really want to know. Did you find the body?"

I put the key in the lock, not turning toward her. Ileana wasn't a body, I thought. She was a beautiful young girl. Whoever did this, whoever left her naked and hanging was . . . unforgivable. That the police were suspicious of me was almost too farcical to be considered. "Please get off my lawn. I have already made my statement," I said. I'd heard that in a movie somewhere; it sounded official.

"Ms. O'Connor."

I opened my door. "Good night," I said, and closed it in her face. Somewhere all the Southern belles in my family, of which there are dozens, rolled over in their graves. I stood in the hallway for a minute, waiting to hear if she drove off. Nothing. I dropped my bag onto the shelf of my 1920's halltree, and walked through the living room to the kitchen.

From the doorway of the tiny, L-shaped room, I could see

the nervous flashing of my answering machine. The attached
caller ID told me twenty-two people had called. The thought
of having to listen to them, much less respond to each, was
enough to send me to the closest Motel 6. Dear God, would
this day never end?

Anyone important would have called my cell phone, I
rationalized as I opened the fridge door. I retrieved an English
cucumber and some date-and-cherry-pepper chutney. Then I
drank half a Shiner Bock, feeling the icy cold beer go straight
to my head. Now I could listen to my messages. As I unscrewed
the chutney bottle lid, I hit the answering-machine button,
listening to call after call.

Half were from my family—but no one mentioned the
murder, so maybe the news wasn't out of Dallas. I laughed out
loud at a call from my buddy Kreg. He was in San Francisco
at a cardiologists' conference, and hadn't made it back to his
hotel last night. He'd left a sheepish message from a cell phone
somewhere on the PCH, telling me that he and a new "friend"
were going to breakfast in Monterey.

If I were freelancing, I thought, I could be breakfasting
in Monterey. I sucked chutney off my fingers, then sliced the
cucumber. A message from Leo, also from a cell phone, flew
by.

"It's about damn time," I said as I jumped at the machine,
then stabbed the key with a sticky finger to replay it. Why
hadn't Leo just called my Nokia? Slapping my sandwich
together, I listened to the static-filled recording.

"(Garble) we need to talk. I have to get out of town for
(garbled) but the (garbled, garbled). Anyway, I will be out of
touch, but I need to see you. Soon." It was curt to the point

of being rude, especially considering I'd left him at least ten messages to call me—no matter what.

"Should have been more specific about where to call me," I muttered, as I dialed Leo back. His cell phone went straight to voice mail. I scrolled back on my caller ID gizmo and found the phone number he'd called from. Unavailable. Great. It was getting to the point where he was going to hear about Ileana through the news. I didn't want him to have to—but maybe he already had? Was he on his way to her family or something? He was acting very strange, especially when I considered what close friends we were.

Though come to think of it, we'd spoken hardly at all the past few weeks. Both of us had been extremely busy. The last time I had seen him, about two, three weeks ago now, he had been almost embarrassingly affectionate. He'd dropped by on a Tuesday night, having just returned from New Orleans. I'd just gotten home from the shoot and had put my feet up. Too tired to open the door, I'd just shouted for him to come in when I heard his knock.

"Dallas, darling, you should be careful," he said, lugging in bags and boxes. "I could be just anybody, intent on harm."

"I heard your car," I said, not moving. He had leaned over and we exchanged a quick kiss. "How was your trip?" I asked.

He sat down and began rubbing my feet. "I've never known such a tenderfoot as you," he said. "It's a bad decision to be a stylist when your feet are so delicate."

"You gave me this career," I said, or rather moaned, as his masterful fingers brought life back into my feet. I had promised anything if he just wouldn't stop. When I finally felt like I could stand again, I offered him dinner. "It's probably going to be leftover eggplant lasagna," I said. "But I have a nice wine."

"I just returned from the city that never stops eating," he said, "and I brought all sorts of goodies." A former male model who had always watched his weight, now Leo gleefully carried around about fifteen extra pounds, proof of his love affair with food.

"How was your trip?" I asked again. "You're back early."

He paused to look at me, the lines of his face only slightly softened by age, his eyes penetratingly blue, black hair waving back from his temples and forehead, and olive skin that contrasted with his white dress shirt—100 percent linen—rumpled from the flight. He'd stuffed a tie in his jacket pocket, and he was still wearing his airplane slippers. He'd gotten them in Turkey and wore them because he said people expected eccentrics to travel in first-class. A little wired, a little tired, but still handsome and funny. My Leo.

Drawing the word out, he said, "Interesting." From his bags he produced sausage—which I don't eat; four kinds of cheeses; baguettes, beignets, coffee with chicory, and a Hurricane mix that just needed alcohol and a blender. "Rock my world with a Hurricane or three, and I'll make an omelet with hollandaise and tell you all about it."

We cooked together well, but Leo appreciated silence while he cooked; it was religion to him. So I took orders to chop and slice and add oil in a slow, steady stream. We returned to the couch with trays.

"How is business?" I asked.

"The new office is doing well," he said. "Other agencies are discovering New Orleans now, so I'm glad Alliance got there first."

He told me about the office ("to-die-for Louis Quinze"), the hotel where he'd stayed ("the most darling little B&B, right in the heart of the Garden District"), the newest jazz sensation ("like sex on a baguette. Absolutely perfect") and the upcoming season ("simply stunning").

"And your big new deal?"

Laying a finger to the side of his nose like a vaudevillian actor, he said, "I don't dare confess, but my darling girl, you are going to be sooo surprised at your Leo." We laughed, but the expression in his eyes was serious. We'd been talking for about two hours when suddenly he looked at his Gucci watch. "It's almost eleven! I have to go," and rose in a flurry of carrying things to the kitchen.

He hugged me, kissed my cheeks, and thanked me for being such an amazing friend. Leo had glanced at the clock and then looked back at me. "Before I forget, here are some croissants," he said, handing me an enormous bag I hadn't seen earlier.

"There must be a thousand in here," I exclaimed, preparing to open the bag. He knew I couldn't resist bread. Though I could cook, I seemed incapable of baking.

He put a hand on mine, stopping me. "Trust me, they are there. You don't want to let air in and dry them too early," he said. "They're a little treat for those days when you miss me, when I can't come by, or meet you for lunch."

"That's sweet," I said, kissing his cheek again. "You are a darling man."

He hugged me again, tightly, for a long while. "You're a good friend, Dallas O'Connor. In another lifetime I would have married you."

"Except for the problem with my being female and blond," I said, laughing.

"That matters less than you think," he said, his blue eyes suddenly glassy, but then he laughed, too. Suddenly he had shrieked at the time and, trailing bags, returned to his car. After listening to his BMW pull away, I put the big bag of croissants in my fridge's freezer.

"What was that about?" I had asked the empty kitchen.

I listened to his abrupt message again. Maybe he was in New York? He had three houses. I looked at the clock. Calling this late was breaking every rule of good manners I'd ever been taught. Then again, he was going to learn his favorite client and protégé was dead. Better to learn from a friend.

That settled it; I opened my Dallas Datebook and called Leo's New York house. An answering machine assured me he'd return soon. I called the Miami duplex and left the same hopefully-not-heart-attack-inducing-but-still-urgent message, and called the Dallas house one more time.

It was almost dawn, and the alcohol was barely keeping pace with my exhaustion. At least I could sleep in tomorrow— Gary had given a day of rest. By some miracle, between four trips to the airport and running the crew ragged—including the famous Pierre-Alain—we'd finished the D&G spread. And I hated to admit how amazing the Diva had been. There was a reason she was still working. A legitimate one.

Metamorphosis was done, or at least the shooting was. Now we just had to edit the film and get the FPOs, the rough scans to lay out the shots, done. On Friday, maybe Gary would even be back. Thank God my job was almost complete.

I ate the last bite of my sandwich, turned off the light, and picked up my beer. Bed.

A rustle at the front door preceded the sound of a car driving away. That reporter had been here the whole time? I crept to the front, peered through the stained-glass inset, and saw no one. Furtively I opened the door, my beer in one hand. She'd left a note. I wadded it up and stuffed it in my purse on the halltree. It was already overflowing with empty water bottles, Zero candy-bar wrappers, and half-eaten Power bars. Maybe after breakfast—at two in the afternoon tomorrow—I'd clean my purse.

Upstairs I ran a cursory toothbrush over my teeth, then stripped down to skin, leaving my clothes in a pile on my bedroom floor. With a groan that was pure pleasure, I slipped into my wrought-iron bed, with pressed 420-thread-count sheets.

This extravagance was longer lasting than sex, better for you than chocolate. The faint scent of Opium clung to my pillow, and starlight fell on me from above.

I was home.

And now someone else was in my home, too. The Spanish psycho had found me. "And now we gotta get outta here," he said in his accented English.

"Could you just throw me something," I pleaded. For the sake of my Grandmama, I had to be wearing something when the police discovered my body. Unlike Ileana. My bones felt icy inside my skin. This man had done that to her, this smooth-talking, flannel-shirt-wearing man. I suppressed a shudder.

"Oh my God, you gotta be kidding. You got no clothes

on at all?" He sounded stricken. A shirt landed on my back almost immediately. "I'm sorry. I didn't mean to hit you."

Was he going to apologize for killing me, too? "Could I have the pants?"

"Oh I'm sorry, of course."

The sweats landed on the bed, just beside me. And he hadn't shot me yet. I looked over my shoulder again. "Could you, uh, please turn around so I can put this on?"

"I'm sorry, *chica,*" he said. "I can't let you out of my sight, you know? Not even for a minute."

What did it matter if he saw me naked. He was going to kill me. It just so happened that he was a friendly murderer, with an artistic eye. I sat up, facing away from him, and pressed the shirt to my breasts. Could I break out the window and jump before he got me? Kick the gun away and hope he didn't squeeze the trigger first? My gaze roamed the desk across from me. This was the time to have a boomerang.

"Why did you do it?" I asked in a trembling voice I didn't recognize. It was corny to want him to tell all, but it was a twofold impulse. "There better be a damn good reason to do this to me." Especially if this hellish day had been my last. That sucked.

"I need your help, you know what I mean?"

"Funny way to ask for it." I pulled on my short-sleeved turtleneck as I spoke.

"What could I do? I was holding the knife when you found me."

I tugged on my sweats. "You did it?" Wouldn't the Dallas police feel stupid when they caught him and he confessed, since they didn't believe my testimony that he even existed. Of course, I would be dead, which was a high price to pay for being right. I touched my throat, my memento of my last brush with death.

"Admit what?" he said. "What are you talking about?"

I spun around. "Did you or did you not just wake me up by saying, 'I'm sorry, but'?"

"Oh no!" he said, gesturing with the gun. "Not that. No, no, I'm sorry for holding a gun on you. I'm sorry for that. Man, my English gets confused when I get—"

The Walther in his hand remained trained on me. "What about the 'you gotta go'?" I asked.

"You gotta go, I gotta go. We need to leave, 'cuz you know, the sun will be up soon."

I squinted to see his features more clearly, but the cap, and now he wore glasses, were good at shielding his face. "Where are we going?"

"You have to help me."

A sneaky thought tickled the back of my memory. I could smell the pungent sweat of fear and knew it was mine. But maybe . . . ? "—so you didn't kill Ileana?"

"Oh man, why would I kill her? She was so beautiful, so full of fire, very brave, and man, did she have a body."

He hadn't answered my question. Why else would he have been there, though? Unless . . .

I stood up on the far side of my bed, getting my plan in order. He was standing about three feet away, holding the gun. He knew how to hold it, but he wasn't comfortable doing so, that much was obvious. I stepped around the foot of the bed, slowly walking toward him. "Then why did you chase me?"

"You were going to call the police."

"Well, I'd found a man with a knife and a knifed woman in the same room. In the dark. What would you have done?"

"Oh man, I'm not blaming you, but I couldn't let you call the cops. They aren't on my side, you know?"

"Where did you get the knife?"

"It was on the floor."

"When you got there?"

"Yeah, just lying there."

"Well then, why on earth did you pick it up? What kind of idiot are you?" Not the way to speak to a kidnapper holding a gun, Dallas.

"I tripped on it. In the dark," he said.

"Why were you in the studio?" I asked, rubbing my eyes. "Stumbling around in the dark? How did you even get in?"

"The door was unlocked. And I carry a little flashlight. It's tiny, it fits in my pocket, you know?"

"Do you often just walk through Deep Ellum, checking out studio doors?"

"No, I had a meeting."

"At six in the morning?"

"I was supposed to meet someone there," he said defensively.

I was getting a weird feeling. "Who?"

"I did some stuff for someone," he said stiffly. "I'm an artist."

"Who were you supposed to meet?"

He waited a beat. "You."

"Raul Domingo?" I squawked.

"Yeah, man, but I didn't see my painting, so I was like looking for it, you know?"

Ah hell, I thought. This made all the sense in the world, while at the same time it made no sense whatsoever. Raul

Domingo was the artist I'd planned to pay this morning; he was Cuban, not Spanish. He was supposed to be there.

Based on his portfolio, I'd commissioned him via phone to do some backdrops. He'd done them at his studio, then had them delivered to ours. Though I'd never met him in person, but this was Raul Domingo, and he wasn't the murderer.

At least, I didn't think so.

"You can put the gun down," I said. "I guess this means you got my message about meeting at six instead of seven."

He didn't put the gun down. "Yeah, I guessed it was you, later, when I was in the front, waited for you and Calvin—" he explained, his accent more pronounced the faster he spoke. He sounded different from on the phone.

"Kevin—"

"Yeah, Kevin, was talking." Raul still hadn't put down the gun.

I was about two arm's lengths from him now, staring into his eyes, but watching the Walther. "If you didn't kill her," I said, trying to sound calm, "why do you need my help?"

"Man, I can't go home. And I can't talk to the police, you know? It would be bad, real bad."

"Welcome to my world," I said under my breath. "Why can't you go home?"

He sighed. "It's a long story, stupid and sad. I screwed up when I was a kid, you know? And the cops, man they never forget."

"I seem to have time for a long story. Since I'm not getting any sleep." Or being murdered.

"Oh. Sorry. We're taking your truck. That Chevy's nice, you know. Very slick. We gotta go to my studio."

If I tackled him, the gun would aim toward the ceiling

and I could roll away, then get downstairs. I finally heard him.
"What? Why?"

"Jacob James's studio, actually. He's pretty cool, lets me
use it sometimes."

"The photographer?"

"Yeah. Man, is there another Jacob James?"

"I work with Jacob all the time," I said. "I've never seen
or heard of you before."

Raul sighed. "Sometimes I assist," he said. "But really,
I'm an artist."

"But you moonlight as an assistant?" He wasn't paying
attention to the gun anymore. One—

"Not always at night, sometimes I work in the day," he
said. "But man, we gotta go to the studio. I don't have—"

"Why go there, unless you need to get your gear before
you go on the lam?" I asked, half-sarcastically. My mother
always knew I had no sense. Two—

"No, but I need to get some films I made."

"Ah, for your portfolio? That will be handy in prison."
Two and a half . . . although he outweighed me by at least
sixty pounds.

"No, man. For evidence. I didn't do it, I didn't hurt
Ileana."

He brought me up short at "three." "Evidence, how?" My
stomach rumbled.

"Man, I think I was the last person who saw Ileana alive."

CHAPTER SEVEN

"You are the killer." As the words left my mouth, I dived for his knees, spinning so that my back took the brunt of the impact. I didn't hear the gun go off as I rolled away and clambered down the stairs, crawling and stumbling, hoping I hadn't locked all the locks. I was on the third one, fumbling with the mechanism, when I heard a click.

The safety was off the Walther. "Oh man, you shouldn't have done that," he said. "You gotta be kidding, I was being nice."

"There's nothing nice about holding a gun on someone in her own home," I snarled.

"Step away from the door." His voice had more steel now, and my thoughts of this being a friendly kidnapping vanished. "Man, what I meant was I was the last person, besides the killer, who saw her. I took her picture."

Instantly, I was incredulous. He was a painter, not a photographer. More than that, he was nobody. Even Jacob James, for all his local influence, was a nobody. Ileana was hot stuff, she was the newest face. People like Steven Meisel and Patrick Demarchelier wanted to photograph her. Local boys didn't stand a chance.

But why would Raul lie?

"Turn around," he said. "Slowly."

I did, watching myself in the mirror. This was too unreal. My hair was matted and my skin looked dark in the half-light. Fortunately, "bedhead" and makeupless makeup were good looks—not that it would matter if I were in jail.

"We gotta go. We're gonna be late," he said.

"For what?"

"Because we are breaking into a studio, man. We gotta do it before dawn."

"You've done enough breaking and entering that you know the peak hours?" I asked, as he walked to the door, opening it behind me. "Wait, I don't have any shoes," I said. "I can't go anywhere like this."

He looked at my feet, the Walther unwavering. "This isn't a fashion show," he said.

"No, but it's winter," I said. "You're crazy if you think I'm going barefoot."

Raul swore in Spanish, looking around. "Then wear those, man," he said, pointing to a pair of Anne Klein pumps by an armchair. "They're nice."

"With sweats?"

"Okay, how about those tennis shoes?" he said, pointing to a pair of ancient Stan Smiths.

"They have holes."

"And those?" He pointed to my new Adidas.

"I haven't broken them in."

"Man, you got a lot of shoes," he said, looking around. "Those?"

"They're zebra-print. They don't even match."

"Man, what do you wear with those pants?" He looked out the door. "Wear those tennis shoes," he said, pointing, "or nothing," he said. "C'mon, we gotta go."

I grabbed the Polo sneakers and shoved my feet in—they had no padding. My soles still hurt from running through the studio, so I hoped we weren't going to be doing much walking.

I picked up my bag.

"Drop it," Raul demanded.

"It's my purse," I said. "You're not going to let me take my purse?"

He eyed my oversize Prada backpack skeptically. "Man, what do you carry in there? Weapons or something?"

"No." But by definition of size and weight, it could serve as a weapon.

"You aren't going to pull any other funny stuff on me, are you?"

I hesitated a moment. The safety was still off. "No."

Raul draped a stocky arm around my shoulder, and pressed the gun against my side with his opposite hand. He looked like a very affectionate boyfriend. It was still surreal. A continuation of My Most Bizarre Day.

As I locked the door behind me and walked across my front lawn, I eyeballed my next-door neighbor's house. He always showed up when I looked like death, or when I was running late. Now, now that I needed his meddlesome ways, he was nowhere around. Even the old lady across the street appeared to be sleeping.

Through my flippancy, I was sweating.

"Are you hot?" he asked as he opened the driver's side. "You are perspiring."

I looked over my shoulder as I slid across the leather bench seat. "Some maniac is holding a gun on me," I said. "It tends to test one's antiperspirant." He got in beside me, hit the power locks, then started the engine.

Immediately, country music blasted us. Raul swore, ordering me to turn it down—or better—off. There was little traffic on Greenville Avenue this time of night. It was silent and still, bright with neon. No police. We turned onto Ross, heading downtown. Raul stared out the window as he drove. "You actually listen to that stuff?" he muttered.

"What stuff?"

"Country music. Songs about jails and run-over dogs, and drinking. Man, you really like that?"

"I'm Texan," I said. "I identify with it. At least part of me does."

He glanced at me, and I tried to make out his features in the passing streetlights, so I could pick him out of a lineup later. "You work for The Store and think you can identify with some dude who's lost his job, his girlfriend, and his truck?"

I shrugged. "Not every single song, no. However, a lot of them are about universal things, like love and goodness and wanting to enjoy life."

We turned onto a side street, close to Fair Park, five blocks from Mere Illusion. Any minute now we should see a police cruiser. How could I get its attention, but not wreck my Chevy?

"Man, what does enjoying life mean, you know? How can you know what's good, what you really want." Raul asked. We pulled into a parking lot at the rear of a two-story stucco building. Lights illuminated cargo doors centered on the back wall.

"If you only go around once, shouldn't you enjoy it?" I asked. My God, I was debating philosophies with a kidnapper. Had I lost my mind? "Why are you kidnapping me if you aren't the murderer?" I asked.

Raul unlocked the doors and undid his seat belt. "Man, life is about giving something to your people, you know? They need stuff like art, books, music, medicine." He motioned for me to open my door and slid out behind me.

The gun was still in his hand.

"And family, man," he continued, motioning me forward with the weapon. "Every dude has to have a family. It's the way, you know what I mean?"

Only a psychopath could have a conversation about the meaning of life while holding a gun on someone. I couldn't say anything else. Fear had me by the throat. Raul pulled me close and walked us around the side of the building. JJS was etched on the left window, and steps led up to double doors. To our right were five covered windows.

Raul opened the door, though I didn't hear any keys jingle. He pushed me inside first, holding me in the foyer while he disarmed the alarm system. He produced a flashlight. "Man, are you gonna behave?"

"Yes," I said quickly. I guess he wasn't going to answer my question.

"You promise?"

My hesitation must have been too long, because he unwrapped a few inches of duct tape.

"I can wrap this around you, and you won't have any say anymore, you know?"

Panic filled my throat. "No, no, I'll behave." He turned the flashlight on in my face. "Turn it off," I said. "I'll be good."

"You won't go outside? You won't try to get away? You promise to me?"

What's a promise to a kidnapper? "I promise."

"On the soul of your mother?"

I glared at him. "Whatever."

"Then c'mon," he said, directing me forward. The beam of light focused on a door marked, PRIVATE. As my eyes adjusted, I could see indistinct shapes that might have been furniture, and rectangles on the walls, presumably Jacob James's work.

Raul tucked the gun in the back of his jeans, hidden by his flannel shirt. Now was my chance, but between fear and curiosity, I didn't run.

Again, the door swung open. Again, I hadn't heard keys. Raul pushed me inside, then crossed to a file cabinet and opened it.

From somewhere in the depths of the studio came a muffled thud. "Did you hear anything?" I asked.

"Nada." He had slipped on glasses and was looking through slides, viewing them in front of the flashlight he held in his mouth.

"What did you shoot?" I asked.

"Ileana."

"Not who, what. What kind of film?"

"Oh. Oh, color negative," he said. "It's easier, I'm not

that good; of course you know it's because it's not what I do. I'm an artist."

"Did you do it here?" I asked.

"Yeah, I just used Jacob's setup for lights, you know. She wanted it that way."

I heard a thump somewhere in the back of the studio. "Are you expecting anyone else?" I whispered, standing beside him. "Like Jacob?"

He reached up and turned on a small light. "Man, you gotta be kidding. Jacob's woman wouldn't let him out of bed this early."

Well. That answered one of the questions about the enigmatic Jacob James. I grabbed Raul's cap. "You're blond?" I said in astonishment. "What kind of Cu—"

Another noise. Raul froze, then lifted his head to listen.

"You heard that." I whispered, getting increasingly nervous, putting on Raul's Hilfiger cap.

"The building," he said, now flipping through prints in the drawer, "man, calm down. It's just breathing. Man, old houses in Havana do this all the time."

I inched backward, closer to the door. The only sound was the rustle of paper as Raul searched. Perhaps I could get out the office door? Once out, it was a straight path through the foyer to the door. Were there any locks on this side that would slow me down?

"Don't forget, man," Raul said, glancing over his shoulder as he slammed one drawer shut and moved to the next one. "You promised. So move back, closer to me. In fact," he said, gesturing with the flashlight, "sit there." He pointed to the desk.

"It's o—"

"Sit down, Dallas," he repeated.

I walked to the wheeled chair and sat down, facing Jacob James's desk. It was impressively neat. A blotter, filled with beautiful cursive script, covered the top. Phone numbers, dates, and names were interspersed with animal sketches, logo designs, and diagrams that looked like they were from an engineering text. A free-form Venetian glass platter displayed a collection of shells.

"Did you do that?" Raul asked.

"Do what?"

"Man, don't touch anything."

I deliberately picked up a shell.

"Damn," he said. "They aren't here."

I spun around. "What are you trying to find?"

Raul slammed the cabinet shut, turned off the light, and grabbed my arm as we walked out—he was wearing plastic gloves. When did that happen?

He locked the door behind us, and then we broke into another office. He rifled through those drawers faster. This time I distinctly heard metal on metal from the back of the studio. Cargo doors opening? Should I scream for help?

Dragging me along in the darkness, he opened another door, and we stepped into the smell of chemicals. The darkroom. First he flipped on the red light, then he climbed a ladder to the high shelves where photos were drying. "Wouldn't color negative film be on a contact sheet" I said loudly. At the same time, I wondered if I wanted to be overheard.

He hopped down, a spring of at least six feet. The man must be part cat. "I don't know, it could be slide or print, or contact sheets," he said. "And I—"

The entire building shook as the cargo doors slammed shut. We stood, immobile, listening.

"I don't think we're alone," I whispered.

In seconds a low, rushing whoosh became a crackling roar.

CHAPTER EIGHT

We opened the darkroom door and Raul peeked out; the Walther was in his plastic-covered hands again. My eyes were watering. "What's that burning smell?" I asked. It was hot all of a sudden.

Raul cursed as he pulled me forward. The air was thick and cloudy, filling my lungs. Weird lights and shadows flickered on the ceiling. The crackling sound was louder, underscored by a dull roar.

The studio was on fire.

We dropped to our knees, coughing, crawling forward. I followed him as we moved across the concrete floors. At least they were cool. I tried to breathe through my nose. Tears streamed down my face, and mingled with sweat. Raul stopped and sat up. "Both exits are blocked," he shouted to me. "I'll get the window."

I was blind with tears. Despite having pulled my shirt over my nose and mouth, I was still coughing. Fire was loud. I'd never realized that before. My hair felt wiry, electric. Somewhere in the smoke I heard the smash of glass.

Raul grabbed my arm and pulled me forward. "Watch out for that glass, man!" he shouted.

I couldn't see; only feel. Straddling the window frame, I moved my hands over the edges as I searched for remaining pieces of glass. I stepped onto the outside grass, and had barely lifted my other leg over before Raul jerked me onto the lawn.

Falling to my hands and knees, I gasped at the outdoors, the delicious rain-soaked air. Behind us, the studio was bright with red-and-orange light. Smoke poured from the windows, and flames danced behind it. We were both coughing, spitting black phlegm on the poured-concrete sidewalk. The fire was deafening. Mesmerized, I watched the blaze lick away at the building.

The first rescue vehicle squealed up to the site. White, red, and blue lights strobed the building. Raul grabbed my hand and yanked me to my feet. We ran, or rather he pulled me, to the back, across the parking lot. Fire trucks were pulling up, impeding our way out. Police cars, lights flashing, were forming blockades.

We didn't talk; I got into the driver's side of my truck, keeping my head down. People were shouting around us, but I couldn't discern their words. I gunned the engine and cut over the curb, my tires slick on the road.

Raul was still closing his door as I turned onto the street, racing toward the freeway. No thought, just flight. I drove around a cop car, over the median, and then remembered to turn on my lights. A sharp left curve forced me to swerve to avoid a head-on collision with another police car. The truck fishtailed. I turned into the spin and took an unintentional right, ending up on the freeway's access road.

The police car made a U-turn. We were busted. I slowed down, preparing to pull over. "Drive!" Raul shouted. A split second of hesitation, and his booted foot slammed down on my canvas-covered one, squealing the tires and kicking us onto the entrance ramp. I screamed as his foot crushed mine, and narrowly avoided smashing us against the walls of the overpass. My oh-so-expensive rain tires clung to the road as we screeched around the curve at 80 mph.

"Stay in the right lane," he said, moving back on his side.

No cop cars behind us.

Once on the freeway I drove with my left foot, obeying Raul's directions. Who was this freakin' madman? Where was my head? Why hadn't I tried to get away? Police cars and ambulances and fire trucks, sirens blaring and lights on, all passed us going the other way. In the rearview mirror I could see the plume of smoke from the fire. Jacob James didn't have a studio anymore. I hoped, for his sake, that he had insurance.

"Exit here," Raul said.

Skyscrapers lined the streets as we drove through downtown. The clock on the dash claimed it was six-thirty. The sky was already blue, just a few streaks of dawn remaining.

"Turn left," he said at Reunion Arena. We crossed the viaduct from downtown to Oak Cliff, Dallas's south side, predominantly black, suburb. The road split, and Raul told me to take the right branch.

My stomach growled. "Man, I wasn't expecting that," Raul said. "I never been in a fire before."

"In a set fire," I said darkly.

"Set? What do you mean?" Raul turned to me, his eyes squinted behind his round glasses. I got my first real look at him and swerved.

I'd been kidnapped by a geeked-out Ricky Martin.

"Be careful," he said.

I looked at him again from the corner of my eye. Square jaw, white teeth, firm lips . . . and light-skinned. Maybe twenty-two. "You're Cuban?" I blurted out.

"My father's Cuban. My mother's German." We drove a moment in silence. "You think the fire was on the set?"

This guy should be in front of the camera, not doing backdrops. "No, I think the fire was set," I said.

"I don't understand."

"Planned," I said. "It was on purpose." I glanced at him; he was frowning. "I thought I heard someone in the studio. Don't you remember? I kept asking if you heard noises."

"You gotta be kidding me. Man, we should have smelled something," he said. "Gas or chemicals."

"We did, they just all belonged there," I said. Studios were filled with combustible stuff. I drove in silence for a few minutes. "These pictures you took of Ileana. When was that?"

He turned to me, still frowning. "Maybe last weekend, maybe a few days before."

"Ileana was here last weekend?" Why hadn't she called me, at least to cancel leasing my duplex? "This past weekend, like four days ago, or the weekend before?"

"The weekend before."

"Have you told the police?"

"No. No police."

"But their investigation, they don't know when—"

"No police."

My little sister had the same emphatic "no." When she said it, it meant neither hell nor high water was going to convince her. I wondered how to get around Raul's no.

"Yeah, you know it was kinda weird. I was supposed to get the film, then we were gonna get together, you know, look at it."

"So you had the film? Then why were we looking for it at Jacob's?"

He seemed to almost hunch his shoulders. "Man, I'm a little, uh, I don't have cash right now."

Ah, he wouldn't have been able to get the film back from the lab.

"I think I left it in an envelope that Jacob made, you know, with his address and phone and stuff on it," he said.

"Did you ask Jacob if he has it?"

"Not really, no," he muttered.

"Why not? You work for him. That would certainly be easier than . . . this," I said, brushing at the soot on my arms.

"Man, I just didn't," he said. "Lay off me, you know."

I slammed on the brakes. "I've had it with your non-answers. What is going on?"

"I don't want Jacob to know," he said. "Man, it wouldn't be cool."

"Oh, that is so much clearer now." I stamped on the gas and screeched through the green light. "So you left the film in the studio, Jacob got it developed, picked it up, and now you don't know where it is."

He shrugged.

I stopped for another red light. "Ileana never called you after the shoot?"

"No."

"Tell me again, how did you end up working with her," I asked. This should be good.

"She heard about me, and she said she kinda had a thing for Cuba, you know? Anyway, I had this idea, and I needed a model to do some testing. So, she called me—"

"She called you? From where? When?"

"Man I don't know, but here, I think. Something about Duchesse."

"When?"

"It was a Sunday," he said. "More or less."

I wanted to scream. What was more or less Sunday?

"So I called her back, 'cuz I was outta town when she called. I wanted to do some testing, and she said she had some stuff she wanted to do, so we'd just trade, you know? Like friends."

"Where was she staying?"

"I don't know, but I have the number."

I glanced over. He wasn't holding the gun on me anymore. And I was driving. Now was the time for my getaway.

Except for a few things. Raul, even though he knew how to get into and out of locked buildings, or hold a gun, was no murderer. Though I had nothing except my instinct for confirmation.

It was quiet for a moment as we sat through light after light. "Doesn't it seem coincidental?" I asked.

"What?"

"That the film you want is missing, and that you get caught in a fire at the same time?"

"The film isn't missing, I just don't know where they are."

"That's called missing."

"No. Misplaced." He looked at me, flashed a smile. "English is a very detailed language, you know? Missing and misplaced are not the same."

I wanted to growl. "Doesn't the timing strike you as odd, then?" I asked, making sure my words were exactly what I wanted them to say.

"Man, if someone wants to hurt you, fire is a stupid way. I mean, just get a gun."

"True," I said. "So maybe it was just to scare you?"

"Or you," he said, looking at me.

"Either way, someone was there," I said. "They set that fire, knowing we were inside."

"Man, I think it was just a mistake, you know," he said after a moment. "Really."

"Are we going anywhere in particular, or just driving in circles?" I asked, as we waited for the millionth red light.

"Man, do you know anyone who lives around here?"

Gary did, but he wasn't home. "No."

"I'm hungry. I have money, too."

Just not enough to get your film back, I thought.

"Let's eat," he said.

We pulled into a diner with a packed parking lot, which was always a good sign. His stomach growled. "C'mon, I'll buy you breakfast. Just please, don't do anything. We'll just eat, call a truce."

I was ravenous and mystified—but he wasn't the enemy. "Yeah, okay."

We spent a few minutes dusting each other off, trying to look as smoke-free as possible. Ozarka water from my bag rinsed our faces and hands. We were a little smoky, but presentable.

It was a shabby, local hangout, and we were the only

white people. I pulled my baseball cap lower. The smell of frying bacon wafted from the kitchen, down the narrow aisles, over the old, autographed framed photos, to the antique cash register. We blended with the bacon.

A mirrored bar covered the front wall, booths lined the other two walls, and tables for four filled the floor. We followed the waitress to a booth with patched Naugahyde seats and a Formica tabletop. She filled two cups of coffee before she even said hello.

Televisions blared from three different places, one on ESPN, one on a local station, and one on CNN. We were both doctoring our coffees when the top of the hour news came on.

"A four-alarm fire this morning in Deep Ellum still blazes out of control," the newscaster said. Raul and I stared at each other, hardly breathing, listening. "The building, in the 3700 block of Main, caught fire at approximately 6 A.M. Unconfirmed sources say arson suspects were seen fleeing the scene." From the TV we heard the sound of sirens, and fire.

"Two suspects were seen fleeing the scene. This man and woman—" I couldn't help it, I looked up at the TV. "Ohmigod," I whispered and immediately ducked my head. "—are wanted for questioning."

I ripped off the baseball cap and whispered to Raul. "It's us."

CHAPTER NINE

"Are y'all ready to order?" the dreadlocked waitress asked, her expression bored but pleasant. Thankfully her back was to the TV. Somehow the cameras had caught me and Raul: his plaid shirt, and my fleeing figure. At least my hair was covered. The waitress waited, pen and pad in her purple-manicured hands.

This was perfect: I was probably a murder suspect and now wanted for questioning regarding arson. Cops, just exactly who I wanted to tangle with.

"Uh, what is your special?" Raul asked, his head averted from her. I needed to give him the baseball cap.

"Three eggs, choice of meat, grits, and Texas toast," she said mechanically.

Had the restaurant quieted, or was that my imagination?

Were they looking at us? I was sweating as I swigged half my coffee.

We were a long way from the front door.

"Uh, that sounds good," Raul said.

"How do you want your eggs?"

"Scrambled. No, no, could you poach them? You boil the water, swirl the egg—like you have with eggs Benedict."

"Sure," she said. "And for you, ma'am?"

"Great," I said. I didn't care about food. I just wanted out of here. We were on TV! Oh my God, my family was going to find out.

"Country fried steak, bacon, or boudain?" she asked Raul.

"Steak," he said.

"You, ma'am?"

"Same," I said, drinking the rest of my coffee in one nervous gulp. I'd never ordered steak in my life. How had we gotten caught on tape? Especially so late—or early, depending on perspective. I didn't remember any lights, but maybe the fire had been bright enough. Obviously it had, Dallas.

"Would you care for more coffee?" It was a different waitress. I nodded and set my mug down. She refilled it and walked away.

"How did they get film of us?" I whispered as I reached for the sugar. "Put on the cap." I pushed it toward him.

"Uh-oh," Raul said under his breath. "Don't look up."

How on earth did the media get there so fast? I tried to run my hand through my hair, but it was too matted.

"Howdy, Officer," one person said behind me. A cop. Ah, hell.

I glanced back to see an older black gentleman wearing

a pressed shirt, houndstooth fedora, and plaid pants with two-tone wingtip golf shoes.

"Hey, Harry. How ya doin'?" I heard the booming response.

"Mighty fine. Can't complain," Harry said.

"Mornin', Monty. You lookin' might' debonair this mornin'. Where you goin'?" our waitress asked the officer.

Purposeful steps came closer.

"Just comin' here to see your pretty face," he said, laughing.

"Well while you are swoonin' over me, can I get your usual?"

"Please, pretty girl."

"More coffee?"

I looked up. Our waitress, carrying a fresh carafe of coffee in her hand, was staring at me. "More coffee?" she repeated.

I'd drunk another whole cup and not realized it. "Uh, please," I stammered.

She brushed by the policeman, who was middle-aged, black, fit, and standing a foot away. He could catch me easily. Our gazes met, and he smiled and nodded his head. "Mornin', ma'am."

"Good morning," I said automatically. His glance slid to Raul and then the cop turned to an older gentleman in Dickey's coveralls and cap, sitting with his back to us.

Our waitress placed our food in front of us: scrambled eggs, grits, batter-covered steak, and enormous pieces of bread, fried in butter. She put little bottles of Tabasco, ketchup, and Worcestershire on the table. "Anything else?"

I looked at Raul, who was looking at his eggs with dismay. He opened his mouth, and I kicked him under the table. This was not the time to call more attention to ourselves. He shook his head, and she walked away. Over the sound of my heart pounding, I heard the policeman talking to the man at the table behind us. On the news, they had moved to another story. I pulled my grits toward me and salted them.

"Buddy, how're you this morning?" the cop asked.

"Fine, fine," the coverall-wearing man said.

"You plannin' on stoppin' by the service station anytime soon?"

There was a pause. "I know you wouldn't be askin' me if there wasn't a reason."

"Inspection sticker, Buddy. You're a month past due." The officer shook his head, his hand on the man's shoulder. "It wouldn't be good to get caught without it."

"Thank ya for remindin' me. I'll get that taken care of right away. Right after I finish my coffee."

"Well, don't rush that good coffee, Buddy, but do get it done real soon."

"Thank ya, Monty. Thanks mighty bunch."

The officer walked by again, touched the brim of his hat, and I heard him sit down at the counter. Raul's plate was almost clean, so I slid him mine. We had to get out of here.

"That reminds me," Raul said, pouring sugar into his coffee, "I need to get my inspection sticker, too."

I looked up at him. How could he be so normal? We were wanted criminals. On TV no less. And here we sat, not three feet away from a cop. In the same clothes!

"That's why we have your Chevy," he said, then shoved my eggs into his mouth. "At least, it's one of the reasons. Man, is that all you're going to eat?"

"You know the number where Ileana was staying, when

she was here before?" I whispered. He nodded. I glanced at my watch. "We need to go there," I said.

"I know the number, man. I just don't know where it is."

The downtown library would be open at nine. "I will, but we have to leave here first." Without getting caught.

Paying the bill meant standing six inches away from the cop, who was cheerfully eating cobbler and drinking milk at the luncheon counter. He could see the whole restaurant in the mirror. Did he see the little glass shards on Raul's cap?

"Are you ready to go, then?" Raul asked. I nodded, and we stood up, walking to the cashier. Not only were we the only whites, now we were the only people under fifty, except for the cop. Terrified of anyone recognizing my profile, or seeing my face, I kept my head ducked and shoulders hunched.

The cashier took the twenty from Raul, looking at him. "Do I know you from somewhere?" she asked.

Raul chuckled nervously. "Been to any local galleries recently?"

"You an artist?" she asked, slowly trickling change into Raul's palm.

He shrugged as she counted the singles. Slowly.

"What kind of art?"

I was about to scream a confession, any confession, just from tension.

"This and that," he said, taking her hand and dumping a single and the change back into it. "For the waitress." He took my arm, smiled at the cop, and the two of us strolled out, looking like lovers.

"I'll drive," he said, holding a hand out for the keys.

"They're in the truck," I said.

"Man, you should be careful, you know. Someone could steal them."

I ignored him. Advice from a fellow suspected felon.

We got in silently, and he pulled out of the parking lot and into the stream of traffic. The clock read 7:44.

"I'm real sorry. I didn't realize this would become such a big mess."

"Oh no, it was just going to be a friendly kidnapping, breaking and entering, arson, wanted by the police kind of scheme, but your plan went awry? What the hell is going on? You show up with a dead body and a knife. You run from the police. They don't even believe me that you exist! We break into the studio to steal something, photos or whatever, it catches on fire, and we're suspected of setting it. Twenty-four hours ago I was a normal person with a normal life. Now I'm wanted by the law—for two felonies!" My brother would be so proud.

"I'm real sorry," he said, turning back toward the viaduct that would return us to the city. "Just drop me off at the bus station and I'll . . . vanish. It's not your concern."

"They are splashing my photo on TV," I said. "With you. Believe me, it's my concern."

"Maybe nobody saw it."

I pulled my phone out of my purse. "Thank God I don't have to be at work today," I said as I dialed.

"You have the day off? That's good." He looked over at me. "Who you calling?"

"My answering machine—to see if anyone has noticed I'm missing," I snapped.

I dialed my number and listened in shock to the assortment of messages. I pressed the END button and put it carefully into my bag. "You were wrong about nobody watching it."

He turned onto Main Street. "Man, why do you say that?"

"Because my creative director wants me to call him about my 'extracurricular activities' as soon as possible."

"You're kidding me. Okay, man, I'll just get out at the bus station," he said. "It's on the way."

"Wait a minute," I said. "Who is going to clear my name if you go?" I asked. "You're my only alibi. You know that we didn't set the fire, or kill Ileana." Just saying it made me squeamish.

"The films are my only alibi," Raul said, weaving his way through downtown's one-way streets. "I think I'll just slip out of here on the bus."

"You can't leave me like this," I protested. "And leaving isn't going to help you either." We pulled up to the Greyhound station, and Raul unbuckled his seat belt. "Wait," I said, laying a hand on his knee. "Look."

A squad car was parked across the street. As we watched, a policeman approached a Hispanic teen in a plaid shirt. He laid a hand on the boy's shoulder and withdrew his badge. "You aren't going anywhere by bus," I said. "Let's get out of here."

"Where am I going?" he asked.

"The main library," I said. "And I'm driving." I glanced at the clock; it wouldn't be open for at least a half hour. I handed him my Nokia, then we crawled across each other to trade seats. He kept dialing Ileana's phone number, and I braced myself to speak to someone about her. As we drove around downtown, killing time and wasting gasoline, we got the same response, again and again:

Busy signal.

When they unlocked the library's doors, I was the first person to slip by the drunks and panhandlers to get inside. Once there I went to the reference section. Within minutes, I was back outside. "Did you ever get her on that line?" I asked.

"All the time. Now where?"

"It's not listed, and it's still busy," I said. Technology was outpacing the reverse directory. He drove the same loop we'd been following for an hour. "So you need to find the film, to prove you didn't do it," I mused.

"Yes."

"And I need you to testify that I didn't do it."

"You could have," he said. "You could have done it before I got there." He looked at me. "In fact you might have, and that's why you changed the time we were meeting." He looked genuinely concerned.

"Oh please," I said. "You can't really believe that." He was silent. "The film," I asked after a moment. "How can it help?"

"It proves my innocence."

"How?"

"Just trust me."

That's rich, coming from a would-be kidnapper. I tried another angle. "Who was it for?"

"Ileana, I think."

"Did she see the Polaroids?"

"Yeah, she liked them."

"Did she seem worried or anything out of the ordinary?" I asked. "I mean, was her face broken out, had she been crying—" I had no idea what I was looking for, maybe some sense that she knew she was in trouble. Ah Ileana, I sighed.

"No man, she was great. Laughed, smiled, we had a great time, you know."

I sighed and tried to figure out what was going on. I could really use Leo's wits about now. Where the hell was he? I was getting angry with my friend; when you call and beg someone to call you back ASAP, you expect them to do it, not just leave a message. "So you think Jacob picked up the film?" I asked. "That's why we went through Jacob's office and darkroom?"

"Yeah, maybe it's at Jacob's house."

"And why aren't we just asking him, flat out?"

Raul looked at me. "Man, would you talk to people who had burned down your studio?"

"But we didn't! We were . . . just there," I finished lamely. "So he has a home office," I asked a moment later. "What about the labs? Have you called around?"

"You think I'm stupid? Man, of course I called other labs. First I went to the lab we usually use, in Deep Ellum. They didn't have film for JJS, or me."

"Maybe Ileana picked it up?"

"Man, I don't think so. Once she was back to looking like herself, you know, she was outta there."

"And why is this film so important, I ask for the ninety-fifth time?"

"It proves I couldn't have done it. We have to find it, otherwise . . ."

"Otherwise you have fingerprints on the knife and I have opportunity and means?"

He flashed a green gaze at me. "You said it, *chica.*"

We were bumper-to-bumper on Main—I had time to make some decisions. "You were doing a test, you said?"

"Yes."

I watched him change lanes, checking his mirrors and over his shoulder at least three times. "Are you going to tell me what you were testing? Lighting? Makeup? New gear, what?"

"A new idea."

"Which was what?"

"Man, I gotta keep my secrets, you know."

"You sound like a petulant three-year-old," I said. "Exit here. What kind of new idea?"

"My idea."

"I'm not even a photographer," I said. "You can tell me."

"Mixing art and photography," he said darkly.

I had the feeling that was all I was going to get out of him on the subject. "And she did this for you from love because y'all had worked together before?" Sarcasm dripped off the dashboard as we joined the traffic heading east through Dallas.

"I told you, we traded," he said. "It was her idea."

"Talking to you is like trying to find a live armadillo," I groused. "What, exactly, did she have you shoot?"

"Old stuff, what's the word, vintage. It was in hatboxes, you know, old ones. She had this big hat with flowers, a jeweled necklace, a white shawl-thing. It was very cool stuff."

Traffic was stopped. "Could you draw me a picture?" I said, pulling out my notepad. With a few simple strokes he showed a light-haired woman, with heavy eye makeup and light coming from the left, highlighting the angle of her cheekbone. We moved with the stop-and-start traffic and I stared at the drawing. There was something familiar. . . .

"Now, add flowers," I said. Raul took the picture back and put a sixties-style bridesmaid's hat, with daisies around the crown, on the woman. Then he sketched in a peasant blouse, slightly off the shoulder.

We moved forward with the traffic, and I stared at the drawing, asking him to tell me about the colors, the other props. As he spoke of the rhinestone dog-collar necklace, the hand-knitted shawl, they took form and shape in my mind, moving from imagination to memory. I sat upright, my heart pounding. "You have this picture with light hair. Was Ileana's hair burgundy when you did this test?"

"Yes. She had a wig. She was blond. Hot, hot, hot, you know what I'm talking about?"

"She never called you back after this? Didn't you think that was weird?"

"Models, you know. They can go out of town in a minute, so no, I didn't," he said. "I think we should go to Jacob's house. Maybe that's where the films is—are."

"At least you know they weren't burned up in the fire," I said. "What about the Polaroids? The makeup artist, the hairstylist."

"It was just us. She did her own makeup and hair."

"That's weird," I said. Blond, a hat with flowers. So between doing that and showing up on my set, she had her hair done, from blond to red. "Is Jacob home?"

"No, man, I don't think so. Probably filling out insurance forms and stuff," he said. I winced; how could I have forgotten about his studio? Poor guy.

"But I have the key," Raul said.

"Okay, we'll go to Jacob's."

* * *

Jacob James lived in one of the hidden treasure troves of Dallas: the Peninsula on White Rock Lake. Cape Cod houses, tucked behind flowering bushes and beneath towering trees, made this part of Dallas seem lush and green. We passed three cottages, then Raul told me it was the house with the feng shui red door. "Pull up in back," he said. "That's where his home office is."

"Are you sure he won't mind us being here?" I asked, though I was really thinking, are you sure he won't shoot us if he finds us here. Despite working with Jacob a lot, I still didn't know five things about him. He was the type of person who deflected questions about himself and drew the other person out, all the while seeming to tell endless, entertaining stories. Not mysterious, but reserved.

Raul shrugged, a response that didn't fill me with confidence.

"Who's here?" I asked, as I pulled up the front driveway. A brand new Mercedes 230 SLK roadster, in taxi yellow, blocked a Porsche convertible in the open, three-car garage. Two mountain bikes, a motorcycle, and a collection of skateboards were piled up in the other space.

"I don't know," Raul said, peering forward to look at the Mercedes. "Man, isn't that sweet? I guess Jacob bought a new car, you know. Business is good."

"Sure, everyone needs three vehicles," I said, throwing my truck in park. "Do you think he's here?"

"No, he's in the SUV," Raul said. "He comes up the back way, so we'll have plenty of time to get out the front. But really, he won't mind." We got out and Raul led me to the outside stairs of a smaller, half-Cape-styled building. "Upstairs is a loft," he said. "The office is down here."

He unlocked the door, and we stepped into an obsessively neat space, decorated solely in black and white. A darkroom took up the back half of the room, opposite a wrought-iron staircase that spiraled to the loft. "I can find it in just a minute," Raul said, kneeling before some filing cabinets. "You can go watch for his car from upstairs," he said. "But really, he won't mind."

I had a big picture of the intensely private Jacob James "not minding" we were ransacking his home, but I said nothing. Climbing the stairs, I emerged in a cozy loft, the harsh black and white exchanged for a warm gray-and-lavender palette. The walls were weathered, as though they were taken from New England, the quilts on the futon were handmade. A collection of carved seabirds was shelved on one wall, opposite a tiny all-white kitchen.

A lavender terry-cloth robe was draped across a stool, in front of a makeshift vanity. A bottle of Joy, just taken from its box, sat beside a silk tie and pair of pearl studs. Who was living here, I wondered. A man? A woman? A cross-dresser?

"Man, you see anyone?" Raul called up.

"No. Why?"

"I just thought I heard a car door," he said.

I dodged to the window, and looked out over the backyard. The huge garden was half-weeded, and a track led through it to the back side of the garage and the front door of this building—presumably Jacob's other road. Slightly to my left was a little desk, with phone, fax machine, and computer. I glanced out the window. No one was outside. "How's it going?" I called to Raul.

"Man, I just can't think where he would have put it," Raul shouted back. "Jacob is so precise."

We'd been in the house almost ten minutes. I leaned against the window, wondering why Ileana had sneaked into town and not told anyone. Had she stayed at a hotel? Why keep it a secret at all? Damn Leo for this silent routine. He wasn't the only one grieving, and I could use some answers.

I wandered back to the dresser and picked up the tie. Something, wrapped up in it, clunked onto the table. A cursory glance showed the tie was Armani, apparently a sample. It had been folded around a mini-cassette recorder. Without thinking, I pressed the Play button, and listened.

"(Garble) we need to talk. I have to get out of town for (garbled) but the (garbled, garbled). Anyway, I will be out of touch, but I need to see you. Soon."

My body went icy cold, and I rewound and played it again, looking around the room with a different eye. This was Leo's voice. In fact, it was the message he'd left me. Who had been staying here? Who wore Joy and pearl studs? What did they have to do with a man's tie? I turned it on the third time, listening to the message, until the sound of gravel caught my attention. An Infiniti SUV was heading up the back road. "Come on," I said racing down the stairs and running through the studio. "He's here."

While at Micky D's, because Raul had had too much coffee, I called my machine.

I had three new calls. Damon wanted to know where I was. Apparently Gary hadn't mentioned he'd given me the day off.

My mother wanted to know if it was the beefsteak tomatoes or the Roma tomatoes that made the best mozzarella salad. The third call mystified me.

"Hello, I'm from Lost Luggage, calling about three suitcases from American Airlines flight number three-one-one from New York. These bags have been unclaimed for two weeks. They have no name. However they were addressed with 2220 Madrid Street, Dallas. If we receive no return phone call within three days, this luggage will be declared unclaimed and the contents confiscated. Please call."

New York? With my street address and no name? I was mystified.

I called Lost Luggage, got their address, and when Raul got back in the Chevy from his pit stop, I was sitting in the driver's seat, still baffled. He buckled his belt, and asked what was next.

"We're going to pick up some luggage," I said.

"That's really nice," he said, "but I have luggage, you know. Not the great kind of stuff that you would take in first-class, but good enough for the bus station."

I glanced at him as I headed toward Central, to go north. "What on earth are you talking about?"

"I don't need new luggage," he said. "Though, if you have a few more twenties, I could use them."

"This isn't for you," I said. "We're looking for clues."

"Where?"

"In someone else's luggage."

"Oh. What are we looking for?"

I didn't know. I was making it up as I went. "We'll know it when we find it." I cranked up Brooks & Dunn and headed to 183 and Beltline, the home of Lost Luggage. "Oh man, are we going to Irving?" he said, enthusiastically. "There is the little restaurant, and man, they make the best churros. I didn't eat any lunch. Can we stop there, maybe?"

Oh to have the metabolism of a twenty-two-year-old.

The setting sun coming in through my front-bedroom windows poured rosy light over the items laid on the floor: the contents of Ileana Karagonis's three suitcases. Models, the way I figured it, had to live like pod people. Anything and everything the person might need, the person had to carry.

First there was the travel uniform: jeans, white T-shirt, jacket, and a small zippered bag with necessities like cold cream, lotion, nail file, eyelash curler, tanning cream, Handi-wipes, sunblock, Carmex, and a crushable hat. That Ileana had gone anywhere without her necessities bag was ominous.

Then there were the electronics: CD player and head-phones, five CDs ranging from Phil Collins to the Spice Girls; Sky Pager, and Pokémon.

She had her portfolio, vouchers, national gym member-ship card, Polaroids, passport, comp cards, and phone card in one slick bag, with water, Donna Karan mules, another hat and her sunglasses on the other side of it.

So far, her luggage could have belonged to any of a hun-dred different girls. Then there was the small photo album with pictures of a chubby-cheeked, dark-eyed baby smiling at the camera. Then pictures of Ileana with her mom and the whole Greek clan of Karagonises. My eyes filled. Little Kalista would never want for anything, but she would never know how Ileana had fought tooth and toenail to give birth to her and rear her.

I rubbed my eyes, staring at the stuff. Not a clue in sight.

The Polaroids were from last year; Ileana had gotten her

hair cut since then. All her vouchers, which are how the models get paid, were in order, ending when she booked herself out. But there was no Palm Pilot or other form of calendar, or any credit cards. Even her driver's license was missing.

"I wonder where her cell phone is," Raul said. "The number just goes straight to voice mail."

I sat bolt upright. "Voice mail! Maybe that's the key. Maybe that will give us an idea—" as I was speaking, I was reaching for the phone. Raul dialed and held the phone away from his ear, so we could both hear.

"Welcome to AT&T wireless services. The customer you have called is unavailable or has traveled outside the coverage area—" He hung up. "She mustn't have paid her phone bill after all."

I looked at him, puzzled. "Or it could be the battery died after . . . however many days of no juice," I said. "Besides, why wouldn't she pay her phone bill?"

"She was having money troubles, you know."

"On a salary of five to ten grand a day?"

He flashed green eyes at me. "When you make good money, you spend good money."

Heroin was the most obvious way I could think of to spend money that fast, but a habit of Manolo Blahnik and Giorgio Armani would also do the trick. Having not made good money in quite a while, I didn't know any of the current toys for the rich and famous.

"So now what?" Raul asked.

Since I had the phone in my hand, I dialed Leo again. Lindsay hadn't seen him in days, which wasn't unusual, but I hated to think of him alone and mourning. We'd been to a lot of funerals together—I needed him in order to make this one. I hung up when I got to his machine, since there was no more room for messages.

The phone rang in my hand, but I decided to screen the call.

"Dallas, it's me. The usual suspects are at Stefano's at nine. See you."

The so-called usual suspects are my best friends. We're all in the business; Lindsay's a booker, Coco is makeup and hair, Julie is a model; we're all tall, straight, divorced, and thirtysomething. Except for Lindsay, who is bi, extremely starry-eyed about marriage because she's never done it, and five-three.

Straddling Cedar Springs gay neighborhood on one side, and crack houses on the other, Stefano's had once been a respectable bar. Now it was filled with garage-sale furniture and lamps, a pool table, the tackiest rooftop bar in the city, with a dollar well and wine drinks. It was our favorite dive. They didn't serve food, nor was it a hangout for the beautiful people, though they crashed in from time to time, leaving a wake of limo air-conditioning and expensive cigar smoke.

"Was that Coco's voice?" Raul asked.

"You know Coco?"

"I painted her house."

"Inside or out?"

"Both, actually."

"The fresco?"

A year or so ago, a Florentine phase had overtaken a lot of the people I knew. Suddenly everyone wanted their ceilings painted with stylized Italian motifs. I'd escaped, but only because fat little cherubs made me feel guilty about eating Häagen-Dazs, even standing over the sink.

"The angels, yeah man. Those were mine."

"Oh. Well, uh—"

"But I don't want to crowd into your party," he said, turning away to look at Ileana's things again. "I'll just wait—"

"No, you won't," I said decisively. "We're going to Stefano's; just let me change clothes."

After trading my sweats for black pants, turtleneck, and leather jacket, we walked out the back to my parked truck.

Stefano's was packed with bikers, cross-dressers, SMU students, and a few philosophy-discussing artists and writers. We bought our wine, and the bottle, and traipsed upstairs to the rooftop bar.

Dallas is miserable in the summer, but for the rest of the year you can live outside. In January, we drive around with our convertible tops down. You can dine on the patio in almost any restaurant year-round. Running, riding, sailing, these are all things that are most popular in winter and spring.

March, the coldest month, was being unseasonably pleasant. I unzipped my Armani—gift from my grandmother—jacket as we climbed the stairs.

The group had overtaken the roof. Coco and Lindsay were there, but Julie was missing. There were also a few additions: some photo assistants, another makeup artist whom I didn't know, and, surprisingly enough, Jacob James.

After the customary cheek kissing and hugs, Jacob rose and pulled a chair out for me, then Raul and I sat down. Jacob didn't say a word about his studio to either of us. As a group, we raised a silent toast to Ileana, then the gossip began. I felt very awkward, sitting next to the man whose studio had burned to the ground. While I was, however reluctantly, present. I was sure he had seen the television footage.

"How are you doing?" he asked. "I understand Ileana was a friend of yours?"

The conversation, speculation about Ileana's loves and ambitions, continued on around us. Raul watched silently, which surprised me. "She was," I said.

"Were you two close?"

I couldn't see Jacob's eyes in this light, but I felt the intensity of his focus on me. It was a little nerve-racking. "I didn't know she was in town, so I would say no," I said, surprised at how not being close enough for her to confide in, hurt. "Leo was both her agent and friend. They were very close. But Gary was closer still."

Jacob shifted, jostling my wine. "Sorry," he said, touching my hand.

"No problem." We listened to the conversation around us, but I was intensely aware of him, though he appeared very calm, he seemed honed in on something, hyperaware. Did Raul notice? I glanced at him, but he was talking to Coco, and I recognized a few Sherwin Williams paint names thrown about. Maybe it was time to replace the angels fresco?

"So she was closest to Gary? He was her dearest confidant?" Jacob asked, sipping at his wine. He was drinking blush, something I would have never guessed of him.

"In the course of her career, yes," I said. "Leo discovered her, but Gary was the one who saved her life."

"Right. Back in '98?"

"Yes." It had happened right after she'd been on the cover of three international *Vogues*—Ileana had cracked, attempting suicide through an overdose. Her boyfriend at the time, a one-hit wonder pop star, had freaked out. Rather than call 911, he'd called Gary.

From the set of his shoot, Gary had made sure the police, ambulance, and Leo arrived. They took her to the most exclusive and highest-rated rehab ward in the country. And didn't let her out until she was clean of drugs, alcohol, and the depression that was slowly eating her alive.

She'd emerged happier, clean, and six months pregnant.

Gary and Leo had shipped her to some relatives to have the baby. Then when she refused to place the child for adoption, they had convinced her to at least leave Kalista with her family, who had finally gotten around to forgiving her. Since then she had worked clean and hard, doing any and everything to provide for her child.

"I heard a rumor that she was getting ready to sign an exclusive contract," he said.

One of the group jumped in. "I heard the same thing. She was going to take the Diva's, oh sorry Jacob, April's, position at Duchesse."

"Yeah, ever since the takeover, they've been going for a different demographic," someone said. "Out with the old and in with the new."

Jacob seemed to grow a little bit stiffer—after all, he was April's friend.

"I don't know," Coco said. "She looks incredible for her age. Hell, she'd be incredible if she were my age! To be that thin, move like that. Wow. I can't imagine. She just needs to get more sleep, protect her eyes so the blood vessels don't break."

"That's not from rough living," Jacob said. "It's a freckle."

"In her eye, the white part?" Coco asked. "Are you serious?"

He nodded. "Just turn her a little to the left, and I bet no one here has ever even noticed. April is excellent at what she does, and she takes good care of herself," he said. "No one can be responsible for every little genetic blip. It shouldn't matter."

The whole table sat in uncomfortable silence for a moment. Jacob rose. "Well, I think I will be saying good night. Thank you for inviting me to your little soiree." He rose, throwing his denim jacket over his Eddie Bauer shirt. We all wished him well and waited until he'd gone downstairs before speaking again.

"Do you think we offended him?"

"I don't know, but I do know that he and April are pretty tight."

"Poor guy, it was his studio that burned to the ground today. On top of Ileana, man. . . ."

"Was he involved with her?"

"April or Ileana?"

"Man, April does have amazing genes," someone else said. "I wonder why she hasn't had children. Who wouldn't want to continue those chromosomes? Man, if they weren't so old, she and Jacob could have beautiful kids."

We all agreed: April was almost genetically perfect. At five-eleven, lean, though still a full B cup, with naturally wavy hair, porcelain skin and exquisite bones, she was staggeringly beautiful. Clothes draped her body perfectly, whether they were Kmart or Korshak. If she were less demanding, she could have been the biggest model, maybe ever.

"It must be sad to be that old and not have anything

else," one of the youngest women said. "I mean, she bypassed a family and husband for her career, and now . . . well," she shrugged.

"So was he involved with Ileana?"

"I don't know," Coco said. "She wouldn't work with him at all, lately. I heard Duchesse was going to have to let him go if they signed her."

"That makes no sense," I said. "I thought they were great friends. He did a ton of her book."

My friend shrugged. "Ileana could be weird."

"Why was she in town early?" someone else asked.

"Maybe she just got to the studio that morning and ran into the serial killer or something."

"That's comforting," someone else said.

"She didn't make her flight, at least that's what I heard," a woman offered.

"Because she was already here, maybe? Where's Leo, he should have some answers," someone said to Lindsay.

I finished my wine in one gulp as I met Lindsay's gaze across the table. What was the deal with Leo?

We got back to my house about one-thirty. After we'd dissected Ileana and April, Jacob had become the topic of conversation. No one really knew much about him, other than he was charming, attractive, and a damned good photographer. Where he was from, what his family was like, no one knew. "He's just one of those people who never answers a question directly," one of the assistants, a female, said. She'd asked him out, and he'd refused her, but continued to be friendly.

He certainly lived well, I thought, remembering the Porsche and new Mercedes. Very well.

Raul checked the lock on the front door, then stood in my living room, tinted by the shades of glass in my table lamp. Oh yeah, he needed a place to sleep. "Let me get you some blankets," I said. "The downstairs futon is really comfortable."

"I don't guess, no, probably not," Raul said.

I was tired and slightly—okay more than slightly—tipsy. "You don't guess what?"

"That I could stay with you?"

"You are staying with me," I pointed out.

"No, in your be—"

"No way," I said, cutting him off. He might be gorgeous, and even Latin, but he was a minute older than jailbait. And blond.

"Okay."

I turned to walk up the stairs. "I'll throw the linens down to you."

"Okay. Good night."

"Good night, Raul."

CHAPTER TEN

"Dallas, you're on TV."

I bolted up, staring at the blond man at the threshold of my bedroom.

"C'mon, wake up," he said. "They are showing you on TV."

As I staggered downstairs, pulling on a robe and tying on a neck scarf, my grandmother's litany went through my head: "Fool's names and fool's faces often wind up in public places." She never wanted her fifteen minutes of fame—and I was beginning to understand why.

I got downstairs just as they were finishing the segment and returning to the studio, for the top of the hour. I needed to hop in the shower. "What did it say?"

"They were enacting the past few days," he said, not looking at me. "You never told me Ileana stole from you."

I felt my face go ashen. "What did they say?"

"That years ago she took $50,000 from your savings account and the two of you had a falling-out, and that she refused to be on any shoot where you were."

I straightened the scarf at my throat and tightened the sash of my Polo robe, not looking at him.

"They think that is a good motive for murder."

Turning on my heel, I climbed the few steps to the kitchen. I would have liked a straight shot of whiskey, but I'd settle for an extra creamy hazelnut latte and some of Leo's croissants. I had just poured the freshly ground beans into the coffeemaker when the telephone rang.

Caller ID—the Dallas Police Department. The dripping of the coffee was the backdrop to Diana Mansfield asking me to call in, she had a few more questions.

The telephone rang again. Gary.

"You're popular this morning, darling," he said. "All three networks are showing you. Seems they've dug up that old chestnut."

"Tell me about it," I said, pouring my fresh coffee into the cup and lowering the heat of the warming milk. Where had the media gotten hold of Leo and why had he talked to them? How could he have betrayed my confidence? I tensed my jaw. Leo had a lot to answer for whenever he deigned to call back.

"I just got in, I'm headed to The Store. But Dallas, I think it's a bad idea for you to show today, what with the news and all."

He was silent for a moment while I added the latte to my latte, then sugar. I stirred quietly, feeling vaguely ashamed and extremely cornered. "Damon's going to fire me," I finally said.

"He can't fire you if you don't come in."

"He's looking for a reason."

"You got the film, right?"

"Right," I said, sagging against the counter, looking at the kitchen clock.

"Well, let me run some interference for you for a change. Just stay out of trouble, and maybe this will be old news by Monday."

"Thanks, Gary."

"Thank you for letting me spend time with Mother," he said. "Gotta run. See you Monday." I hung up the phone slowly. No work today, again. Almost immediately the phone rang, with a long-distance area code. I saw movement from the corner of my eye—Raul was standing in the breakfast area.

"Dallas, it's Christi. Don't call me back. I just wanted to let you know that there is a BOLO out, for you and Leo Pastriani, with no special regard. Isn't he a friend of yours? Anyway, a lousy photo of you is all over the wire. Oh yeah, BOLO means Be On the LookOut for. What the hell is going on? No. Wait. Don't answer that. I don't want to know, 'cause then I'd be able to tell Mom. You never heard from me."

I deleted Christi's call in an attempt at protection. "I'm wanted officially now," I said to Raul.

"You gotta be kidding?"

"That was my sister Christi, who is a cop in San Antonio, calling to tell me."

"Nice sister."

I chuckled, the sense of unreality engulfing me. "She feels guilty for having the most normal name."

Raul frowned, puzzled.

"In my family we're all named after Texas cities. My parents are full-on history buffs. My sisters have always been jealous that Christi has the most normal name, even if she is named after the body of Christ," I said, stirring my coffee.

Raul was silent for a moment, thinking. "Corpus Christi?"

"E-yup."

Raul took a step closer, "Her first name isn't Corpus, is it?"

I laughed. "No, just Christi. But compared to Dallas, Augustina, and Ojeda, it's good." Augustina had a pretty name, it was just a mouthful.

"Dallas is good."

"It's taken me a while," I said, "since it's usually a guy's name, but now I think so, too."

"So you think the police are coming here?"

"It would be logical," I said, sipping my coffee.

"Should we maybe go then?"

"Run away? Again?" I took a big slurp of coffee, staring out the window. "I don't have anything to hide. I'm not running."

Raul stepped to me, took my cup, and carefully set it on the counter. Then he took both of my hands in his. "Dallas, you are a good person. A good American. But you don't know how things can get confused, even if you are innocent. Once the police take you in, man, the marks are against you."

"If they have to search for me, it will be worse . . . won't it?"

"Not if you can find out who really did it." My heart was pounding, and he squeezed my hands. "Go get dressed. We're going away from here. Just for a few days."

"I don't think—"

"You are too innocent," he said with something that sounded like pride. "You have shielded me, *chica*; let me protect you for a while."

I didn't know about that, but I did know that I couldn't do anything from inside a jail cell. Not to mention having to explain to my family how I got in a jail cell. My phone rang again.

"Dallas honey, it's Houston. What in the Sam Hill is going on? Call me, young lady." The phone was slammed down.

Sibling number two checking in.

Mechanically I dressed in indigo jeans, Doc Martens and a three-quarter-sleeve white turtleneck, then threw a few things in my backpack. Within minutes we were out the door, safely in my truck, with Raul in the driver's seat. Where we were going and what we would do once we got there, I couldn't imagine. "What has happened to my life?" I whispered as we drove out of the M Streets.

Four police officers—one patrol car and two motorcycle cops—passed us. My God, the police were coming to get me. "Why aren't they stopping us?" I asked. "They must have my Chevy's plates."

"I changed them," Raul said, turning onto Fitzhugh from Ross.

"When?"

"Last night."

My head was starting to ache with twisted information. "Where are we going?"

"Do you play pool?"

I looked at the dashboard. "At nine-thirty? In the morning?"

"It's where assistants who aren't working go until the bars open. C'mon."

Never in my life have I played pool. Or had anything to drink before noon. Or, for that matter, been the subject of a BOLO, so today seemed as good as any for all three firsts.

Raul introduced me to a few of the assistants, who were indeed drinking and smoking. They scanned me, but not with much interest, before turning back to their game. Raul put all the balls in a wooden triangle, then another of the guys split it apart with the white ball.

"What do you think of Ileana?" Raul said to them, rubbing chalk on the end of his cue. There was some jargon I was learning.

"Man, that's a bad scene," a black-haired, multiple-tattooed guy said. His shorts hung from below his underwear elastic to below his knees. Tommy Hilfiger would be so proud. He wore a bright yellow Hawaiian shirt open over a Marilyn Manson T-shirt, and an Egyptian ankh the size of my foot hung from a leather thong around his neck. "I wonder if that old agent guy did her in. I mean, I know he was a model and cool and everything, but he'd gotten kinda hefty and he was old, ya know? Why do the great chicks go for that, man?"

"Maybe 'cause they have the cash and we're playing pool instead of workin'," said his friend, who was in baggy jeans, Teva's, and a bowling shirt with "Ernie" embroidered over the pocket.

"Man, are you talkin' about Leo?" Raul asked, putting three striped balls in the pockets.

Baggy jeans bent over to take a shot. "I caught 'em boffing in the pool when I had to deliver some prints to him once," he said. "That guy could sure move for an old guy."

What? Leo and Ileana? It wasn't possible. This kid must be wrong.

"And no one has been able to get hold of him for days," Shorts said. "I been to his house to drop off prints three times. Man, he ain't there. What's with that, you know? She's dead, and he's gone? Sounds like *America's Most Wanted* to me." Shorts continued putting solid balls in the pockets until only the black ball was left. Raul watched as Shorts lined up his shot, then he hit it so the white ball went in, too.

Shorts swore.

"We'll just play the table out," Raul said, then he cleared the rest of the balls off the table, finishing with the black ball in the corner pocket. "You guys want to play another round?" Raul asked.

Shorts and Baggy Jeans said no, they both had to work at noon and needed to eat first. "You," they said, then glanced at me, "and her, want to get some food with us?"

"Where're you goin'?"

"It's Friday. So that means Jamaica."

Raul looked over at me, and I shrugged. Sure, fine, whatever. These guys thought that Leo and Ileana were lovers? That Leo had killed Ileana?

For a moment I wondered . . . was any of it possible? It could explain some things but—surely not.

Once we were seated at lunch, crammed into a tiny booth in a supermarket-cum-restaurant on Martin Luther King, Jr. Boulevard, I asked Baggy Jeans, whose name was Raymond, why he thought Leo would kill her. It hurt even to say the words.

"She went behind his back," he said around a mouthful of jerked chicken.

"Doing what?"

Raymond and Scott, who was Shorts, exchanged looks. "With Duchesse."

I laid down my fork. "What are you talking about? And how would you know?"

"I drive models all the time," Scott said. "I pick 'em up at the airport, I take 'em to hotels, or apartments, I get them food. And they talk to me. Usually they're lonely, and kinda young, it's nice to have someone their own age to talk to. So they tell me stuff."

"Ileana confided in you?"

"No. She's a cool one. No, the secretary at Duchesse who made the appointment talked to me." He grinned. "She's pretty hot."

I sighed. This was going nowhere fast. I picked up my fork again and stabbed at my Jamaican peas and rice.

"Ileana went to Duchesse, the cosmetics company, in New York. Demanded to speak to the president, but was told she's down here in Dallas. So Ileana hotfoots it here, not telling anyone what she's up to. Meets with the president and offers to be their face. Exclusively. 'Cuz you know, they've been trying to get a new one, behind April's back."

Well that rumor was somewhat confirmed. "Okay." It sounded like something April Alexander would have done in her heyday. "When was that?"

Scott and Raymond looked at each other, trying to figure out the day. They concluded it was after the beginning of the month—which could have been before or during the two weeks Ileana had booked herself out.

"Then, the secretary said, she offered to call ahead and check Ileana's flight, 'cause she was real curious where this woman was going next. Was she making the rounds and visiting Revlon and Max Factor, too? Or was this just Duchesse. But Ileana kinda smiled, the secretary said, and said that she was just going back to the airport to be picked up by her boyfriend."

Scott finished his plate and sat back, his arms crossed over his chest.

"Who is, was, the boyfriend?" I asked.

Raymond chuckled. "I was driving her that day. She was fine, I liked to watch her move, so I hung around the airport until she was picked up. By that old agent guy."

"Leo?" Raul asked.

"That's the man."

"Did you see him? Specifically see Leo?"

"Well, some guy was driving, but it was definitely Leo's car. I've seen it enough at the studios and stuff."

"But did you actually see Leo?"

Raymond thought about it. "No, I can't swear it was Leo. He didn't get out of the car, just pulled up, and Ileana got in.

"Did she have luggage?"

"No, that was the weird thing. Her purse wasn't even big. Most models I've seen carry a shitload of stuff, but she just had this skinny old purse. Gucci, but small."

"Have the police talked to y'all?" I asked, dumbfounded at all they knew. Then again, they were the errand boys. Probably not many people paid attention to them. I usually didn't, but that was going to change.

Scott held up his hands, as though warning me away. "I

don't mess with the cops. They don't bother me, I don't bother them."

"Me neither," Raymond said. He looked up at me. "You look better in real life than on TV, you know."

I felt my face redden.

"Anybody want dessert?" Raul asked.

CHAPTER ELEVEN

When I called in to check my messages, the police had inquired if I'd seen Leo Pastriani. Raul scoffed. "It's luring you," he said. "They trick you to coming in, answering the questions, then pounce." He was shaking his head. "They're crafty, those cops are."

"You sound like you know a lot about how the police behave," I said. "Any particular reason for that?"

He turned on the blinker as we headed east through downtown Dallas. *"Nada."*

We sat in silence for a few more minutes; obviously he'd said all he was going to say. I heaved a giant sigh. This was exhausting. "I need to talk to some people, see if anyone can confirm what those guys said."

"Who are you going to call?"

I looked at my watch. "Calling is pointless. No one

answers, or if they do, they are on the shoot and can't really talk. No, I need to see them."

"Don't forget, the cops know what we look like, you know, have pictures of us?"

I looked at him sideways. "I'm not going to forget soon." We drove for a few more miles, and suddenly I began to recognize the neighborhood. "Pull into that thrift store," I said, gesturing to the right.

"We're going shopping?"

"They have dressing rooms."

"We need new clothes?"

"We need new everything."

Raul's eyes widened. "Man, I don't know—"

"Trust me. I'm a stylist. I live in a world of fooling the people." Raul shrugged and drove the hundred or so yards down the road. "Step into my parlor," I said, hopping out of the Chevy and climbing up into the bed to my TrukBox.

I opened it and Raul let out a long, low whistle. "You really like to fish," he said with a smile when he saw the tackle boxes I had. Five, to be exact.

"I have the bait," I said.

"What's in these?" he asked. "I always see stylists carrying around these boxes, but I never looked in one."

I pointed to the zebra-striped one. "Makeup."

"Bait for a man, huh," he said.

Next to it was a hot pink box and a green one. "Those are props."

"You prop style, too? I love to watch prop stylists, man. They are so interesting, all the stuff they have." He turned green eyes to me. "What do you carry?"

"You name it," I said. "Champagne glasses, picnic blankets, beaded moccasins, cigar cases, the list goes on and on."

"Bow and arrow? To go with the moccasins?"

I laughed. "Yeah, and I have the Lone Ranger's gun, too."

"What's in that one?" he asked, pointing.

"Lingerie. I can make any garment fit any model," I bragged. "Too long, too short, too loose, too tight, wrong color, wrong neck, wrong length—I can do it all. I also carry contact lenses, wigs, hairpieces, breasts, butts, anything you can put on, to change a body."

"That scares me a little," he said. "What women can do to their bodies."

"Don't think that's limited to women," I warned.

One of the boxes held tools; everything from pressing hams for perfect French cuffs, to silk ivy and a terra-cotta pot for an instant, do-it-yourself, topiary. "That one is clothes," I said, pointing my foot toward the metal one. "Shoes, wacky outfits that I carry, just in case I'm doing a shoot and they don't have props." As I talked, I pulled out a wig, some hair tint, Catwalk hair styling spray, my smaller tackle box of on-site makeup, and a few of the lingerie items. "Do you have any cash?" I asked, since Raymond and Scott had paid for lunch.

"Change from the diner."

I nodded and motioned for him to follow me inside. This particular thrift store was enormous and usually had great things—though it required a lot of searching to find the perfect items. We didn't have time, but we did need style.

On top of selection, they hired teenagers who didn't care how long you took, and didn't make you check your purse. "Let me get to the rest room," I said. "Watch where I go, then come join me in say"—I looked at my watch—"twenty minutes."

Raul stood stock-still, staring, then whispered to me. "What do I do for twenty minutes?"

"Find another pair of pants and shirt," I said. "Preferably change shoes, too. If you get really bored, they also have books." I headed to the lavatory.

Twenty-two minutes later I heard a hesitant knock. "Who is it?" I called. Before Raul started apologizing, I opened the door.

"Oh, I'm sorry miss, I—"

"It's me," I said, pulling him in and locking the door behind him.

He blinked. "Dallas?"

I nodded.

"What, what did you do to your hair?"

"Cut it, colored it red, and shaped it. In twenty minutes."

"Uh. Wow, I—"

"Raul, it's a wig."

"Oh. Oh, whew, that's amazing, you know? You look completely different. I'd never recognize you."

I turned around, adding a few more touches to my face. I'd gone from a faux-tanned, long-haired, brown-eyed blonde, to a pale-skinned, blue-eyed redhead with short, asymmetrical hair. I'd exchanged my jeans and shirt, for a wool, double-breasted knee coat over an acid green tank and black-velvet flared jeans. With a nose ring and gobs of silver jewelry, even my ex-husband wouldn't recognize me.

Someone knocked on the door. Raul opened his mouth, but I forestalled him by imitating a very sick, very loud woman.

I flushed the toilet a few times, then heard the person mutter, "excuse me" and go in search of another facility.

"What did you get?" I asked him, looking through his selection. A seventies' black jacket, good; electric blue pants, usable; and a white poet's shirt that laced up the front. "Do you want to be gay or straight?" I asked.

"I like women," he said, mildly outraged. "I would have showed you last night, but you—"

I glanced up at him. "Then we'll make you gay," I said. "It's a disguise."

"I don't want to be gay."

"Tough. We're trying to hide you. What better way to hide a straight guy than as a gay guy?" I laughed. "Especially in Dallas."

"I am not dressing if you are making me gay. And don't touch my hair."

"Shut up," I said as I pushed him down on the commode.

He muttered in Spanish and pulled away from the first bottle I opened. He was wise. "What is that?"

"Do you want to go to prison? With your looks, you would be very popular."

He glared at me, then reluctantly looked in the mirror. I stepped behind him, "Let me do what I do best," I said soothingly, reaching for the peroxide with my left hand while I rested my right on his shoulder. "We need to find out who was Ileana's boyfriend and why he had Leo's car."

"Maybe it was Leo?"

"Impossible. So, only a few people will have the insight we need." My model friend Julie would know. "They will be starting happy hour"—I looked at my watch—"at Cafe-TwoOneFour, in forty-five minutes."

"So you think I'm good-looking?" he said, meeting my gaze in the mirror.

He was sold. "Yes, of course I do. You have great bones, pretty eyes, nice smile." I looked pointedly at my Movado.

"So turning me down last night—"

"Oh please," I said, opening the bottle.

Raul took off his baseball cap. "You promise you are a professional?"

"I promise," I lied.

"You lied!" Raul shouted, standing in the bed of my truck, looking at his reflection. Fortunately, he hadn't seen himself full-length until now. He no longer looked like a Ricky Martin playing a preppie lumberjack. Now he looked like a staffer from Velvet Goldmine. His feet were small—or mine are big, a matter of perspective—so he was wearing my black platform ankle boots with black jeans—$3; a mesh, spandex, long-sleeved shirt—$5, over his own white tank undershirt; and a suede shirt from my kit, since the poet's shirt had looked a little too gay. I'd kill him if he got anything on my clothes.

The biggest changes were physical, however. The dirty-dishwater blond-haired, green-eyed, tanned Cuban had become a smoky blue-eyed, bleached white blond with a razored crew cut. With a few earrings and rings and a pair of racer eyeglasses—$1—he looked like Anne Rice's version of a surfer dude.

"You said you were a professional," he huffed.

"Professional what?" I retorted. "I style clothes and rooms, not people's hair or makeup."

"Remind me, the point of this was?" he asked, gesturing toward his image. "I look like Halloween."

"Something about not going to prison," I snapped. He looked good; how dare he complain. "They can't put you in prison if they can't find you."

"My mother wouldn't recognize me. What did you do to me? I do look like I like boys. Completely changed."

"Which is exactly why you should be thanking me instead of bitching." I hopped down to the ground. "Be careful in those heels," I said, as Raul gingerly tripped his way to the tailgate. He stepped down and walked around to the driver's side. "Do you know where we're going?" I asked.

"No," he said, still miffed, though whether that was because I lied or because he'd never had anything done to his appearance before, I didn't know. He threw the keys at me, more at my head than for me to catch, as I walked to the driver's side. We got in and I gunned the engine and aimed for the high-rise skyline. The event of Friday night happy hour at CafeTwoOneFour would be starting in ten minutes. We'd be there in twenty.

Tactfully, tastefully on time.

I removed my glasses, and it took a moment for my eyes to adjust. CafeTwoOneFour was the place for the fashion and advertising industry to see and be seen. "Be careful," I whispered to Raul, thinking of him in my high-heeled boots. "The floors are ramped." Then I remembered that he wasn't wearing his glasses. "And split-level," I added.

"*Jesus*," he muttered.

Black-marble floors, black-leather booths and white starched tablecloths were the backdrop for lean, beautiful females and ripped, handsome men. And the rest of us. To the right, sunlight poured in through the stained-glass windows with the numerals 2-1-4, giving us a view of the south-facing patio. Unscented white roses were arranged on the curved bar. One wall was mirrored, one was a mural, and the other was covered with interpretations of what 214 meant.

The hostess, Janice, was six-two without her three-inch platform heels. Though she wasn't a model, by the end of the month she would be hired as one. That's how it happened at the TwoOneFour. Women worked here for practically nothing, just because of the potential of "being seen."

Janice told us there would be a wait, as her gaze fell to my unmanicured hands. I felt very strange not being myself, in a world that was mine. Janice knew *me*, but she didn't recognize the woman standing before her.

Which, technically, was good.

Raul asked for a menu, and she handed it to him, smiling.

The Store's staffers were seated on the patio. It was Friday, and they were already on the second round of martinis. Kevin, the photo assistant from that fateful morning, sat in a booth talking on his cell phone. Maybe he had killed Ileana? But why.

Hartford's, whose employees usually stayed north of Loop 635, took up four booths, dining on poblano and shrimp nachos, and swigging imported beer. In a side booth, two stylists were sitting, feet up, drinking 214 margaritas. A group of models were picking at salads and doing sorbet shots—they would be sorry for that later. A table of employees from another agency were looking through *W* while sipping lattes. Spiked, I was sure.

"What is monkfish with pumpkin-seed scales?" Raul asked me as he read the menu.

"It's monkfish with roasted pumpkin seeds placed on it

like scales, served on a pear-yam galette on a sea of raspberry coulis," Janice responded. "That comes with 214 salad or cole-slaw."

Raul grunted. I didn't see Julie anywhere, but it was Friday, so I knew she would show up. Sooner or later. Though she no longer had to work the scene, since she was so in demand, she was savvy enough not to rest on her size four laurels.

"Have you dined with us before?" Janice asked Raul.

"No."

"Well, I'm sure you'll enjoy the experience," she said, her voice a little huskier than before. "At lunch we have three daily specials and a blue plate special."

"What's that?"

"Today it's either veal and porcini mushroom meat loaf, blue corn polenta cakes with mahimahi, or orrechiette with Picasso spears."

"Why is it on a blue plate?" Raul asked.

"How long have you been in this country?" I whispered. He looked at me, bewildered, then turned back to Janice.

Her recitations reminded me I had been in and out of eating establishments all day—but not eaten much. No wonder I was hungry.

By the bar I saw a pair of green-plaid golf pants topped by an orange sweater vest over—I was certain—a cashmere T-shirt. Julie. She hadn't worked today, so she was without makeup. Still, she was a stunner.

Julie, with strawberry blond hair and cream skin, was one of the few people who could wear orange successfully. Since it was the "rage" color for autumn, she had been working nonstop. She drained her glass, and I glanced at my watch.

Julie had the world's smallest bladder and she drank water

like a thirsty camel—hence her perfect complexion. The result was that she spent a lot of time in the Ladies' Lounge. That's where I needed to corner her. But I didn't dare leave Raul alone. He was sweet, handsome . . . and a dingbat.

"Man, I really love the art in here," he said, looking at the murals. "Who did this? Do you know?"

Seven minutes had passed, and Julie was walking to the rest room.

"Don't move. Don't talk to anyone. I'll be right back," I said, following Julie in. The rest room was a mosaic cube, each stall a different color. Julie slipped into the yellow one. Two other women were repairing their makeup and gossiping. I stepped into the blue stall and closed the door.

They chattered on and on. I watched Julie's feet. At least she was still here. I glanced at my watch and prayed Raul was behaving. Julie stepped out. The women were still there. I flushed and opened the door, just as they were leaving. Julie was drying her hands.

I spoke in a stage whisper. "It's Dallas."

CHAPTER TWELVE

The door opened, admitting two more women.

The second between Julie turning, and the women recognizing her, our gazes met in the mirror. As I left, I hoped she was putting the pieces together. At the hostess stand, Raul was talking to Janice. She could rest her elbow on his head, if she were so inclined.

Our table still wasn't ready. I kept my back to the rest room, hoping.

Julie went back to the bar, lit a cigarette, and continued speaking to the clients she was with. Then, she glanced up, saw me, did an obvious double take, and squealed.

Acting as though I'd just seen her, I minced across the slippery floor. "Julie, darling!" I cooed, holding my arms wide. Automatically she hugged me, her gaze searching mine as she tried to figure why on earth I was a pierced redhead. I kissed her on the cheeks three times.

"How is LA?" she asked, smiling. "It's been so long. Everyone has been asking about you, wondering whatever happened to you. And *July*," she said.

Around the room, men and women heard her question and instantly made a thousand assumptions about me. After all, I was from LA. Julie walked with me to the suddenly available table.

July? I glanced at her and laughed, walking to Raul. He rose as we approached. "You remember Fred, don't you?"

"How is the music business?" she asked him, kissing his cheek. "It's been so long since I've heard your little birds sing."

He laughed, too, but I started thinking. Yes, Julie happens to be beautiful and photogenic, but she also happens to be as sharp as the proverbial tack. My brain was whirring, trying to figure out what she was talking about. July? Birds sing? The whole restaurant was eavesdropping; who had the police talked to, who would love to turn me in?

I made sure to laugh, trill, and generally act like every obnoxious and inaccurate representation of a fashion person that I'd seen.

Our waitress interrupted with a list of the day's special drinks. "Can we get some food?" Raul asked. She went away to get menus.

"You probably don't know," Julie said in a tone of high drama, "but Ileana Karagonis was found murdered."

I jabbed Raul with my elbow before he started explaining anything.

"And," she said, leaning closer—the whole restaurant leaned—"do you remember Dallas O'Connor?"

Raul did not look at me, but instead muttered something about having met her in LA, and I nodded. "Well, the rumor is that she found the body."

"How terrible for her," Raul recited.

"Apparently, Dallas held a grudge against Ileana because she, Ileana, not Dallas, stole a hundred thousand dollars from her—that's Dallas, not Ileana." Julie lit a cigarette, puffed it, and blew the smoke over her shoulder. Some of the patrons were about to fall out of their chairs they were listening so intently.

The waitress stood at my shoulder. "Rumor also has it that Ileana was about to dump Leo Pastriani," she offered. "Now Leo's missing and Ileana, God rest her soul, is dead. What can I get y'all to eat?"

I felt ashen. Whether or not I looked it, I felt it. I waited silently while she uncorked the wine and poured. Raul asked questions about the menu, and Julie smoked. "What makes you say that?" Julie asked the waitress.

The girl, a tall skinny brunette, smiled. "Some people were in here for lunch. I overheard them. Apparently he had a meeting with Duchesse Cosmetics' president yesterday, and didn't show."

Leo would never miss a meeting with Duchesse. I felt the wine at the pit of my stomach. "People miss meetings," Julie reasoned.

The waitress raised an eyebrow and asked for our orders. With difficulty I swallowed some wine.

"What about this, the word going around that Leo and Ileana were lovers?" Julie asked her. "What do you think?"

A stylist, who usually did commercial film, popped her head into the conversation. "How are you Julie? Are you doing the BR shoot on Saturday? I couldn't help but overhear you, and well, Ileana was ambitious," the girl said, her eyes serious behind cat-eye frames. "She wouldn't be the first model to make a lover out of her older, more experienced agent or photographer."

"Yeah, all five of the straight ones," I said.

"What would you like to order?" the waitress asked us. Raul was focused on the menu, and the stylist was reminding Julie they'd worked together before.

"I'll have the prison special," I said. Raul ordered the blue plate special and the waitress went back to the kitchen to place our orders and get limes for Raul.

"Fred here *was* her photographer," Julie said. "One of them, anyway." A photographer in the music business, I guessed.

The stylist looked at Raul more carefully. "He's not the one I'm thinking of."

"Did you ever meet Ileana?" I asked Julie, for the sake of our audience.

Her blue-green eyes narrowed. "We did a cosmetics thing together, a year or so back."

"I've often wondered what fragrance she would wear, doing a cosmetics thing and all," I said. "I mean, how does one keep from offending the clients or appearing to brownnose them?" If this stylist would just go away, we could converse like normal people. I could get the information I needed in half the time.

The waitress came back to apologize for giving us the wrong menu; only appetizers and dinner were available. She refilled our glasses and went to get the correct menus.

The stylist, Missy, had joined us, bummed a cigarette,

and leaned in to get our attention. "It's funny you should ask, because I saw her at the headbook party, for Alliance, around the first of the month."

"March 3," I said, before I remembered I was supposed to be from LA.

"Whatever."

"The one at the Samba Room?" Julie asked.

"Yes, exactly." Missy looked at me a moment. "You weren't there, were you?"

I shook my head, hoping she didn't look too closely. I had been there. In fact, I'd been there with Julie and her boyfriend.

"It was a crush," Julie said. "Perfect weather, perfect food. I remember your dress, Missy. You looked stunning."

Missy smiled, simpered, and continued speaking. "Well, Ileana smelled like that really expensive fragrance, and I remember thinking it was too mature for her. I mean, my God, the girl was only eighteen, or seventeen, or something."

Another person jumped in, a gay art director. "She was nineteen, I'm sure of it. Poor dear."

"Which really expensive fragrance?" Raul asked. "Chanel?" The man had a fixation.

Julie raised one perfectly shaped eyebrow at him. "Chanel is, one hates to say cheap, but certainly extremely affordable."

"It's one word," Missy said. "What is it?"

I sipped my wine to keep from shouting out *"Joy."* The waitress handed Raul the right menu. "Hey, are the lobster quesadillas any good?"

"They're fabulous," the gay AD said, casually laying a hand on Raul's shoulder. I glared at Raul so he wouldn't flinch.

"Happy? No, that is the Clinique perfume. Umm," Julie took another puff.

"Or maybe the blue corn polenta cakes?" Raul said.

"Excellent choice, especially with a 214 margarita," the AD said to Raul.

I finished my glass of wine and resisted the urge to look at my Movado. In my head I heard the theme from *Jeopardy*. The waitress came, took Raul's order for fried calamari with mango-fig salsa, and poured another glass of wine for me.

"You'll be very pleased," the AD said, pulling up a chair and joining our little group. Introductions were made around, and he started grilling "Fred the Fashion Photographer slash musician" about his life in LA.

We were headed for disaster. I finished my glass of wine, still wondering what July and singing birds meant.

"Joy," Missy crowed, like she'd just won a thousand dollars. "Yes, that stuff is what, eleven hundred dollars an ounce? Way too old for Ileana." She put the cigarette back in the ashtray.

The AD, Patrick, swiped a cigarette. "Ileana was an old soul, had been in the business since she was eight or something."

"Still, it was strange," Missy insisted.

"Which photographer did she have a thing with?" I asked.

"The photographer was nothing," Missy said. "Her agent Leo was the man."

I sat back. Leo and Ileana? This was everyone's answer, and I couldn't buy it. It wasn't the age question, or even the "appropriateness" of mixing business and pleasure; I just knew they didn't fit. "She was with Leo when she . . . died?"

"Well, she had just left Leo," Patrick said, "to date a cowboy."

"A Dallas Cowboy?" Raul asked.

"No, a real, West Texas, rolling-in-cash cowboy, the lucky wench." Patrick inhaled deeply. "Maybe the cowboy did her in."

"Or maybe Leo did, and that's why he's vanished," the waitress said, setting down some sweet potato chips and tomatillo salsa.

"Everyone is blaming Leo," I blurted. "It's not fair; he's probably somewhere crying his eyes out over her, and here he is being castigated."

Missy took a long drag, then put the cigarette in the ashtray. "I didn't know he was thick with people from LA. As far as we, here in Dallas, know, he's vanished. Poof. Unless you've heard from him."

"No, I haven't, but isn't vanished a little . . . extreme?" I asked her.

Julie spoke solemnly. "Leo didn't show up for a meeting with his biggest client—on a topic of unbelievable importance to them both. He didn't respond to his pager, his cell phone, or a couriered message." Her eyes were soft, sad.

"There," Missy said, sitting back and crossing her arms. "You tell me."

"Well, those are just the rumors, and they are flying thick and fast. So until Leo himself shows up with an explanation, they will probably remain." Julie rose abruptly. "I have to get back to my party."

We kissed each other's cheeks again, and Julie whispered, "In case you are interested, a police cruiser just pulled in behind your Z71."

I swore. "Are they still there?"

"Yeah, looking around."

Missy and Patrick were laughing at something Raul said.

"Need a car?" Julie asked.

"Ju—"

"Or a place to stay? Or both? Look, I leave for Vegas in two hours, and I'll be gone all weekend." I couldn't go back to my house—though why I was avoiding the police, I didn't exactly know. Except if I could stay free, I might find out just exactly what was going on. Leo?

"I was going to go to a hotel," I said.

"On a credit card? When you're hiding?"

She had a point. I was stupid to not have thought of it earlier. I never had cash; I lived on plastic. "Are they still there?" We'd been hugging a really long time and were starting to get looks.

"Writing down the number." I motioned for Raul to join us.

He draped arms around our waists, "What's up, you gorgeous ladies?"

"I thought you changed the plates," I said.

"Plates? Blue—?"

"On the truck," I hissed.

"Only the front," he said. "I only had one."

"So did you change the other, or just leave it off?"

The blood rushed to his cheeks. Swearing, I turned to Julie. "Okay," I said. "I'll take your offer. Both of them. What are you driving?"

"The red Miata. Parked on the other side of the Dream Cafe," she said, naming a restaurant at the opposite end of the building. "Your disguises are perfect, but—"

"That doesn't matter," I said, glaring at Raul.

"I'm sorry," he said. "I just forgot. Completely for—"

"Then you'd better hustle," Julie said. "Here come the interlopers."

"Now?" Raul asked.

"What's the buzz?" Patrick said, putting his arms around Raul and Julie. "Anything exciting?"

Missy got up stiffly and wandered away.

I hoped there was a back door by the rest rooms, behind the bar. We disentangled ourselves and I grabbed my bag. The waitress set down Raul's food. He looked over at me. "We're leaving, aren't we?"

"Unless you want to eat in jail," I hissed in Spanish.

"My spare key is in one of those metal keyholders, above the right front tire," Julie said. "I'll pick up your tab. Go!"

Dragging Raul, I ducked behind the mirrored bar, then walked down the hallway by the bathrooms. We narrowly missed smashing into Janice as we raced through the kitchen and into the parking lot.

"This is getting ridiculous," I said as we crossed the lot. The cops had just stepped into Ken Knight's store, right next to the café. I fumbled for the key on the Miata and got in. We pulled into Friday afternoon traffic.

No police followed.

CHAPTER THIRTEEN

"Do you have a key?" Raul asked, as we stood in front of Julie's ivy-covered, brick façade, apartment. Flowers overflowed from pots on her porch that overlooked the parking lot, and the shopping and eating strip of Knox-Henderson. Beyond that was a small green where Julie walked her dog.

Her dog. I'd forgotten about Phideaux, but I didn't hear any barking from inside. "She keeps the key under one of these," I said, peeking beneath potted geraniums and pansies.

"She's crazy to leave keys out. For her house and her car," Raul said. "Man, doesn't she know this is a dangerous world, and she's an attractive woman. She could have all kinds of—"

"She's an expert kickboxer," I said. "And it's not here anyway." I sighed as I leaned against the ivy. The wind had cooled, and it was almost dark. I was bone tired and bewildered. "How many days since the fire?"

"And since we became outlaws? It's Friday. That was yesterday. Do you want me to open the door?"

"Do you have a lockpick kit?"

He stepped to the door. "It's a family secret."

"Whatever. Just get me inside."

His back protected his family secret from my wandering eye. We stumbled into the hallway, and I reached for the light.

"Where's her furniture?" Raul asked.

Julie lived simply. Spartan. One could call it minimalist.

The room had hardwood floors. Rugs hung on the walls, potted trees formed her interior walls, and a few cushions provided comfort. "The study is better," I said, leading him through miniature lemon trees to the other room. It was fairly normal, with a desk, chair, printer stand, TV, and VCR, and a leather chaise longue. That was where I wanted to be, face-down on that piece of furniture.

"Do you need to call your answering machine?" he asked.

I shook my head and turned on the TV, hoping for news, since it was approaching six. "Are we going to eat?" Raul asked.

"The food is in the kitchen," I said. "Be my guest, though she is as Spartan in her cooking as in her decorating."

"Stories your *Eye on Texas News* is following up now," the male newsreader said. I turned off the volume, but watched the shot of Raul and me running across the parking lot of Jacob's studio, and pulling out in my silver Chevy Z71. I felt ill.

"They are still talking about us." His tone was subdued.

I didn't want to phone my house. My sister and brother already knew, and it was just a matter of time before the whole clan was involved. I groaned aloud—the last thing I needed was O'Connors, with their Irish tempers up, asking questions and pulling strings. I covered my face and turned the sound on.

The weather predicted it would get warmer and the sports-caster told me more than I wanted to know about the Dallas Cowboys' illegal activities, and not nearly enough about how the Dallas Stars were playing.

How had the media gotten to the scene of the fire so quickly, I wondered again. Or the cops, for that matter? How was it that someone was a step ahead of us, all the time? My brain hurt from thinking, and I ripped off my wig as I turned off the TV. Raul didn't say anything; he just left the room. With a groan, I lay down on the chaise, stretching my arms above me.

"Wake up, sleepyhead," a man said.

Startled, I sat upright. My heart was pounding, my head was swimming. Standing over me, a tray in his hands, was my bleach job on legs. I should never be allowed to touch chemicals again. "Are you okay?" he asked.

I nodded, rubbed my face, and backed up against the chaise. "What time is it?"

"About three, maybe a little later. Here, eat." He opened the white takeout box and tore open the plasticware. "I haven't seen you eat—"

I wanted to cry with joy. "It's the prison special from CafeTwoOneFour," I said.

"You wanted it earlier, so I thought maybe, you know, it was your favorite."

"It is my favorite," I said. I just hope I don't find out

what prison is really like, I thought as I scooped up some black beans seasoned with za'atar. "Did you get anything?"

"I ate while I was there. With Janice."

Dipping my pita bread in hummus, then layering on some Spanish rice, I glanced up at him. "So that's how you got the lunch menu for dinner." I bit into the bread, savoring the spices. "Smitten?"

"She has a nice face. I'd like to paint her."

"Does that line actually work on women?" I asked with a grin.

His smile was fleeting, but canny. "The trick is, never use it on anyone you don't want to paint. Because if she said yes, oh man, then would I be in trouble."

My disorientation was fading. "That's right, I forget that you are both painter and photographer. How did you diversify? Have you painted long? How did you meet Ileana to begin with?"

He sat down on the edge of the chaise, leaning forward, his elbows on his knees. "It's not that I'm avoiding your questions, but there is something I didn't tell you." His green eyes were serious. "You know, about finding the body."

I dipped my bread again. "Actually, if you would start with why you won't go to the police, that would make things considerably easier," I said.

He shook his head. "That doesn't matter, you know. The only thing now is what to do."

"What do you have to tell me?"

He stood up. "Eat your dinner first, because once you hear it, man, you might not be hungry anymore."

Sitting alone, I had a few more forkfuls of black beans, then closed the top of the container. I couldn't eat with those provocative statements floating around. I wiped my mouth and my hands, and called out to him. "Talk to me."

Raul came back in the room and handed me a Shiner, then opened one for himself. "Ileana was killed by someone in fashion, you know. In the industry."

"Why do you say that?"

He scratched his neck and blinked a few times. "Part of my job when I assist is to uncrate the merchandise, hang it up for the presser."

"Who will come in a day or two before the shoot and prepare the garments," I said. "I know this. And?"

"The clothes. They're not perfect, right?"

"Rarely."

"They have, like cutouts, and writing on them, and stuff."

I stared at him. A lot of them have a triangle cut out in the back, and above that triangle was stamped "Mutilated," so that if the clothes were taken out of the country, there wouldn't be import/export issues. Also, they were marked and stamped that way if they were samples. It made them effectively unwearable. "Yes?" I said, hesitantly.

"Were you wondering where the blood came from?"

A chill passed through me. Once again I saw Ileana hanging there, blood dripping off her heel onto the floor. There had been no wounds that I could see; in fact she had been ghostly pale, almost tinged with blue.

Drained of blood. "Are you telling me . . . ?"

He laid a hand on my icy-cold one. "She'd been stabbed in the throat, drained, you know. But Dallas—"

I tried to pull away, but he held my hands, forcing me to look at him. "She had a triangle cut into the small of her back."

*   *   *

An hour and forty-five minutes later, Raul knocked on the bathroom door. Though the rest of her home was spare, Julie catered to luxury in here. Candles, incense, African violets, plush towels, a CD player, and a thick terry-cloth robe set off the jewel of her extralong, extrawide Jacuzzi bathtub. Tears had left me feeling drained, so I'd poured oils and powders into the steaming hot tub and gone to nirvana for a while.

It was too much to know. A sample triangle? Cut into the flesh of a person? Dear God, I hope Ileana had been dead already. I shook my head, trying to clear the visual.

Raul knocked again.

"What do you want?" I asked. My voice was still thick; my face hurt. It couldn't have been done by someone in my industry. I didn't know anyone who would, who was cold enough to be able to do such a thing.

While I worked in a world that was admittedly shallow, it was a world that had great respect for beauty, individuality, and personal space. Pettiness was only skin-deep. People genuinely cared for one another. Fashion was a team effort. Corporate, in the most fundamental use of the word.

The thought that anyone considered I could have committed this heinous act, or the suggestion that Leo might have done it, made the urge to clear both our names almost overwhelming.

Or should I be getting an attorney? No dammit, I had done nothing wrong! I wasn't going to behave as though I had. Maybe it was a random killing. I wasn't sure which scenario made me angrier. Either way, some sicko was going to get busted for what he'd done to Ileana.

Poor Ileana. Inadvertently I jerked in the water, splashing it over the side.

"Are you okay?" Raul called through the door.

"Fine."

"I thought you were tougher than that, you know. Man, I'm sorry."

Just because I knew how to skin a deer didn't mean that I was impervious to blood. "I hope I'm never that tough," I said bitterly as tears welled in my eyes again. "Whoever did this was a monster."

After a beat, Raul agreed. "How long have you been in this business?" I asked, flicking a bubble in the candlelight, watching the prism of colors shift.

"A year, maybe two."

I wet my lips. "Ileana was like so many others I've known. A hundred others. Young, beautiful, and intoxicated by their sudden success. To see her potential, that excitement snuffed out—" I gritted my teeth. I couldn't believe it had happened, and just as Ileana was finally getting her act together. "I'm sorry, you must be hurting, too, being her friend and all," I said.

"You uh, want your dinner? I nuked it to be warm."

I watched my reflection in the bubble smile. "You are awfully thoughtful for a kidnapper," I said.

"Yeah, well, you are my first."

Arranging the dying bubbles over me strategically, I called for him to come in. I hoped he didn't take it for an invitation. Though he was Latino, he didn't seem to have the same sort of allure I'd fallen for in other Latin men. And he was way, way too young.

"Wow," he said, glancing at me. "I won't disturb you." He waited a minute. "Unless—"

My expression must have communicated my resounding "no," because before I could say anything else, he'd left the takeout box on the floor and closed the door behind him. I heard his boots—my boots—in retreat to the jungle room. The sound of boots came back. Short knock on the door before it opened. "Thought you might like this," he said, setting a Shiner on the bath's edge. He escaped again.

It was already opened. I raised a silent toast to Ileana. "We'll find who did this to you," I said, feeling tears mingle with sweat on my face. "We'll find him, and he'll pay."

CHAPTER FOURTEEN

L eo's house might have the answers, it might even have a clue as to where he was; I had Leo's house key. These were the thoughts that woke me at 10 A.M. Saturday. Raul was stretched out on the floor in the jungle room, fully dressed and snoring. I promised him breakfast, and we took off in Julie's Miata.

I wondered if the police had impounded my truck.

Leo lived three streets over from me, but those three streets made all the difference. My parents had purchased a house back in the sixties, when it became obvious they would have children all over the place. This way, if we attended SMU or worked in Dallas, we wouldn't have to pay rent. It was a great idea, and one of the better-executed schemes they'd come up with.

So I lived in a lovely duplex that I'd never be able to

afford otherwise. And if I could get a renter for the other half, I could pay for all the needed repairs. It would probably help if I called some of the applicants back.

Though my address was nice, Leo's was downright ritzy. His three-bedroom house was Deco-Italianate, with porches, curved doorways, and stained glass, surrounded by a huge lawn. He was always having parties, and I think he also rented his guest bedroom to traveling models.

Over the years we'd become good neighbors.

He'd walk his dog to my yard to fertilize my rosebushes; I'd hang out around his pool in the summertime, drinking beer or red wine since I hated margaritas.

Every January he would start a new exercise regime and drag me into it. In-line skating, running, biking, skateboarding. Each one lasted for about ten days, then he'd start with excuses, and our meetings would become lunches again: usually pasta and garlic bread to fortify ourselves against the "cold" weather.

Mostly he enjoyed working on his house—a built-in hobby for those of us who lived in these older, beautiful homes. As we drove by now, I saw his lawn was a blanket of green. Already. Mine still looked like the fur on a mangy dog. I hated Leo at times. "Aren't you going to park here?" Raul asked as we passed Leo's house on the second drive-by.

"No. Let's park a few blocks over," I said, just in case. Raul was still a blond, though he no longer had all the earrings. I'd left the wig at Julie's, my hair was under a scarf, and I had on the velvet jeans from yesterday, with one of Julie's bulky sweaters. Orange.

Would the cops recognize us? They couldn't know we'd traded vehicles. But I did have a sense of being watched, though whether that was real, or imagined, I couldn't guess.

Raul drove three more blocks over. Now we were six streets from my house.

It was an overcast Saturday. March in Texas is like a woman with PMS: mood swings are the norm. By 2 P.M. it could be snowing, one never knew. But now it was blustery and cool. Raul still wore my suede shirt, since his plaid one had been all over Dallas TV.

We hopped out of the Miata and started down the street. People walking, with dogs, children, and each other, abounded. They smiled, stared, wished each other good morning. Raul and I didn't stick out exactly, but we were most noticeable since neither of us was appropriately casual. What irony. We turned onto an emptier street. At the far end I saw a police car.

Sweat broke out beneath my sweater. "Let's cut through."

We wedged ourselves through fences and crawled under bushes. From the alleyway we opened Leo's gate and entered through the backyard. I fished for my keys and unlocked the door. "It's not breaking and entering if I have a key, right?"

"Right."

"And we're here because Leo might have some clue as to what happened, right?"

Raul looked over his shoulder. "Right. Hurry."

We stepped into Leo's sunroom, and instantly I knew that something was wrong. Leo had prided himself on a very English-style conservatory. It was usually as humid as Houston in here, and heavy with the smell of orchids. Today everything was drooping and brown, and only the faintest floral scent remained.

My sense of foreboding grew as we walked through the dying greenery and let ourselves into the main part of the house. Dust covered everything. I'd never seen dust in Leo's house before. Even if he was in Milan, or Miami, or LA, for a day or a season, he had a woman who cleaned for him. However, he had to call her; but he could do that from anywhere.

That he hadn't done so proved he'd left unexpectedly.

Unless, I shivered at the thought, he couldn't call at all. Had he really skipped town. Why? He loved his life, he loved Dallas. Maybe he'd been in trouble with someone. I shook my head; this was not a Mafioso movie. Leo had a reasonable explanation. I just wish he'd show up to give it.

Raul stood in the foyer, staring at the ceiling. "That is really something," he said.

Oh yes. One of Leo's lovers had been an Italian model who fancied himself the next Michelangelo. He'd used Leo's house as his palette, picking some of the more titillating stories from Roman mythology as his subjects. Bacchus feasted on the ceiling, with a selection of very disproportionate guests. "Stop staring," I said, tapping Raul on the shoulder. "His bedroom and office are upstairs."

Raul commented on the sensibilities of the art, the luxury of the carpets, the style of the furniture. I noticed that everything was just a little off-balance. A painting hung a half inch askew, a pillow wasn't exactly placed. Flowers that were once fresh were beyond dead, the water either evaporated or reduced to green slime in the vase. Leo hadn't been here in a long time.

His bedroom was in the same state of untidiness—bed unmade, clothes on the floor, and toiletries strewn throughout the bathroom. "Has he been robbed?" Raul said. "Or is he just a pig?"

The clothes were crumpled, the socks dirty. "Maybe he had just unpacked," I said, thinking aloud. I went back into the bathroom and looked at the shaving kit. Complimentary shampoo and conditioner from his New Orleans hotel were nestled against his hairbrush. I looked over the bedroom and a chill settled in my blood. "Let's look in his office."

Someone had been in his office, and recently. The dust that covered everything else was missing here. More telling, the books were slanted, the chair was tilted, and the trompe l'oeil door to the hidden WC was slightly ajar.

"Oh my God," Raul said in a dazed tone. "That's exactly what we shot." He was staring at a 32-by-48 framed print. It was a copy of an ad campaign for Duchesse Cosmetics, featuring a young and exquisitely beautiful blonde. She wore a huge picture hat, dripping with daisies, and a tiny peasant-style shirt that revealed glowing brown shoulders and the slightest hint of cleavage.

Raul crossed his arms and stared at the photo critically. "Even the makeup was the same," he said. "Those long eyelashes and that, like Egyptian or something, what do you call that black stuff?"

"Eyeliner."

"Yeah, that. Man, it looked just like that."

"That was about 1970," I said. "Do you know who she is?"

"I wasn't even born," he muttered.

I glanced at him: baby. "April Alexander, when she was about seventeen. The center of Leo's life."

"I didn't know they were married."

I laughed at how Raul translated what I said. "No. I mean yes. Well, he was both. First he was her husband, then he was her agent. She made his career, and he made hers." As I spoke, with mental apologies to Leo, I opened his desk drawer. There, sitting on top of his files, was a contract from Duchesse.

Speaking of the grand Diva herself. "Why isn't that filed?" Raul asked. I stared at this further proof of chaos in Leo's life, feeling the blood pounding in my throat. Something was wrong.

"Oh my God," Raul said, flipping through the file, marked "M" for "millions" on Leo's desk. "I didn't know he was agent for all these models. Look, Paulina, man she was hot. And Elizabeth Hurley, *muy caliente*. And oh my God, Shalom. The way she walks, it makes a man think of sin. Man, he was really big-time."

I started opening drawers, just randomly. What could I find? What would help me figure out where Leo was and if he knew what had happened to Ileana?

Because my other thought, when I woke up this morning, was that Leo realized somehow he would be implicated, so he vanished. When was the last Leo sighting?

"Tyra Banks? Man, this Leo was some rich dude I guess, yeah?"

"Yes and no," I said, sorting through files. Leo had the screwiest filing system on the planet.

"I don't see April's name or Ileana's," Raul said. "Hey, none of these contracts are signed by the woman, only Leo. He has a really nice signing," Raul said.

"Signature," I automatically corrected him. "That's because you are looking through his fantasy file," I said. "None of those models was his. They were wishful thinking, superstition. Leo did it for luck.

"When he met someone he wanted to represent, he would

make up a contract for her, in hopes that it would pull her to him. He had contracts for everyone who ever became anyone." I shut the drawers. "Nothing here."

We traipsed through the house to the model's suite and opened the door. The room was pink and black, with framed vintage film posters and circa-1930s armoire and vanity. A bathrobe, which I had actually picked out to be the "loaner," in pink chenille, with big black heart outlines, was thrown across the end of the wrought-iron daybed. A straw hat, festooned with daisies, was lying on top of an old train case.

"Jesus," Raul breathed against my back. "That's the hat."

Downstairs, the doorbell rang. Raul looked at me, frozen, and I shrugged. "They'll go away."

Knowing that we shouldn't touch anything—hell, we were doing this without gloves, which was stupid—I crouched in front of the hat. Whether it was a retro piece or a reproduction, it looked exactly like the photo. "You sure it is?"

"I'm positive, man," he said.

The doorbell rang again, but we ignored it. "Ileana had this hat, less than two weeks ago when she saw you," I clarified.

"That's it. I'd swear to it."

I picked it up with my fingertips, then carefully opened the train case. The interior was black satin.

Knock on the door again.

Creeping past the shadows at the front door, we went back to Leo's office. "It *is* the same," I said, standing at the threshold, looking at the print. "How did it get here?"

"Maybe Leo had the films!" Raul shouted.

This time the knock was accompanied with shouting. "Dallas po-lice! We need to speak to you, Mr. Pastriani!"

"Police?" Raul and I mouthed to each other in unison. We

bolted out the office door. "Damn," I said. "They'll probably be around the back, too."

"Po-lice! Open up, Mr. Pastriani." They pounded again.

"Can they come in if he doesn't answer?" I whispered.

"Back door?" Raul asked.

The police beat the door again. "Mr. Pastriani, open up!" We heard the key in the lock.

"Omigod, they have a key," I said, halting. Raul banged into me.

"Back door?" Raul repeated.

"Back window," I said, and ran across the hallway to the guest room. It was decorated with Ralph Lauren's take on country life, in gingham, denim, and eyelet. A big window framed a view of a bigger tree. The downstairs door's dead bolt slid open with a loud click.

Raul opened the window. "What do we do?" he asked, staring outside.

"There's a tree, we climb down it," I said, then perched on the ledge and jumped for the branch. At least working for The Store I had health insurance, I thought as the branch wobbled. I swung my legs up and over the top, grimacing at the sound of velvet seams ripping, then inched down toward the trunk. "C'mon!" I hissed at Raul, who was still standing in the window. I looked around to see if any neighbors were watching.

He was pale. "I hate heights," he said.

"Would you prefer prison?" I threatened.

Glaring, he jumped and the whole branch dipped, almost unseating me. I scooted backward, against the trunk. "Close the window!" I whispered.

I think he cursed at me, but I couldn't hear him above

the sound of the wind rustling the budding branches. In a city renowned for its lack of green, this was one of the few neighborhoods that still had big trees. Thank God. I hugged the trunk, giving Raul space to climb over after he closed the window.

When the cop looked out the window, I was embracing the tree and Raul was lying on the branch like a well-fed snake. We stayed stock-still as the policeman looked at the ground, then stepped back into the room. Fear had me paralyzed, which was good because Detective Diana Mansfield looked out the window next.

The back door opened, and two more cops stepped into the yard to look at the grass.

My feet were beginning to slide on the bark, since these shoes were made for tennis on Martha's Vineyard, not escaping the Dallas police by hanging like a monkey. I dug my fingers into the bark of the tree, grateful for those hours at the gym. I didn't dare look at Raul—in fact, I was afraid to look at the cops. I've always been able to sense when someone was watching me. Maybe they could, too. I held my breath.

The back door closed, but I could still see movement inside the second story. As soon as it was still, I threw myself on to the other branch, scooted down it and fell—six feet—into the alleyway. I rolled into an azalea bush, wincing and cursing in its relative protection.

Raul leaped down beside me, again landing on his feet like a damn cat. "Let's go."

"I can't move," I said.

"Sure you can. You got here."

We heard men's voices. I bolted up, stifling a yelp because it really did smart. Gravel was stuck to my palms, and my knee

ached. I started down the alleyway, then thought a minute—
we needed to disappear. Cars approached. I grabbed his hand
and we walked to the back gate of someone's house. I reached
over, unlatched the gate, and we walked in as though we
owned the place. Raul shut it behind us and we strolled to
the back patio.

Fortunately, the woman who was planting on the same
back patio had her back to us. I pulled him into a crouch
when I spotted our reflections in her glass back doors. In the
alleyway, a car stopped.

Without a word, we ran to the opposite gate, let ourselves
through the front, crossed the next two streets and got into
the Miata. As I started the engine I wondered if the neighbors,
who had seen us leave and return, would tell the police.

"Where should we go?" Raul asked after a few moments
of tense driving through the neighborhood. We were at the
corner of Greenville and Vickery, with restaurants stretching
out north and south. Across the street, waitresses at Terilli's
set tables for their expected lunchtime crowd. Next door to
that, the waitresses hosed down chairs at the GBG. Two Mexican restaurants faced each other across Goodwin, one of the
streets that wove through the west side of the M Street district.

"What do we do now?" Raul asked, stretching his arm
along the back of my seat. I didn't know; cops were everywhere.
If Leo's house had any answer, it was that he was not in a
position to respond. What had happened?

"That photo is the same as the one you took?" I asked
Raul again.

"Exactly. Even signed with Jacob James's studio logo."

I did a double take. "Jacob did that shot of April?"

"I think it was his first big job," Raul said. "The lighting was the same, exactly. Couldn't you see?"

"Of course," I said, realizing what had been familiar about the print in Leo's office. That lighting style was Jacob's signature.

Patrick Demarchelier's work was easy to identify, because a square showed up on the model's pupil, from his specific ring lights. Jacob did a strange side lighting with Chinese umbrellas. He'd done it for years. "I'd never really looked at that photo," I said. "In fact, I'd just assumed that a big 'name' had done the shot. What do you know, Jacob James." Maybe there was more to him than I thought. I licked my lips, thinking furiously. "And those shots of Ileana, looked just like that?"

"Right. Same lighting and everything."

A car honked behind me, and I realized we'd been sitting at the stop sign forever. I started toward Central. "It makes no sense to recycle an old ad series," I muttered. "To take a young, new model and make her look like an old, dated model. What's the point? But anyway, Leo signed the first model."

"You say so."

"And rumor said he was going to sign the second."

"I didn't see a contract," Raul said. "Did you?"

"It would be at Alliance's offices," I said. "But these photos, the film that looks just like an old picture. Why is it missing?" I tapped the steering wheel as I thought. "What's the point?"

"Leo is missing also, *chica.*"

And Ileana had been linked with Leo by everyone.

"If we could find those films," Raul said. "I don't know where they could be. Jacob didn't say anything, so he probably didn't find them."

"That's another weird thing, why didn't Jacob say anything the other night? He had to know we were at his studio when it burned. God, half of Dallas did."

Raul shrugged.

I zigzagged through Uptown, with its trendy restaurants and shops, aiming toward Harry Hines Boulevard. We drove past Parkland Hospital, heading north.

Ten minutes later we pulled into the parking lot of Mecca, a perpetual breakfast hole-in-the-wall. I didn't have my styling kit, and my jeans were wrecked, so I took some enormous safety pins from my purse and haphazardly pinned the seams. With some gel I rasta'd my hair, then replaced the assortment of earrings and nose rings I'd worn the day before. The Polo shoes were stripped of their laces. Finally, I put black eyeliner on the inside lower lids of my eyes and painted on heavy maroon lipstick—insta-Goth.

"You look completely different," Raul said in a less-than-flattering tone. "It's amazing how women do that."

"A little bit of makeup, and change of hair, and you can fool anyone," I said, closing my door. "Do you have any cash?" I asked. "If not, this is going to be a skinny breakfast."

"Don't worry. I have money."

There was a step I always tripped on, so my gaze was focused on the ground in an effort to miss it. "I thought you had no money," I said.

"I stopped by the ATM on my way to dinner last night."

I looked up and promptly tripped. Raul steadied me with his hand on my elbow. "That's right. How did you drive without—"

"Janice brought me back."

"At three in the morning? How did you get there?"

"I walked."

"From Knox-Henderson to the Quadrangle?" That was a twenty-block walk, by any standard, but a distance that was especially unheard of in a city where no one walked. Except from a car to the air-conditioned building.

"It was good to clear my head."

"That was nice of her to bring you back," I said, then I added the pieces together and felt my cheeks turn red: Three o'clock. CafeTwoOneFour closed at one.

"Two," he told the aging waitress. She led us through the Texana kitsch to a booth and poured two cups of strong coffee. After ordering their famous cinnamon roll and listening to Raul request every form of meat they served, I pulled out my Nokia to check my messages.

Kreg had called from California. Would I mind watering his plants? I laughed out loud.

Raul looked expectantly at me. "A friend of mine wants me to water his plants," I said, moving to the next message. A few other acquaintances; an irritated Damon; my mother. No Leo.

Raul waited until I had hung up. "What is funny about his plants?"

The waitress placed a series of steaming plates in front of Raul, and a mountain of hot cinnamon pastry, glazed with melting butter, before me. She refilled our coffees and moved away.

"It's a code," I said to Raul.

"Ah, a code."

"Water his plants means he's staying longer, but the person he is with doesn't know it. Yet. And it's funny because: a: he doesn't have plants, his whole house is steel and glass;

b: he's too high-maintenance to give anyone except his concierge his key; and c: he's allergic to anything that requires a commitment, be it plants, animals, or live-in lovers."

"Is he your live-out lover?"

I looked at Raul a moment.

"I'm just curious," he said.

"Kreg is a dear friend," I said. I refused to admit my grandmama called me Snow White and the Seven Queers, since I didn't know one, unmarried, straight, male. The more wonderful, educated, well dressed, and tasteful they were—at least in this city—the more likely that they wanted to date each other.

This was a common topic among Coco, Julie, Lindsay, and me. We teased Lindsay that she was bi, just so she could get a date in Dallas.

"He's a lucky man."

"We're both lucky," I concluded. "Except," I said, around a mouth of superheated pastry, "if I don't find out what happened, I'm going to go to jail. Which won't be lucky."

Raul was bent over his food, eating like a machine. "She was killed by someone in fashion," he repeated with his mouth full.

"Or someone who knew enough that he or she wanted to make it look like a fashion killing," I countered.

"Then frozen. Like a Popsicle."

CHAPTER FIFTEEN

"How, exactly, do you know that?" The hair on the back of my neck rose. Could he—

"The news," he said. "It was on the radio. She was frozen after being killed."

Do you have a deep freeze, Ms. O'Connor? The echo of that reporter's question resounded in my mind: How could I have forgotten that? Quickly I told Raul about Carla at the *Morning News*.

"You have a deep freeze here?" he asked.

"Of course I do. It's Dallas. Where else am I supposed to sleep in the summer?"

He wasn't amused. "What did you keep in it?"

"Food. It's a freezer."

"But what kinds, you know?"

"Mostly vegetables. And pastries that are too tempting to keep in the kitchen."

He gave me the look of a man who's never experienced food temptation. "Then why worry?" He took another bite of steak.

"You mean if the only forensics they find in there are for Brussels sprouts?" He looked baffled, and I guessed he didn't have Brussels sprouts in Havana.

"You are innocent, the freezer will prove that," he said. "Searching will work in your favor. You should invite them to your house. When you are gone."

"You know an awful lot about this process," I said. "Any particular reason why?"

He shrugged. *"Nada."*

We ate in silence for another round of coffee. "Was her body frozen to confuse the time-of-death question?" I asked, then caught myself. "I can't believe I said that."

"Why?"

"It seems so corny, I mean people on TV talk like this. Not real people." Murder doesn't happen to real people, I thought. "I feel a lot like that character Angela Lansbury played for years."

"Jessica Fletcher?"

"She was the murderer," I said.

"I loved Jessica," Raul said. "She was very hot for an old lady. And she always solved the crime."

"That was easy. She was the murderer."

"Not my Jessica!"

"Didn't you find it mysterious that wherever she was, people died? She was a serial killer."

"Not my Jessica," he said, then stabbed his last bite of steak.

A few minutes of silence passed—surely he knew I was joking? "So was the body frozen to make it hard to pin the time of death?"

"Probably."

"The last time you saw Ileana was how many days ago?"

"It's Saturday? I saw her thirteen days ago."

"Hmm," I said. Julie had seen her on the third. I dialed Lindsay's cell.

"Dallas?"

"I know you're a professional and guard privacy, and I know the police have probably already talked to you, but please tell me, did Ileana show up for the job before *Metamorphosis?*"

She sighed. "No, she canceled it. She was sick, she said."

"Where'd she call from?"

"I don't know, Dallas. God, it's Saturday."

"I know, Lindsay, but—"

"But you're on TV, and not looking good," she said. "So I'll bend the rules, especially since you are one of Leo's dearest friends. Ileana booked herself out for two weeks, and was quite iffy about working past that. I think perhaps that contract negotiations with Duchesse were going on, and she didn't want to commit herself until she knew the status."

"Are you sure of that?" I asked, picking at my cinnamon roll.

"Of course not. Leo wouldn't have said anything."

"Where is Leo?"

"I was wondering if maybe you knew."

"I haven't seen him since he got back from New Orleans."

"That was more recently than I," she said. In the background I heard the doorbell ring. "Gotta run, love. That's my date."

"Male or female?"

"It's Dallas," she said with a laugh. I guess that meant female.

"Wait, one more question. When did her two weeks of being booked out start?"

"The weekend after the headbook party."

"Have fun," I said, and hung up. Raul was still eating.

Ileana had been found, dead, on Wednesday, twenty days after the headbook party. She'd booked herself out, which meant she had called in to take time off, for two weeks before that. At some point she had flown to New York, stormed through Duchesse, then flown back and done the same thing with the client here. According to Raul, less than two weeks ago, she was photographed, looking like a young April Alexander.

"Really," I said to Raul, playing with the edge of my roll, "if you think about it, Leo's been out of sight since before Ileana. Almost three weeks." I cut a section from my cinnamon roll. "What do you know about Jacob James?"

Raul shook his head. "Whatever you are thinking, you're wrong. He's the best person in the world. Quiet sometimes, but he wouldn't hurt a fly. He would go before a, what's in English, firing squad, before betraying a friend, or breaking a promise."

"How did you start working with him?"

"I painted his house, first, and we got to talking, then he saw some of my stuff. First he commissioned a portrait of his sister, then one day he was desperate for an assistant—"

"—so he hired you?" I winked.

"To train, yeah, he started then."

"How long have you known him?"

"Five, six years."

"But you don't know if he and Ileana were . . . ?

"He never says anything about himself. It was a year before I knew he'd been married and had twins. He just doesn't talk much about himself."

I leaned back and stared at an autographed photo of Troy Aikman.

"Man, I wish we'd had time to look for the films—film," he said. "I bet they are in Leo's house."

"No they're not. He hasn't been there in weeks. That place was a dust barn," I said, cutting the final quarter of my cinnamon roll. I tugged at the bandanna around my throat, thinking. "There is one more hiding place of Leo's." I grabbed my purse. "And it's a drive, so c'mon."

"Turn left," I said, wincing at the grinding of gears. "Where did you learn to drive?" I asked. "Between breaking my foot—"

"I did not break your foot."

"You're right. Between *almost* breaking my foot—"

"That's better."

I sighed. "You are difficult to argue with, mostly because you get me confused. What was I saying?"

"Do I turn here?" he asked.

We'd already gone through the town of Glen Rose, with its Dairy Queen, strip malls, and motels. Before that we had passed three subdivisions, featuring the finest of fairway living. We were almost to Fossil Rim Wildlife Park. I debated telling Raul I didn't know exactly where to go, since I'd never been to Leo's hideout. I just had a good idea, sort of, where it was. Heavy on the "sort of" part.

However, if there were any place Leo was—either in the flesh, or hidden, undeveloped film—Glen Rose would be the place. "I get so weary of the grabbing, glittery world," he'd once said, "so I bought a little hideaway, nestled in the backside of beyond, completely rustic. The people are so homey and quaint."

His roots were from some Southern backwater, but he'd buried them deep.

"Sure," I said to Raul. It really didn't matter. We didn't have anywhere else to go, except maybe jail. We flew by the western Texas roadlife—smashed armadillos, stinkweed, bluebonnets, and Indian paintbrush mixed with sticker bushes and fire ant hills. I was a little crabby.

"Havana," Raul said.

I looked back at him, blond and tanned with sci-fi glasses on, wrecking Julie's transmission, and had to laugh. "What are you talking about?"

"I learned to drive in Havana. I was seven years old."

"Haven't improved much, have ya?"

"We haven't gotten caught," he reminded me.

Yet, I thought morosely. "Wait! That's it!"

He slammed on the brakes, throwing me forward. "Where?"

"Back there—" but before I could suggest we U-turn or go around the block, he'd reversed through oncoming traffic and taken the turn. The poor motorists couldn't react fast enough to his rude driving even to honk. "Great," I said. "That's a surefire way to sneak us through town, not attracting the police."

We were at the top of a hilly subdivision, roads, and construction projects poking up through the mesquite trees, and spreading over the wildflower-covered hills.

"Do you think Leo did it?" Raul asked.

I was staring at the houses, trying to remember what Leo had said about his house, how to identify it. Each residence stood on half acre or more lots, the houses set far back on the property, giving the illusion of spaciousness. Leo had said his house backed onto a creek bed, or cliff. It was on the second highest hill in the area.

"Killed Ileana?" I had been asking myself the same question, against every instinct I'd ever had.

"He is missing," Raul said.

"Well, to most of the world, we're missing, too," I said. "But we are innocent." I looked over at him. "At least I am."

Raul drove up the hill slowly. "Did he do it, you think?"

"There!" I said, pointing to a two-story house with a wide second-story balcony. Following the winding, uphill driveway, we pulled up to the carport at the back of the house. No sign of Leo, or any form of habitation.

"Are you sure? I mean, this doesn't look like the same kind of house, you know?" Raul asked, as I craned my head up.

"Yes," I said, pointing up. "Leo said he bought the house because of the tree house." Across from the back of the blue-and-cream house, stood a tree house in matching blue-and-cream paint, the branches of the tree on a level with the platform. "It even has a ladder."

Raul turned off the Miata and let the quiet of the country settle on us for a moment.

"Raul, I don't know you at all," I said slowly. "But I know

you aren't a murderer, because I sense it." I tugged at the bandanna around my throat. "It's the same with Leo. Oh sure, he could have gotten angry enough to kill someone, I think anyone can. But then I think he would either panic and hide the body, or confess all to the first available officer. More importantly, why? He loved Ileana. He's been through a lot with that girl. She was the embodiment of his ambitions."

I looked at the sloping lawn, sprigged with yellow, pink, and white. "Despite his being an agent, dealing in fooling the people, Leo is up front. He knows the modeling business because he'd been in it, and been good. He knows the benefits and the pitfalls. I just . . . I can't make it make sense. Leo is what you saw. I don't think he would be so . . . cold," I said. "Disrespectful of someone's body, especially dead. And . . ." I trailed off. "With the details you told me last night, well . . . no way did he do it. No way."

"What about passion? He was a good-looking man, you know?"

"You're asking what if he had been Ileana's lover and she jilted him?" I guessed. "That's impossible," I said flatly. "Impossible."

"You are certain."

I opened the convertible's door and got out. "I know my friend," I said, before shutting it.

Leo's lot rolled down to the gate for Fossil Rim. Why Leo hadn't built the porch on the back, I didn't know. A Coca-Cola-logo stained-glass window indicated the landing on the staircase.

I gestured toward the door. "I don't have keys, so work your magic."

"Did you knock? Maybe he's here."

For five minutes we beat on the door and got no response. "Now will you open it?"

"Are any of the windows unlocked?"

"I haven't tried."

"Do you have a credit card?" he asked.

"Yes," I answered. "Is that how you always do it?" I asked. "Is American Express your family's secret?"

"Let me see the card," he said.

I gave it to him, he turned to the door, then turned back to me with a Ricky Martin smile.

The door stood open.

I stepped into Leo's private lair. "Jeez. He did take this country-house thing seriously," I said, staring. It looked like a set for the El Paso Trading Company. Mexican blankets, distressed furniture, and animal heads?

"You sure this is the same guy's house?"

Maybe I didn't know Leo as well as I thought.

"Do you think he has any food?" Raul asked, heading for the kitchen. "That was a long drive from Dallas."

"Aren't artists supposed to starve?" I called, moving toward the office. The home-on-the-range, cowboy flavor was replaced with ordinary office furniture, complete with gray-metal file cabinets. I would have never guessed. I opened the top drawer of one of the cabinets and began looking. For what, I wasn't sure.

"Do you like Tabasco?" Raul called.

"I'm from Texas," I shouted back—which should be answer enough. Nothing was filed under I, nothing under K. Where else would he keep contact sheets for Ileana? I looked up and saw that that same older Duchesse advertisement was sitting on his desk, framed. "P," I said to myself. "Pictures, of course."

Outside, a car backfired.

"Do you like pork and beans, or chili better?" Raul shouted.

I opened the P file, and found the folder labeled "Pictures" and another with "Portraits." I shouted back, "From a can, or—"

Downstairs, I heard glass shatter.

CHAPTER SIXTEEN

That's not a car, Dallas. That's a serious, 12-gauge shotgun. The front windows were being shot out, one by one. Raul burst into the office. The folder was empty, and I threw it as we ran down the stairs and raced for the garage. We rolled beneath the slowly opening automatic door, then jumped into the convertible.

The front of the house was silent, anticipating. The shooter was waiting for us to give ourselves away. Whoever it was knew that he, or she, blocked the only drive out of here. Why someone was shooting at us, I'd worry about later.

I looked around more carefully. The parking area was an island of concrete on the edge of the slope, with meadow at our backs. There were still no sounds from the front. I slipped the keys into the ignition and put the car in neutral. Raul got out and pushed it downhill silently. Momentum took over about the same time shots started again. He hopped into the seat.

We started sailing down the hill, bumping over rocks and into holes. I fought the powerless power steering to avoid the bigger obstacles—like mesquite trees. "Faster, *andele!*" Raul shouted. He fired his Walther at the Suburban.

A Suburban?

I pressed the clutch, put it in third, and popped it; the engine started. Raul banged against the dash, then slammed back into the seat. "Put on your seat belt!" I shouted, weaving down the hill.

At the bottom, there was no road. Only the wired fences of Fossil Rim.

"Are they shocking?" Raul asked.

Electrified? It hadn't occurred to me. Raul was swearing in Spanish as he sat up again. The driver of the Suburban fired after us again. He was a lousy shot—thank God.

For just a second the wheels of the Miata stuck in the gummy mud. I gassed it until they tore free, then cranked the steering wheel to avoid hitting the fence. The Suburban followed us, but couldn't turn so tightly. As we heard the smash of metal on fence, I floored it.

Ahead, I spied a small gate that read EMPLOYEES ONLY. No one was around. Raul hopped out, fiddled with the padlock and opened it. As I rumbled over the cattle guard, he jumped back in the car.

Fossil Rim Wildlife Park. I barreled down a bumpy road, hills above us. Across a half-mile plain was another set of hills. Clumps of trees offered the animals some shade.

There was nowhere to hide. I tore across a small clearing that was sprinkled with roaming zebras. At the base of the other hills, we were stopped short by a minicaravan of cars with open windows, filled with people feeding the animals.

"What kind of maniac would target us here?" I asked. My hands were shaking.

"It's okay," Raul said. "He's gone, you know. Calm down."

Cars one and two moved forward. "Calm down!"

"It's just a gun," he said, putting his Walther in his waistband.

"It's not just the gun," I raved. "I've been around guns my entire life; it's the being shot at part that's unnerving."

The third car, still directly in front of us, was spewing food to a growing crowd of animals. I kept glancing frantically in the rearview mirror.

No Suburban.

I rubbed my forehead, where makeup, dirt, and sweat had formed a paste. "Do you think he meant to be shooting at Leo?"

"Turn there," Raul said, pointing to a sign clearly marked WRONG WAY. GO BACK.

"And go one way the wrong way?"

"We'll hide. He won't look there."

"Shouldn't we just stay with the cars, wouldn't that be safer?"

"I don't think he cares who sees, *chica*. It's the middle of the afternoon, and he's shooting with no suppressor."

I saw the Suburban enter the park. I jerked the wheel, turning left into the restricted area, and pulled up beneath a cluster of savanna-style trees. Two minutes later, the Suburban was driving across the clearing. As it approached we could see that the front driver's side was dented, a headlight was out, and the windshield was cracked.

"How could it still be on our trail?" I asked. "Who are they?"

"*No se*. We need to get out of here," Raul said. "I am very nervous about this."

"I don't know a way out," I said. "I've been here once, for a Liz Claiborne fashion shoot, and we didn't set a wheel on the EMPLOYEE ONLY back roads."

"Just drive, and I'll keep an eye on the Suburban," Raul said.

I put it in reverse and started down a hill. At the bottom I threw on the parking brake, spinning the car around, then moved downhill—the correct direction—in low gear.

"It does remind me of Africa," Raul said. "If I had my camera, man, I could get some good shots."

"I wish I had a .270," I said, pulling onto a twisty road. "I'd punch holes through that thing, like a tin can." We drove through the zebra-and-giraffe compound without incident.

"There it is," Raul said, turning around. Sandwiched between a small bus and a four-wheel drive, the tan Suburban sat on the steeply graded hill, at least a quarter mile behind us. On the flatlands we drove past wandering ostriches and emu, and penned rhinos.

Then we were going up again, with no way, no place to turn. Across the valley, the Suburban was heading straight toward us. Fast. No one was around, no other cars, no employee trucks. Just a herd of grazing ibex.

"Do you think he sees us?" Raul asked, staring straight ahead. I was stymied; the underbrush was too dense to drive through, there were no other roads, our only choices were to back up or to go forward. The Suburban angled, and I saw the driver's side window roll down. A black object was pointed toward us. "Silencer!" Raul shouted.

I pressed the pedal to the floor, just as my windshield cracked from the center to the edges. Ibex ran in front of me as I jigged and jagged across the plain. We couldn't hear the shots clearly, so we didn't know we were hit until something else happened to the car.

Like the tire blowing out.

I turned into the spin, driving wildly until we were in the undergrowth of some mesquite trees, killing the engine. It was suddenly silent. "Are you okay?" Raul asked after a moment. I sat, stunned, my safety belt still holding me flat against the seat. We'd managed to cross the valley and get a little uphill, before spinning out. The quiet was interrupted by the sound of a Suburban, somewhere in the distance, shifting into low gear.

"He's still coming after us," I realized, unhooking my belt. We raced forty feet into the underbrush, with Raul dragging a branch behind us, sweeping the ground from side to side to hide our tracks. We were practically on our bellies beneath the trees when we heard the Suburban's door quietly click shut. He was behind the Miata.

We stood motionless, not even breathing. About four feet away a white-tailed deer walked by.

A muffled shot.

The deer fled.

I pressed my lips together to keep from screaming as leaves rained down on us. He was a better shot when he wasn't driving. I heard another vehicle approach.

The Suburban's door slammed again, and he took off.

The other car halted. "Is anyone hurt?" someone called out. "We'll call the police."

Raul and I looked wide-eyed at each other. Not the cops! The second car pulled away and we raced back to our car. The doors were open, the windshield cobwebbed and the tire exploded. "Is there a spare?" he asked.

Knowing Julie, who was the soul of self-sufficiency, I nodded. Raul popped the trunk while I listened for the Suburban, or anyone else, and tried not to shake. Repeatedly I whispered, "Don't lose it. Calm down. Calm down." It is one thing to live with guns. It is entirely another thing to be hunted by them.

"You might try some deep-breathing exercises," Raul said, slipping the jack beneath the car. I watched him raise up the car. Far off, I heard the wail of a police siren. Raul switched out the tires—it was a midget spare—then released the jack. I wedged the tire in the backseat. "We make a good team," he said, flashing a smile.

I threw him the keys and we drove down the hill, taking the correct turns and finally finding ourselves on the road back to the highway. The sound of sirens was getting closer. If the police had a description of our car, we were finished. To our left, a longhorn munched grass in a field, his horns standing out two feet on either side of his head. The sirens fell silent; they were going another way.

In silence we rode at least fifteen miles, at forty miles per hour.

"So," Raul said, "I don't think so, but why are you sure Leo and Ileana weren't you know, lovers?"

There had been no sign of a beige Suburban. I guessed we were safe. "He's bi."

Raul slowed down for one of the small towns, obeying the signs that I could barely read through the windshield. How was I going to explain the destroyed car to Julie? How was I going to pay for it to be fixed?

"He liked men and women," Raul said. "Very passionate."

"Yes," I said.

"So why not Ileana? Or April? It seems being bi would mean them. To take the best of men and women, would mean them."

"Blondes," I said.

"*¿Que?*" he said, glancing at me.

"Blonde, both Ileana and April were blondes, at least most of the time."

"He didn't like blondes?" Raul sounded horrified.

"It's more than that. He preferred a particular type of woman, and a spectrum of men."

"So he would, uh, be with a blond man, but not a blonde woman?"

I shrugged. "I don't really know. We did stuff together, but we didn't talk about his love life. However, I know he loved Latina types. Blondes left him cold. That's why I can't believe the rumors about a relationship with Ileana." When had she dyed her hair, though? Did the police know to look into that?

"Why tell me this now? Why not before?"

I shrugged. My feeling about Leo's silence was growing worse by the moment. "I wish I had looked over his house more carefully," I said.

"Hard to when you're being shot at, you know?"

"No, I mean in Dallas." I glanced at my watch. We might do a little more breaking and entering when we got back.

"How did the Suburban find us?" Raul said.

"Why did he?" I asked. "Why shoot at us? And what kind of idiot would shoot in front of all those people?"

Raul was silent as we limped back to Dallas at 40 mph.

Raul and I had traded places; I was driving and fantasizing about food, he was checking his messages. It was almost dark as we drove into the city. Storm clouds hovered over the glass-and-metal skyline, the tints of salmon and yellow reflected from earth to sky.

Salmon. My stomach growled.

"Where are we going?" Raul asked.

I didn't have an answer, not that I hadn't thought about it. I had thought of little else for the past one and a half hours as we drove past the many concrete factories and power stations and through early evening traffic. The Dallas Stars were in town tonight, playing at Reunion Arena. "So I've been thinking about it. Do you think the shooter knew who we were?" I asked.

"Yes."

I changed lanes carefully, the window too fractured to see out. "Then why shoot at us?"

"Maybe we know something."

"How did he even know we were there?" I asked.

Raul glanced at me. "Your phone, maybe?"

"It's tapped?"

"I don't know. Could he trace it?" Raul asked.

I looked at my Nokia, jutting up from the black hole of my Prada bag, so green and innocent. "Can you trace cell-phone calls?"

"How else would he know?"

I told Raul to hand it to me, and he turned my purse over in the process. As he stuffed everything back in, apologizing profusely, I saw the wadded-up note from the other night. "Read that," I told him.

"It's kind of dark. Are you sure?"

"Just read."

Dear Ms. O'Connor:

I know that I started badly by lying to you, but I was afraid you wouldn't answer me unless you thought I was legitimate. I am a real reporter, a stringer for the *Dallas Morning News*, and I am on the crime beat. However, until I hit a big story, I will be nothing else. As a good faith gesture, if there is any information you need, test me and make sure that I will deliver it. I need this story Ms. O'Connor. It's my life's dream,

Please.

Sincerely,
Carla Chou

"Who's she?" Raul asked. "Unless I am being ... No forget it. I'm sorry."

"If you apologize again," I said through gritted teeth, "I'll hurt you. Saying you're sorry for taking me hostage would be nice. Everything else is a waste of time." I waited a moment. He said nothing. Good. "It's a note from that reporter I told you about. She's willing to do something for me in good faith, so that I will tell her what it was like to find the body." Raul turned off his flashlight. "She'd really want the story if she knew it had kidnapping, Cubans, and target-practicing Suburbans in it."

On Raul's suggestion, we pulled up in front of a Deep Ellum bar with open doors and blaring music. It was kind of early for Ellum, so parking was easy. A few well-tattooed twentysomethings were clustered on the sidewalk, smoking and drinking. It looked appealing, but I'd given up cigarettes about the same time I gave up being married and gave up living in Mexico City. The temptation only reared its head in a bar.

And this was the second time I'd been in a bar in the past two days. My grandmother would be stricken; I was becoming a barfly.

"Wait a minute," I said, as we got out and crossed the street to a different pool hall from yesterday's. "Whether the phone was tapped or not doesn't matter. We didn't tell anyone where we were going."

"*Jesus,* that's right," Raul said. "Man, we're being followed."

It was a relief to step into the dark of the bar, the anonymity. I ordered an ice-cold Shiner to go with the air-conditioning they had on full blast. "You need to call your answering machine," Raul said. "The pay phones are in back. Do you have change?"

I was about to say I had a calling card, but then I realized that maybe they could trace its use just like a credit card. Not that I was buying the whole phone-tapping scenario, but I was feeling paranoid enough to be extracareful. Shouldering my bag and taking his change, I walked to the back. With an unwieldy stack of quarters and nickels—I didn't know a phone call had gone up to thirty-five cents—I dialed in, used my remote code, and held my breath.

Kreg had checked in from California, concerned that he hadn't heard from me in so long. "Are you shacked up with something dark and romantic?" he asked. Sotto voce he said, "I am," and hung up. I grinned and swallowed some more Shiner.

My mother called. She had just seen a documentary on cell phones, and was concerned about me getting brain cancer. "Hold the antenna away from your head," she said. "And talk on your left side. Save your creative right side, you'll need it." At least she hadn't seen broadcast TV. I guessed this hadn't hit her local paper yet. Now if my siblings would just stay quiet. . . .

Another message.

"Dallas O'Connor, this is Officer Williams from the Dallas Police Department, I'm Detective Mansfield's partner. Call me at your earliest convenience. We need your assistance with regard to Leo Pastriani." He gave the number and hung up.

Was that a lure? He had to know I was wanted. Did he think I was stupid enough to just call back? The next messasge: "Dallas O'Connor? I'm interested in renting your duplex. I'm male, professional, no pets, I don't smoke, and I want to live close to the lake. Please call me—"

"I finally get a normal-sounding person, and I don't have time to respond," I groused to myself, saving the call for another time.

The last phone call was Carla Chou. "Ms. O'Connor. By now you have read my note. As part of the good-faith gesture, I wanted to let you know that if you have any questions, I will be pleased to answer them." Very slowly, enunciating deliberately Carla said: "*Any* questions."

I finished my beer and stared at the graffiti on the wall. Before I could rethink, I called Carla. "Answer this: who is Texas license plate BFW 56-something?"

"Give me a number to call you back," she said.

"No, I'll call you," I said. "Just tell me when."

"This isn't TV Ms. O'Connor—"

"For heaven's sake, just call me Dallas."

"Okay, Dallas. I can't have a response for you until sometime tomorrow. When can we meet and discuss the case?"

"I'll call you," I said, and hung up. Hanging up without saying good-bye was wearing on me. It made this whole hiding, furtive, lifestyle seem that much more melodramatic and ludicrous. I needed to just call the police, drag Raul in to testify for me, and get back to my life.

Since I had one.

Ileana didn't.

I finished my beer in a swallow and called Carla back. "Another question."

"Shoot."

"I just got a call from Officer Williams, the detective's partner. He said he wanted my 'assistance' about—"

"Oh no, he really said that?"

"Yes, regarding Leo Pastriani. Why?"

Carla sighed and lowered her voice. "Usually, that means the person is . . . deceased."

CHAPTER SEVENTEEN

L eo. Leo wasn't missing; I'd felt that in my bones, even though I'd been loath to admit it. Leo was dead. I read the names that were written on the wall, of whom I should be calling for a good time, as I felt the knowledge descend on me.

"You have my condolences," Carla said to my silence. "Anything else?" she asked after a moment.

"No. But,—"

"When can I interview you?"

I stared scanning the darkness of the bar, irrationally afraid that she could somehow see me. "I'll call you," I said, hanging up and sliding to the floor.

Leo, Leo, what happened.

"This is a really bad idea," Raul said for the umpteenth time on the drive. I wondered briefly what "umpteenth" meant, really. Probably something with Latin roots.

Latin was appropriate, because it was Saturday night, I'd missed mass twice today—not news—and I was going back to Leo's house. That was news.

"Make sure and look for the film," Raul said, also for the umpteenth time. "Maybe in his luggage or something."

The image of Leo's bathroom, with those bottles from New Orleans just scattered around, haunted me. Why had he come back from New Orleans early, and who else had seen him since? Only two things had shown up: a contract and a tape-recorded message. That was it.

Why was that cassette player at Jacob's house? What woman had been staying there. Ileana? Why? When? I was driving myself crazy with questions; we needed more information.

Leo's house might have it, and the film that Raul swore would make everything make sense. If I got enough information, I was going to call Diana Mansfield and set the story straight. With or without Mr. Raul Domingo's permission.

He pulled into Starbucks, and I stayed in the car, slouched down, and practiced what I would say to the woman who thought I was capable of a horrific murder. He handed me a doppio latte and a biscotti. It wasn't much, but it would combat the Shiners I'd had. We drove in silence to our tried-and-true parking spot, three blocks from Leo's house. Raul opened the door to get out. I laid a hand on his arm.

"What?" he said quietly.

"You don't have to come. In fact, it might be better if you don't."

"You don't want me along?"

"If there is some sort of trap, only one of us will get caught."

"A trap? Oh man, you gotta be kidding me?"

"No, but I'd rather have a getaway car than someone who wigs out when it comes to climbing down a tree." I winked to show I was, sort of, joking. With one gulp I finished my latte. "I'll be back in a few minutes," I said, handing him my phone. "Take this in case I need to call you."

He nodded.

I paused, slipping on a pair of leather driving gloves. My attempt at discretion. "Are you sure you don't want to tell me why you fear the police so much? Beyond the murder?"

"No."

"Whatever," I said, shutting the door behind me.

It's not breaking and entering, I reminded myself. I have a key, I'm just choosing to climb through the window. I wasn't sure if they were watching the front door, and the back door had been braced with a piece of wood—who knew why. So I was jimmying the window, in the dark, looking over my shoulder the whole time. Finally, it popped open, and I wiggled a leg through, then slid the rest of my body after it.

My velvet jeans were ruined.

The conservatory was rank with rotting vegetation now. Leo, Leo, I thought, even as I prayed that the reporter was wrong about why I'd been called.

Tiptoeing through the conservatory, then the hallway, I raced up the stairs and burst into Leo's room. "What in the hell?" I said aloud. What had been messy before was downright ransacked now. And I doubted it had been the police—to my knowledge they didn't open mattresses with knives.

Careful not to touch anything, I poked my head in the bathroom. Though everything had been tossed, I saw the New

Orleans hotel toiletries. Leo had been unpacking, I was almost certain of it.

Unpacking—wait! I raced downstairs and opened his refrigerator door. Bad milk, sour cream and crème fraiche could have knocked me over. Bacon, still wrapped, sat on the shelf next to boudain sausage. Unopened. Leo hadn't been here since he'd left my house. Oh God.

I closed the door slowly and sank to the Saltillo tile floor, trying to steady myself. Leo was gone. Really gone. No way would boudain sit untouched—I knew my friend too well. With solemn steps I walked through the dining room to the little model's suite on the opposite side of the house. Cautiously, I opened the door.

The smell was overpowering

This room had been trashed, too. The armoire doors were open, cosmetics strewn over the floor with the ripped mattress, all sprinkled with shards of mirror. A broken bottle of perfume had seeped into the carpet. Joy.

Again.

In the bathroom, Pepto-Bismol pink towels filled the claw-foot bathtub. A pair of size small black thong underwear hung from the bathroom faucet. Nothing else.

I moved the mattress and found the hat, now squashed, and the train case. Picking it up, I moved in to the bathroom for light and looked inside the case. Stuffed in the side was a latent Polaroid negative, the black blending in with the black of the case.

Maybe from the shoot Raul did of Ileana? I tucked it in my jeans, then put the stuff back, smashed under the mattress.

Two bottles of Joy. Two women who wore it. I left the room and was on my way out the back when I passed the garage door. "Do you have a deep freeze?" the question rose in my mind. My heart throbbed in my throat as I opened the door and stepped into the dark, humid space. I didn't know where the light switch was, but I knew where the freezer was. It seemed to glow whitely from the wall. Leo's BMW was missing.

Gone.

I pressed my lips together to keep from crying.

The suction that held the top of the freezer down was strong; I had to use both hands to pull it open. Artificial white light threw the contents into brighter-than-life colors. It took me a second to realize what I was staring at.

Blood. On carpet.

The top fell from my cold hands and I fled the garage, kicking the door shut. I raced into the kitchen, ripping off my gloves and scouring my hands with soap and hot water until they were red. My teeth were gritted so tightly together that my jaw ached. "Oh Leo, my God, what happened?" I asked the empty kitchen.

The kitchen that would always be empty.

I ran through the house, desperate to leave it. A few tugs wouldn't move the wood blocking the door, so I ducked through the window. I was crouched there, one foot in, one foot out, when I realized I really did have to call the police now. There was no choice. I went back to the kitchen to use the phone. It took a few tries to dial; I had no control in my fingers.

I didn't have the number; I'd have to call information.

A minute later I was asking to speak to the woman working on the Ileana Karagonis case.

Voice mail.

"This is Detective Diana Mansfield, please leave your name and number at the tone and I'll get back to you as soon as possible. Beep."

"Uh, yes. I have some information about the Karagonis murder—uh—" I said, trying to stop the wavering in my voice. "I want to meet with you." I felt like Deep Throat. I felt the terror Deep Throat must have felt. "I uh, have some information, and uh, I don't want to come downtown." Was it my imagination or was I giving them plenty of time to come get me? "Forget it," I said, hanging up.

I looked at my watch; of course, it was 10:45 on a Saturday night, why should she be there? But I had to tell her, I had to tell somebody about this. An anonymous 911 call? They'd know it was from this house. "Oh God," I whispered, more as a prayer than anything else. Where could I meet her, straighten this mess out?

My mind, after a lifetime of living in or visiting Dallas, was blank. I looked around the room, searching for a clue. No place where anyone knew me. No place where I couldn't escape. No place that was trendy.

My gaze fell on Leo's Rollerblades, tossed in a corner. Skating, that was the idea. Skate in, skate out—much faster than running. But where could I go and not see anyone I knew? White Rock Lake was out, as was Fair Park. I dialed her again: "Meet me at Bachman Lake," I said. "Across from In Flight Chicken. By the bridge. Tomorrow, 9 A.M. I'll be the blonde." I hung up, shaking.

Hoping Leo had my foot size, I picked up his skates, fumbling to hold on to them. I dialed my cell phone and Raul answered. "The alley," I said. "Come get me."

* * *

In Flight Chicken, across from Bachman Lake in the center of Dallas and directly in the flight pattern of the Love Field airport, is the perfect place to not talk. The food is simple and tasty, and the planes fly over approximately every forty-five seconds, drowning out all hopes of conversation.

A man-made lake located on the south side of four-lane Loop 12, Bachman Lake was in a rather run-down part of the city. When my grandparents had lived here in the forties and fifties, Bachman Lake had been the height of respectability. It had been a site for company picnics, romantic dinners, and, of all things, rowboats.

Now it was seedy, though I saw a new drugstore and shopping center had gone up. Maybe they were trying to revitalize it. Whatever. It seemed unreal to me now, compared to the contents of the deep freeze. Seven more Shiner Bocks hadn't faded that memory, though I felt them today.

"Are you sure this is it?" Raul said, as I motioned him into the gravel parking lot next to the restaurant.

"It's perfect," I said automatically. "I'll be back in a few minutes."

He was looking around, frowning. "This is a bad neighborhood, Dallas."

"I didn't want safe, I wanted out of the way," I said.

"Should you eat?"

I glanced at my watch: 8:50 on a Sunday morning. My stomach churned. "They aren't open yet," I said. "Maybe when I get back."

I sat down and strapped on my skates, while he planned what he was going to order when they did open: A plate of roasted chicken, double-baked potatoes, and the best coleslaw in the city. "I'll get you a Coke."

"I'd kill for strong, rancher's coffee right now," I said then, "I take it back. We use that word too much."

A plane flew over, so I pantomimed good-bye and recklessly skated across the street, reaching the sidewalk that followed the edge of the lake. The wind blew over me, and I was grateful for my velvet jeans, despite the holes, and wishing I had a T-shirt beneath my sweater. "Think mundane," I whispered to myself. It felt good to be moving, doing something physical and normal, despite my hangover.

The sidewalk was deserted as far as I could see. If I went right, I would reach the parking lot. A few lowriders, stereos blasting, already claimed that space. To my left was a downhill path that led under the bridge, and up again to the back of a chain hotel.

At least it was morning. Would she be here?

I pushed off toward the hotel. The ducks were already paddling across the greenish gray water.

I slowed down on the hill, approaching the bridge cautiously. As I entered the shadow the overpass made, I took off my baseball cap and my hair fell to my shoulders.

"You're the blond? Dallas O'Connor?" Her voice traveled across the water. She stood twenty feet away, on the other side of the lake.

I shouldn't have been surprised. "Yes," I said, surprised at how strong my voice sounded.

"Do you want to go across the street for coffee, or get killed here by some strung-out teenager?" she asked. "This is a stupid location. This case doesn't need any more melodrama."

"I know," I said. "I'm sorry. I'll meet you at Norma's," I

said, naming a fifties-style diner across the street. I was really growing tired of running. I needed my life back, and her trust in me would be the first step.

"We'll go together," she said. "My partner is behind you."

"No," I said, panicked. I turned around and heard a gunshot beside me.

Behind me, a man shouted as she fell into the water.

Someone plowed into my back, knocking me onto the concrete, shoving me toward the water. I kicked out, then rolled away, regaining my feet. I skated like hell for the road.

"Stop her!" I heard behind me.

Not daring to glance over my shoulder I powered my way to the road, then across it, deaf to the squealing tires and honking horns.

"Freeze or I'll shoot!"

I froze. Hands jerked me back onto the Bachman Lake side and threw me onto the grass.

"Spread-eagled," he barked, kicking my legs apart.

I complied immediately, panting, sweating and terrified. He ran rough hands ran over my body. "You have the right to remain silent. Anything you say can and will be held against you in a court of law—" He cuffed one wrist, then jerked my other hand back to it. Over the sound of tires squealing I heard the approach of sirens.

A police car pulled up beside the road and I was forced into the backseat, the rest of the Miranda warning echoing in my brain. "What are the charges?" I managed to stutter out.

An ambulance tore across the grass. The officer's voice was full of fury. "Assaulting a police officer."

I closed my eyes in terror.

*   *   *

It was impossible to lean back comfortably. The cops in the front seat didn't talk to each other or to me during the ride to downtown. I haven't done anything wrong, I repeated to myself. This was a mistake. A mistake. I ground my teeth together to keep from screaming.

We crossed under I-35, then Industrial, and pulled up to an automatic door. Before us, a metal gate rose and we drove into the restricted parking beneath the Lew Sterritt County Courts Building. They parked the car in the garage and got out, opening the trunk of the car. In the side mirror I saw them take off their weapons. Then they opened the door and let me out.

The underground lot was filled with men in white jump-suits with black letters that spelled PRISONER going down the left leg. They wore orange shoes. I was in socks, since they'd taken my Rollerblades. As we walked toward the doors, I had the nagging feeling I'd been here before.

I'd never been here before, what was I thinking?

Double doors led into a low-ceiling, fluorescent-lit hall-way, too narrow for anything except conducting prisoners.

"Lee Harvey Oswald," I said in shock, halting.

The officer glanced at me. "Good eye. Yes, this is right where Mr. Jack Ruby shot Mr. Oswald. The doors are different, glassed now, but this is the place."

My parents, the psycho history buffs, would think it too cool to see this.

"And above the jail, it's haunted," he said, as they escorted me into the building, and into an elevator. My breath felt tight in my chest as I tried not to breathe in the mingled odors of pine cleaner and urine.

We stepped out into chaos. Who would have thought so many people were going to jail on a Sunday. "We'll put you in holding until they're ready to process you," the officer who'd arrested me said.

"Don't I get a phone call?" I asked, my throat constricted.

"Sure. You can call as many people as you like," he said as we walked past tables where men and women were lined up, their shoes and socks already removed. In front of me I saw the holding cell for men. To my right was the cell for women.

Oh my God. I was in jail.

A female cop grasped my arm, unlocked my cuffs, and pushed me into the room where about twelve other women were seated or standing. "Toilets are to the back and left," she barked. "Phone calls are all collect. We should have you processed in about three hours."

The barred door slammed shut.

CHAPTER EIGHTEEN

Hours later—they had taken my Movado—I still couldn't get hold of the wily Cuban who had my cell phone. That telephone, with its memory full of home and office numbers for my large, scattered family who could actually help me out of here, was MIA.

But then, when I thought about it, I wondered if I really did want to call my family. All those questions, recriminations, all that Irish temper. A friend would be a better choice. Much better.

As I looked around the holding cell, the assortment of females in assorted dress, I was astounded at the quantity of business in a jail on a Sunday.

Back in line for the phones, I waited through another group of women calling boyfriends, fathers, brothers, pimps, and bookies. Contrary to what Hollywood had shown me, people didn't chat. No one cared why someone else was here. It was intensely private, despite us being packed in like chickens.

I didn't know much about jail, but bail I knew. One of my siblings—who shall remain nameless but was born in Houston—had to be bailed out of jail after a rowdy bachelor party. I knew all about bail and about what you can and cannot hock at dawn on a holiday.

So of my friends, who was in town?

I was certain Raul wouldn't have the cash for bail. Coco and Julie were in Vegas, Lindsay's cell was off.

Time slipped by and I watched as woman after woman was taken away. They didn't come back.

The dreaded "processing" was approaching. Unlike the scene of the murder, no one had asked me a thing.

Dialing The Store's corporate headquarters, I got no one. Gary didn't answer at his home. I looked at the line of women waiting behind me. They stared stonily at me. I dialed some more numbers. Mere Illusion's front office rang incessantly, so I called the other extension.

"Darkroom," came a response.

"Finally!" I cried.

There was a puzzled silence.

"This is Dallas O'Connor," I explained. "This sounds awful, but I need someone to find the photo assistant Raul Domingo and retrieve my cell phone from him. It's an emergency."

"Okay, Dallas O'Connor, but why is it an emergency?" The voice was male, but between the clash of metal on metal and the conversation among the women, I couldn't discern more. "Where are you?"

"It's a long story," I hedged. "Please, let me tell you where Raul might be."

"I'm curious about that," he said, "but what is the emergency? Finding Raul doesn't sound much like—"

"I'm in jail," I said.

"I'll be right down."

"I—" but I was talking to air. Who would have been working on a Sunday? I didn't care; I just wanted this day to be over.

"This your first time," a woman said to me. "You look pretty scared for a criminal." Her glance was appraising, making me aware of the differences and similarities between us. We were the same height, same coloration, probably the same age, though I couldn't tell beneath her makeup.

"What are you here for?" I asked, imitating every cop show I'd ever seen.

She laughed. "Does it matter? There's no differences in here, baby. Now are you gonna use that phone, or just waste more of my time?"

I stepped away. Maybe some Hollywood clichés were right. "Go for it."

Ten minutes later, my name was called from the front. I was shaking all over; even my feet trembled. I just hoped it wasn't processing. Raul's comments about how innocent citizens got caught and trapped in the system were haunting me.

I pushed forward through the crowd. The warden, or whatever the female guard cop is called, replaced my handcuffs and I told myself that it was just for a few more minutes. I was going to be free!

I recognized the red-haired, uniformed cop waiting for me. "Officer Williams, how is Detective Mansfield?" I asked.

His eyes were cold. "Stable, fortunately."

Thank God. Then I remembered where I'd heard his name before, and felt sick to my stomach. "You called me," I said, my voice barely a whisper.

"About Leo Pastriani, yes. Would you mind answering some questions?"

I nodded. I wanted out of here, at any cost.

"Then we'll get you processed next," he said, hand on my arm.

"Is that necessary?" I pleaded. "I won't be here much longer."

"I can't question you until you are processed through here. I think you want to tell me about Leo, I really do." He placed me in line and joined two other uniformed cops by the far wall.

The lines before the tables had gotten shorter. I took off my socks and waited, watching. Before me a man was instructed to put his hands on his head. A different female cop, wearing plastic bags on her hands, searched him. Thoroughly.

A woman to my left was taken into a small room. She appeared a few minutes later. "Your turn," the cop said. My breath got stuck in my chest when they clicked the handcuffs on again.

When we emerged from the little room I was fighting tears. I watched stoically as they gummed my fingers with ink, then gently pressed them, all ten, for my fingerprints. While one cop was doing that, another was asking yes/no questions about whether I'd ever been depressed. On medication. Suicidal. My voice shook as I answered.

Williams was waiting for me and walked me to the elevator. "I didn't do anything to Detective Mansfield," I said. "I saw her go—"

"Why did you run instead of helping her?"

"She said her partner—you I guess—was there," I said. "I was scared. I've been shot at a lot in the past few days."

Williams' gaze sharpened. "You've been shot at? Since when?"

"Well," I said, stalling.

"Perhaps at Leo's house in Glen Rose?" he asked me.

I nodded, mute.

"You've been very difficult to reach, Ms. O'Connor," Williams said. "Despite explicit directions not to leave town."

It wasn't my fault, I wanted to shout. However, I didn't want to get Raul in trouble. The elevator dinged, and the doors opened. "Please," I said, listening to the pleading in my voice. "I'll answer all your questions right now. I'll tell you everything I can think of."

"You are waiving your right to an attorney?"

Was this the stupidest thing I'd ever done? But I knew if I went upstairs, it would become significantly harder to get released. "I do."

He pressed the elevator button—going down. "I'll take you downtown then."

Homicide, or whatever they called it, was in the basement of the Municipal building on Main Street, down an oppressive hallway, down two flights of stairs, and farther down a low-ceilinged passageway. The desks were cluttered, the coffee was industrial, and everyone wore weapons. Williams put me in a windowless room on a hard chair, to wait.

At least I wasn't in jail, I thought, rubbing my face against my shoulder—though I was still in handcuffs, and it was almost dark. I rested my head on the table, just for a minute to ease the kinks in my shoulders. . . .

At 9:55 P.M., Williams opened the door and stepped inside, leaving it ajar behind him. I jerked up, stunned out of my sleep, blinking furiously.

"So you want to tell me about the lake?" he asked, as he unlocked my handcuffs.

"I was trying to meet Diana," I said, shocked into honesty, hissing as feeling flowed back into my arms. "I, uh,—"

"What were you doing at Leo Pastriani's house?"

Which time? "I wanted to see if I could figure out where he'd gone," I said. "We're friends."

He nodded. "Did you learn anything?"

I shivered involuntarily. "The freezer," I said, whispered because I couldn't say it louder. "There's some stuff in the freezer."

He stepped outside for a minute, then came back. "Can I get you anything? Coffee? Coke?"

I shook my head. "I just want to go home," I said, disgusted at the catch in my voice. My stomach growled. "What else can I tell you?"

"How much truth is there in the newspaper report about your relationship with Ileana?" His gaze was intense, but it didn't seem as angry anymore.

My lips were dry, and I couldn't hold his gaze. "I think I should have an attorney present before I answer that," I said.

I only looked up when I heard his chair scrape back. He sat down next to me. "Be warned," he said and handed a photo to me. "It's kind of brutal."

"Oh my God," I said, covering my mouth as my gorge rose. That the Polaroid was of a human being at all, took a moment to register.

"They blew his face off," Williams said. "But we had enough left to ID him from dental records." He pointed to holes in the thing's putty-colored skin. "He's been in the water a while. We found him Thursday, the day after you found Ileana."

I felt like I was going to vomit. Williams passed me another shot, the entire upper body and head of the man.

My gaze skimmed over the remains of the face in the photograph—I couldn't bear to look—down his chest to his hands. They were inflated, white, completely bare of hair.

"Do you recognize this ring?" Williams said, handing me a small bag with a white gold-and-ruby ring. I swallowed hard, looking back at the photo.

"Can you see that abrasion there? Well, after the body was in the water a while, it got swollen. Getting the ring off left some bruising on the pinky."

I stared at the photograph, trying to recognize something beneath the bloating, the fish, the gunshot wound.

"Do you know who it is?"

I nodded. This thing can't be you, I thought. I felt an arm around me.

"For the record ma'am, who is the subject?"

My stomach was cramping; tears were running down my face. Williams waited patiently for my response. "Leo Pastri-ani," I said. "But that's not his original name. He had it legally changed when he was twenty-one." It couldn't be: it had to be. Leo had had the most beautiful hands, almost womanly. He was assiduous about manicures, he'd even had the backs of them Epi-lighted so they didn't look like bear paws, he'd said. The ruby ring had been his grandmother's.

"From what?"

I shook my head. "He never said. But he was from a poor, deep-South family. Mississippi or Alabama, I think. Oh God, how did he end up in the water?"

"Some of the workers on the new stadium down by the Trinity River came across the body. We're awaiting final results, but we know he was shot before he entered the water. They weighted it pretty good."

"Results from what?"

"Forensics tests, ma'am." Williams's eyes were brown and long-lashed. "We send them to SWIFS, that's Southwestern Institute of Forensic Sciences, to see what they tell us."

"You say he was in the, the water for a while?" My eyes were closed, the images laser printed on my mind.

"A week or two," Williams said.

"Then he couldn't have killed Ileana."

"We won't know until we get the forensics back on her," he said. "Your friend Leo isn't completely out of the question yet."

Without looking at it, I handed him back the photo. Williams stood up. "Your ride is waiting," he said.

I looked up, still dazed.

"Diana said you didn't shoot at her. She said you weren't responsible. In fact, she said she saw someone else, standing close to you. However, I had to take you in since you were on the scene and there was an outside chance that you had set her up."

I should be mad, fighting for my rights, but I was numb. "She's fine?"

"Doing well. The shooter nicked her shoulder, a lousy shot if he was trying to hurt her. Then she fell into the lake—"

"That's almost worse," I said. "That water is gross." This must be what an out-of-body experience is like. I'm here, but I'm not.

"Do you think it was the same person you claim has been shooting at you?" Williams asked.

"My guy is a lousy shot, or he's right-handed and can't shoot and drive," I said. "She was shot, at least it sounded like it, with a .357 Magnum." The same one that shot Leo, probably. I felt sick.

"You know guns?" he asked, his tone changing a little.

"My granddaddy," I answered automatically. "Part of my education."

"Well," Williams continued, crossing his arms like a high-school coach, "you are under suspicion of arson, car theft, which would be grand larceny, breaking, and entering, and perhaps aiding and abetting a known felon."

I felt nothing. Leo was dead, horribly dead. "That it?" I snapped. It didn't matter. None of it.

"Your transportation is here."

"I can leave?"

"This building, but not this town. Don't leave Dallas," Williams said. "And give me your cell-phone number."

I rattled it off—why not.

"Your ride's out front."

I nodded. Whoever he was, I hope he recognized me. All I could see was Leo's faceless body.

Only one "he" was waiting at the Main Street exit at eleven on Sunday night. Not Raul, not Kevin, not Gary. No, the only person I wanted to see less than the cops, not only because I felt guilty for his studio burning down, but because there were a lot of unanswered questions regarding his relationship with Ileana, and all of them were distasteful.

Jacob James's gaze stayed focused on my face. In his left hand, he held my Rollerblades by their fasteners. In his right was a flask. "You hate tequila, right?" he said, handing it to me. My hands were shaking too badly to hold it, so he very gently and slowly tipped it for me. Jack Daniel's scorched my throat. "Excuse me," I said, fighting tears.

He shook his head, then fed me another sip. "You ready to get out of here?"

I nodded, beyond the powers of speech. His hand on my back directed me through the echoing hallway of the building, out into the March night. I'd missed a whole day in my life. I started shaking.

Jacob helped me into the front seat of his SUV, then walked around to his side. After throwing my in-line skates in back, he turned on the engine and slid into traffic, heading toward Deep Ellum.

Jacob said nothing and neither did I.

We pulled up before the ruins of his studio and he got out, walking to the edge of the yellow caution tape. I had a few more sips of JD, then got out in search of him.

He was crouched at the back of what had been his building. The wind stirred his dark hair, blowing over his face. "How are you," he said, as I crept up behind him.

"How's it going?" I countered.

He chuckled. "It depends if one has insurance or not, I would imagine."

"You did?"

He shrugged. "Whatever."

"Jacob, I—"

Slowly he got to his feet and turned to look at me. Of the men I know, Jacob is the only one I wouldn't mind being locked in an elevator with for twelve hours straight. His dark blue eyes seem like he can see through you. "It's too bad that you were the one who found Ileana. It's a hard thing to face a dead body."

"Leo is gone, too," I said. My voice caught and I looked away. Leo was gone, really and truly gone. The truth of it washed over me. "Excuse me," I said, turning on my heel and stumbling back to the SUV.

"Dallas, wait!" Jacob called.

I picked my way carefully, blinded by tears. As I fought to open the door, I felt Jacob's hands on mine. Then, from behind, he wrapped me in his arms. After a moment he turned me around and pressed my head to his chest, his grip secure around my waist. "Go ahead," he said. "Cry, girl."

All I saw behind my eyelids was the mash of red where Leo's face should have been. "He was shot," I whispered, still fighting my tears, "from behind."

Jacob held me tighter, surrounding me in the clean smell of starch and soap. My fingers clenched in the folds of his shirt as I fought not to lose it. "Tell me," he said. "Talk to me, Dallas."

"They shot him and dumped his body in the river," I said. "Only his hands were . . . recognizable? The gun . . . the fish . . ." If I thought about this, I was going to be sick. "Why be so brutal? Dead is dead—why, why take his face?" I choked. "Leo always wanted open casket," I said. "Now, now we can't—"

* * *

Leo and I had been sharing a banana-walnut-fudge split on Oak Lawn Avenue after another funeral in the early nineties. The fashion community in Dallas had been devastated by AIDS. We'd just returned from a memorial service where the victim was too young, too talented, and too alive to be dead. Early on, Leo and I had made the pact that we would eat a banana split in celebration for each of the lives of the funerals we'd attended.

About then is when I had to join the gym.

"You know the good thing about Clive's funeral," Leo had said, talking with his spoon.

"I can't think of one good thing," I'd said. We were attending funerals at least once a month. It became numbing after a while.

"He was still beautiful enough to have open casket."

"That was the part I found so disturbing. I hate open caskets. It's chilling. Do you know what they do to the bodies? Talk about styling, the magic of makeup. Ugh."

"Dallas, did you know that man was forty-eight?"

I'd paused, the texture of warm fudge brownie and melting ice cream on my tongue. "No way. He couldn't have been much more than thirty-five."

Leo leaned across the table. "I dated him briefly. I assure you, late forties."

"He was definitely still beautiful."

"When I go—"

"Now Leo, don't—"

"No, this is a conversation we need to have. You never know what tomorrow holds. So just—"

"I don't want—"

"Listen to me, Dallas," he'd said, cutting off my protests. "I've thought about this a lot. If I die before you, it is your job to see that everything is perfect."

"Should I be taking notes?"

"They are already in my file, marked 'E' for Eternity."

I'd nodded.

"I want white lilies, I don't care about the cost. Open casket with a nice jewel-toned velvet drape if it's in the fall or winter. I loathe the satin, but if there are no choices for the spring or summer, then try to go light, a blush so that I look tan."

One by one I picked the walnut pieces off the whipped cream.

"I want 'You Light Up My Life' to be sung by Tommy, as Debby Boone, and 'Shall We Gather by the River,' to be sung by a gospel choir. I have a list of choices from Oak Cliff churches," he'd said. "But I want real gospel. I'm from the South, girl, even from Beyond I'll know if they are real."

"Okay."

"You will, of course, give a stunning eulogy."

"I hate talking in front of people," I'd said.

"I'm your nearest and dearest friend and neighbor! You'll do it for me."

"If you are really dead, you won't know." I stabbed the cherry. "This is a terrible conversation."

"Dallas, promise me this."

I'd looked up at him.

"No matter what, you will make sure I look beautiful, right? Healthy, tanned, fit? And not a wrinkle or gray hair showing."

*　*　*

It was that expression, the most emotionally naked Leo had ever been with me, that I saw now in my mind's eye. "He wanted to make those bitches weep when he was gone," I whispered against Jacob's shirt. "But . . . but he's not pretty anymore," I said. Then the sobs came, uncontrollable crying. My dear friend was dead. Someone had deliberately ended his life, taken his final requests from him, and tried to wreck his reputation, too.

Jacob's touch was soothing, and as I cried he rubbed my back, stroked up my spine, then down. He slipped a starched handkerchief into my hand at one point, and I blew my nose, temporarily wrung out. I pulled away, not wanting to leave the security of his embrace, but needing to gulp at the air.

He released me immediately, leaning against the door of the Infiniti. I gestured toward the ruin of his building. "Do the police know anything?"

"The fire department said it was arson," he said. "A Molotov cocktail, through a window. Why were you here that night?"

Damn. He had seen the TV. "Raul," I said.

"Why was he here?"

My brain was too tired, too overloaded to think of anything but the truth. "He wanted to see if you had some film of a shoot he'd done."

"Ileana?"

I nodded.

"No. She'd tried to get me to do it. For some reason, she wanted to be in my studio. I don't like to mix my professional and private lives, so I told her to make Raul do the shoot."

Glancing at him, I said, "You were dating Ileana?" Jacob

was some indefinable age between forty and death. He'd always been around, but he seemed my contemporary. Still, even forty was sickeningly old to be dating a nineteen-year-old.

He didn't meet my gaze. "We ended our association last month."

Ileana had wanted to be in his studio. So she'd used Raul instead. "Why?"

"Because this isn't a book by Nabokov," he said bitterly. "I'm not an old roué."

"Then why was she staying with you?"

If he was surprised, he didn't show it. "She wasn't. She never had. It wouldn't have been smart for either of us."

Which meant another woman, who wore Joy, was. "Who do you think killed Ileana?" I asked.

He crossed his arms, leaned his head back, and stared at the wreckage of his studio. "In a few hours, the police will tell you that I did."

"Raul was the one found with the knife," I said. "Not that the police believe me."

"My knife."

It was a moment before I thought of a response. "What would be your reason?"

"Perhaps that I didn't want her to go? Or that she threatened to press charges against me for statutory rape, since she was a minor when we first met? Maybe she was going to reveal some deep, dark secret of mine." His tone was ruthlessly casual. Chilling. Filled with icy anger. "Or perhaps the truth."

"Which is?"

He pushed away from the car, and his face was hard as he spoke. "That she and Leo screwed me out of Duchesse Cosmetics. My longtime client, my dear friend, both smitten by a young, new face." Jacob gestured to the studio. "That Duchesse fee was the money I was counting on to use to insure my studio."

My blood turned to ice. "You don't have insurance?" How was that possible? He made a fortune, relatively speaking, he had a nice house, three new cars, everything he could want. "No insurance?" I squawked again.

"No. And now I have no gear, no studio, no assistant and every reason to have killed a nineteen-year-old beauty." His tone was mean now. "Be careful, Dallas. While I may have lost a client, and a ton of money, which would be motive enough, the police think her theft of your money is even stronger."

I felt surprise on my face. His expression hardened. "You know, you aren't young, but you can be really stupid." He walked around the car and got in, gunning the motor.

In silence, I got in and we took off with a squeal.

I was deep into the sleep of the innocent and justified, when my phone startled me awake: 3:30 A.M. "Something you might find interesting."

"Yes?" I groaned, trying to place the voice

"The autopsy reports are back from SWIFS. You know that they can tell if someone has used a gun by the powder burns left on their fingers, right?" It was the reporter—Carla. My mind was clearing fast. I sat up.

"Uh-huh?" I didn't know that, but she didn't need to know how ignorant I was.

"They can also tell whose blood has been on what instrument, even if the instrument has been cleaned."

"Okay."

"Think on this. Leo Pastriani's fingerprints were found on the hunting knife that was found at the scene, with Ileana. But," she said triumphantly, "it was Jacob James's knife. He's downtown for questioning right now. It's looking like they'll take him in; they already have a search warrant for his house."

I hung up the phone and lay back down, my head spinning. Jacob had guessed right—or he'd known. After a half hour of trying to return to sleep, I gave up, went downstairs, and started some coffee. I poured a café au lait with extra cream and walked out to my porch swing. It was dark out, and the weather had changed to cold. I pulled a blanket over my shoulders and tucked it in around my legs, swinging back and forth.

Leo's prints were on the murder weapon, the knife that was used on Ileana, but he'd been dead for weeks. When had she died?

Jacob and Ileana had "ended their association" whatever that meant, and the knife was Jacob's originally.

There were rumors about Ileana being in and April being out of the Duchesse. And April was the only other woman—I knew of—who wore Joy. Where had she been during all of this?

Raul was scared of the police and refused to answer their questions, but his prints also had to be on the knife, though the cops hadn't said anything.

Someone in a Suburban had been trying to shoot us.

And the strangest detail, was the cutout on Ileana's back.

Inside, the phone rang. I couldn't talk to Carla again; I needed to think.

I got up and walked to the door, listening for the click, just in case it was my parents. If I didn't answer at four in the morning, they would freak out. I'm thirty-five and have lived my life independently since I was twenty, but they didn't hear that. Instead of a message being left, however, I heard keys being pressed.

Someone was trying to access my messages through the recorder! Outraged, I picked up the phone. "Was there something you wanted?" I asked.

CHAPTER NINETEEN

Click.

What was the code to do an automatic return call? I flipped through the phone book madly, looking for the page that would tell me. The phone rang again and I picked up.

"How are you?" Jacob asked me.

"Fine," I said tersely. "Isn't it early to be calling?"

"Well," he said, "under normal circumstances I would say yes. In this case however—"

"Did you just call me?"

"Yeah, but the line was busy."

Was he telling the truth or lying?

"Dallas, I hate to ask, but could you come get me?"

I waited a moment, "You're in jail, aren't you?"

"Yup."

*   *   *

The media vans were already there, and a nice officer told me I could park out front while the police held a press conference in the parking garage.

I sat, engine idling, and waited for Jacob. They must have dragged him from the gym because he came out wearing sweats and Reeboks. He looked around for me, and I realized he didn't recognize my car. I waved and he walked—quickly—over.

"This beauty is yours?" he said, gesturing to my '67 Mustang convertible.

"Get in," I said, reaching over to help with the door. He did and I pulled out, heading toward I-35.

"Can I buy you breakfast?" Jacob asked. "I really appreciate this, and it's almost six."

"You can tell me the truth about what is going on."

His laugh was caustic. "Truth isn't always the best thing, Dallas."

I accelerated up the ramp. "I just put my car up for your bail, Jacob." Thank God my brother used to work for the bailbondsman, or I'd be on a bicycle now. "I need to know."

We stopped at Barbec's, the down-at-heels but traditional White Rock Lake breakfast joint. We were the only people sitting outside, so we just had coffee, since it was still nippy and they weren't actually serving out here.

Jacob sat silently, staring into the distance. I sipped my coffee and waited.

"It's involved," he said.

"I have time."

He looked over at my car, pristine condition, gleaming

silver in the morning sun. "You put that up as collateral for me?"

"I don't own anything else," I said. I took another sip of coffee. "Your story?"

"There was a group of us," he began. "A gang. We started working together when we were all very young." Jacob ticked the names off on his fingers, famous names, people I didn't know Jacob, Francis, April, and Leo had run with.

In fact, I hadn't realized just how well Jacob and Leo had known each other. I was beginning to wonder just how well I knew—had known—Leo.

I sipped silently.

"We made a pact that we would always work together. They were such golden days, Dallas, you can't imagine. Every shoot was fun, we were so interwoven into each other's lives, money was never a consideration for anything—we were the rulers of our small world."

I fought to keep from fidgeting. How bad would it be to realize the best days were behind you, not in front of you. For the first time, I felt the age gap between us.

"Leo and April were together through most of it," Jacob said.

"I'd guessed as much."

"Leo had stopped modeling by the time he stumbled on April." Jacob motioned for the waitress. "He negotiated her contract with Duchesse, and they rode that glamour train for a while. She started drinking. He had difficulty keeping his pants zipped. After a while he seemed to lose interest in her, personally. April dabbled in drugs, alcohol . . . it wasn't pretty for a while." Jacob fell silent. "Then we lost three of our crowd to AIDS." The waitress came outside and filled our mugs, then left. "After that, things were never the same," he said.

"What happened with you?"

He looked at me, his deep blue eyes sad. "I moved to Italy, married a model, started a family."

I waited. "Are you still married?"

"Widowed."

"Jacob, that's terrible."

He shrugged. "Life really, really sucks sometimes. Anyway, early on Leo and April set up joint everything: life insurance, wills, stocks, everything financial was between the two of them."

"That was almost twenty years ago," I said. "I'm sure they dissolved those agreements long ago."

"Some of them, but remember, Leo represented her until he died. She was Alliance Artists' first talent. Though they had huge romantic conflicts, April and Leo were great business partners. She was almost superstitious about his representing her." He pushed his cup away. "April didn't think much of men, but she loved Leo because he hadn't betrayed her. At least, not yet."

I looked from my cup, into his face. "What are you telling me?"

"How well did you know Leo?"

Leo and I had been friends for almost a decade. I'd started out selling flowers commercially throughout East Texas, and the Dallas Metroplex had been one of my markets. Leo had met me early on, and had been instrumental in getting me placed at The Store after I'd had my third wreck in a year, because I was living in my car on an insane schedule.

"We were great friends. He lived well, but he worked

hard. Besides, if April were so paranoid about his representing her, she wouldn't kill him. Which brings us back to the original question: Who would?"

Jacob stared at me a moment, then shrugged. "What about Ileana? Why kill her?"

"No idea," I said. "What about Duchesse?"

"They've been going through a major overhaul," he said. "Trying to get a younger demographic. But they're doing well."

"You were rooked out of that, you said. What could one shoot be worth, Jacob?"

"It wasn't just a shoot. It was the whole job," he said. "And I've told you all I'm going to, Dallas." He got up, looking at his watch. "I'm ready to go now."

I drove up to his cottage. A black Labrador sat on the front steps, outlined against the bright front door. "Thank you," Jacob said, opening the car's door before I'd even slowed down. "Where will you be today, so I can get you your money? This is too beautiful a vehicle not to know it's yours."

"Thank you," I said. "I'll be at The Store." He closed the door behind him, and I pulled away, but in the rearview I saw the dog jumping in circles around his master.

I opened my front door at seven-forty-five, sweaty from the gym, just in time to hear Damon leaving a message on my answering machine. ". . . we will discuss this in depth at 11 A.M. I trust you will not be late. Failure to appear will result in immediate dismissal." I slapped my hand on the counter. Great.

A quick rewind revealed that the Dallas police had been asking questions. They'd so disturbed my coworkers that word had gotten back to Damon. I was called to a tribunal, essentially, of The Store's managers. At 11 A.M.

The call before that was the Dallas Police Department, with a few more questions. If I would call Detective Mansfield immediately, they would appreciate it. Caller ID showed me ten other calls, but I didn't have the heart or stomach to listen to them. I was exhausted, emotionally and physically. What had happened to my life?

The *Metamorphosis* film would be delivered at eight. I was racing upstairs, stripping as I went.

I had just buttoned up a freshly pressed, three-quarter-length white shirt, when the phone rang. Wearing it, a half slip, and panty hose, I hung over the landing, listening to the message. The Dallas police really wanted to talk to me.

I had five minutes before I had to be on the road, zooming to The Store. My cell phone was still in Mr. Raul Domingo's possession. I'd deal with the DPD after I delivered the film to Damon and faced his interrogation.

The bathroom mirror proved I looked like hell, and I had the beginnings of an enormous zit. One of the benefits of having a makeup artist friend is learning her tricks. I colored the bump with eye pencil, and sent a silent thanks to Cindy Crawford for making moles acceptable, then left the bathroom before I discovered some worse flaw.

DKNY skirt and jacket in place, I had my head in my closet, in search of my new Bruno Magli pumps, when someone knocked—forcefully—on my front door. I froze.

They knocked again, harder.

I found my shoes, tied on an Hermès scarf, and slunk downstairs. Through the tiny stained-glass window inset in the front door, I saw Raul standing on my step, Hilfiger cap, jeans, and still a bleached blond. I ripped open the door. "Where the hell have you been?" The Miata, with four normal-sized tires, a clean, whole windshield, and sparkling in morning sunshine, was parked at the curb.

He held out my cell phone. "Have you had breakfast?" he said.

The phone rang and I answered it. "Damon's on the warpath," Gary said in a whisper. "Don't come into the office. Just go straight to the meeting, and please, Dallas, look the part." He hung up.

I stared at the phone a second, then backed up, inviting Raul in. "I haven't."

"Good. We can eat while we watch the press conference," he said, brushing past me and going down the half flight of stairs to the TV room. "I like my eggs poached, you know?" he said as he settled on the sofa.

The phone rang again, and I answered. "Ms. O'Connor," the female began.

"How are you, Diana?"

"Out of the hospital, thanks for asking. It was just a flesh wound. I wanted to warn you that the media might be descending upon you. We just got back the forensics on Ileana Karagonis—" My land line rang in the kitchen.

"What are the results?"

"Well, she was frozen."

"No way!" Raul shouted from the other room. My answering machine clicked on, and the caller hung up. "Man, you got that wrong! Dallas, man, you aren't gonna believe this—" I plugged my ear and asked Diana to repeat what she'd said.

"It appears that Ileana was killed several weeks before her body was found. That is, found by you."

The kitchen phone stopped ringing.

"You're saying Leo could have done it?" I asked.

"Man, that's impossible!" Raul shouted in the other room. "What kind of crazy cop stuff is this?"

The kitchen phone started ringing again.

"I'm not saying anything," Diana said. "I just wanted to let you know."

Someone knocked on my front door. I heard my answering machine click on again. Raul was shouting in Spanish at the TV. "Thanks," I said. "Oh, Diana, I thought of something."

"Yes?"

"Ileana was scheduled for that shoot, and we all knew her as a blonde."

"She's a natural redhead," Diana said.

"Whatever. What I'm telling you is that someone must have done her hair between the last time I saw her at the headbook party, and, well, when she showed up on the set."

"Do you know her hairstylist?"

"Lindsay at Alliance would," I said.

She thanked me, and we hung up.

I peeked out the door and saw Channel 11 pull up. Channel 4 was already there. I pulled the curtains across the back windows, turned off my answering machine, and walked down the stairs. "What are you screaming about?" I asked Raul, as I locked the side doors.

"Man, it's crazy. They said Ileana had been dead for weeks before she was hung up! Man, I took pictures of her just two weeks ago. You know it's crazy when you can't believe the news."

I opened my mouth, when something dawned on me. I ran upstairs, ignoring the knocking on the door, the calling, and ran into my bedroom loft. My jeans were there, on the floor.

In the back pocket, a little rumpled, was the Polaroid backing. I ran back downstairs and shoved it at Raul. "Is this it?"

He looked at the black square. "It's a Polaroid backing," he said, handing it back to me. "It's useless."

"That's where you are wrong," I said, turning on a light by the couch. "Hold it just right," I said, angling the negative, "and you can see as much detail as in the actual photo."

In reverse, we saw a blond woman in sixties makeup and a peasant blouse. She was looking away, so that we only saw the left side of her face. "Ileana," I said.

"Man, that's incredible."

"Diana said she was a natural redhead."

"Yeah, I knew that. In fact, I took a before shot, just as a comparison to the final shot. Photographers are supposed to."

"When you'd shot her before, was she a redhead?"

"Oh man, I never shot her before. I'd never seen her before."

I looked up at him. "That's the first time you shared that piece of information. You didn't know Ileana?"

"Nope."

"Then why did she call you?"

He shrugged. "She'd heard about me, said she wanted to work with me."

I blinked; the astounding thing was that he had believed her. "So you took photographs of this woman, who was a stranger to you."

"Yeah."

"She showed up with red hair, then put on a blond wig, then took it off again?"

He nodded. "It's amazing how different a woman can look, you know. Her real hair, the red, I guess she tied it up or something, but the blond was a wig."

"You took before shots?" I said.

"Yeah. In the film."

I turned off the ringer on the handset on the table. The knocking on the door was starting to beat through my skull.

"Where did you find this?" he asked, looking at the Polaroid.

"When I went back to Leo's. It was in the train case." I searched through my bag for a loupe. "When did you shoot her," I asked again, looking closely at the backing.

"I'm telling you," he said, after he counted through the days. "It was a Sunday, a week before she was found. I know this, man, 'cuz I'm Domingo you know? Sunday is my lucky day."

"Yet the police think she was already dead?" I said, looking at the negative through the loupe. "Well, she certainly doesn't look dead."

"I'm telling you, I swear on my mother's soul, she was alive."

Ileana, beautiful Ileana, was frozen on the film. I put the negative and the loupe down on the table. My cell phone rang again, the caller ID was *The Dallas Morning News*. I gave up and answered. "You've had a rough twenty-four hours," Carla Chou said.

"Do you have anything on that Suburban's license plate?"

"No, it's coming up blank, like it's being transferred or something."

"I thought this was the great age of computers," I said, looking up at Raul. He was staring at the negative again, frowning. "What county is it registered in, do we know that?"

"Dallas County."

A Suburban in Dallas County—the proverbial needle would be easier to find.

"I have this friend who does PI work, who could meet us at eleven this morning, then we could grab some lunch and talk about the case," she said. I was about to agree when I looked at the VCR clock: 10:45.

I was doomed.

"Why do I always get on this road?" I asked myself in frustration as I sat, bumper-to-bumper, in traffic on Central Expressway. The radio had no answers for me, and I scanned the exits for a clear path to downtown. It wasn't even noon—where were all these people going, clogging up the highways?

We inched forward, and I saw the sign. All three lanes were being narrowed into one in a half mile. The joy of living in Dallas.

I put on my blinker and haphazardly cut through two lanes of traffic, squealing onto the access road. I seethed and fumed my way down Haskell, then Ross, then Pearl and roared onto Main, bypassing The Store and slipping my car into valet parking before the Adolphus Hotel. The Store's executives ruled from the Tower.

The elevator took forever, but it gave me a chance to breathe deeply, fish for some earrings in my purse, put them on, reline my eyes, and step off calmly.

At 11:10.

The receptionist was a fashionably dressed woman who'd

probably had this job for as long as I'd been alive. I gave her my name. She looked at the clock, gave me a reproving glance, then notified Mr. Whitside that I had "finally arrived." Lips pursed, she stomped her way down the hall, and I tiptoed behind her.

The conference room was the real thing; Aubusson rugs, Louis XV antiques, original oils. A table resembling the back of a very large, very well polished turtle, filled one side of the room. Four people sat around it, nibbling pastries and drinking from Wedgwood china.

Damon didn't rise, he was too busy kissing up to the Oracle—also known as the head of the creative division. What she wore, well-dressed women clamored for. Her sense of what was coming in, and what was going out, was so impeccable that she was called the Oracle openly, though her name was Lavinia. She'd been at The Store for decades. A Chanel pant-suit covered her still-lean five-foot-nine-inch frame, a cabo-chon ruby gleamed at her throat, and she wore her dark hair in a chignon.

Damn, I should have worn a chignon, too. Had I even brushed my hair this morning?

"Ms. O'Connor," Damon said.

I nodded.

"Please be seated. Would you care for coffee?" the Oracle asked.

"Yes, thank you," I croaked.

One of the Wedgwood cups appeared before me as we waited in silence. I'd drink it black, since stirring would make more noise than I wanted. The two others were introduced to me: the merchandising manager and the local PR liaison. "Gary is unable to join us this morning," Damon said. "If you would please look at the file before you."

My last hope of having a friendly face died. They looked at my employment file. Damon brought to their attention that I had received several reprimands about my attire. The Oracle didn't even look at me. "She seems appropriately dressed now," she said.

"Indeed, but she shows up for work looking like a hobo," Damon said.

"What exactly does this have to do with her performance?" the PR director asked.

I fought back a smile.

"At The Store, we have an image to uphold. Indeed, it is our image that we sell. It isn't appropriate for an employee of The Store to appear so styleless and . . . casual."

Damon made it sound like I had a disease. The Oracle was looking through the file on me. I swallowed.

"Do you have any response?" the merchandising person asked. "By the way, I was extremely pleased with the downtown windows you did for Christmas."

"The elves?" the PR liaison asked. "You did the elves?"

I nodded. I'd been part of the team that spent last November working on twenty elf mannequins, complete with fantasy makeup, wigs, and costumes. Gary had commissioned a local artist to build giant wrought-iron snowflake shapes for the elves to play on. In fact, working with those elves had taught me how to hang and manipulate mannequins.

"Those were the most inventive windows I've ever seen," the PR liaison said. "The concept was brilliant, 'Christmas: up close & personal.' "

"Record sales," the merchandising manager said.

I didn't dare glance at Damon. This wasn't going the way he wanted it to—it was going the way it should: I was being judged on what I did, not how I looked.

"So, what *do* you wear to work?" the PR liaison said.

"Usually pants and a top," I said. "I'm sure you know my job is extremely active, requiring me to crawl on studio floors, climb ladders, mix stuff, lug props around. It would be foolish for me to wear clothing appropriate for office work to a studio."

"What about when you are in the office?" the Oracle asked.

"I rarely am," I said. "But I think I dress appropriately."

"Perhaps we don't all agree on the definition of appropriate," the PR liaison said. She looked at me. "Do you wear clothing that The Store sells?"

"Of course! Ralph Lauren sweaters are some of my favorites, and I collect Magli shoes. And nothing is more perfect than my CK cargo pants. I use all those pockets. There's one that fits my Swiss Army knife perfectly."

She shrugged and turned to Damon. "Well, I'm satisfied, and I'd appreciate it if you didn't call me to meetings like this," she said with bite as she scooted her chair out.

Damon spoke rapidly. "More important than her previous demerits," Damon said, "is this recent business with the model."

Everyone at the table stiffened.

"The model who was murdered?" the PR liaison said, scooting back in slowly.

"How does this pertain to an employee evaluation?" the Oracle asked.

"I didn't want to bring this up," Damon said, his tone apologetic. "I didn't want to taint your view of an employee, but Ms. O'Connor spent the past weekend in the custody of the Dallas Police Department."

It was dead silent in that room, the hush of the carpets and the floor felt stifling. "Is this true?" the Oracle asked.

"It was a few hours on Sunday," I said in a small voice.

"Regarding what?" she asked.

Damon answered. "The hanging model case. I wouldn't want to start unpleasant rumors, but between us and these four walls, she is the strongest suspect."

I was the only one who gasped. I couldn't believe the police had said that. The managers didn't respond at all. Somehow, that nonreaction was worse. Damon continued. "Given the situation, the negative press that The Store is receiving, due to the fact it was our photo shoot, I think it necessary to terminate Ms. O'Connor's employment here."

My stomach was boiling with acid. This was a nightmare.

"This behavior, or even the appearance of illegal behavior, is inappropriate to the image The Store perpetuates and expects its employees to uphold."

Suddenly gazes that had been sympathetic turned suspicious. No one said anything for a few minutes.

"Do you have any comment?" the Oracle asked me.

I took a deep breath. "For the past month I have worked ten-hour days at Mere Illusion, on the midsummer edition of *Metamorphosis*. I knew Ileana. We were friends. Being accused of her murder is horrifying, even more than discovering her body. Then, to have my employer of the past three years even consider that I would do such a thing is . . . is . . ." I let the tears gather in my eyes. "Completely disheartening."

The Oracle looked at Damon. He stared ahead, unperturbed. "You are the only person with the time to have suspended the body," he said, turning toward me. "And there is the matter of that money she took."

Everyone looked at me, as Damon continued speaking. "I hate to say it, but these are the facts."

For once, he sounded human. From someone else, I might have believed that little quirk of sincerity in a voice. But this was Damon the Demon Whitside, who loathed me.

"I was gone for three hours, which left plenty of time for someone else to ... do that." I took a sip of coffee, just to clear the taste from my mouth. Suddenly I was furious. "If you are finished," I said, rising, "I think we know what the outcome here will be."

"Well I—"

"That would be foolish, Ms. O'Connor," the PR person said.

I picked up my purse. "No. What is foolish is that I was called down here at all. I could no more have killed a human being—"

"I heard you knew the weapon, and also knew that she hadn't been killed there, simply by looking at her," Damon said. "How do you explain that?"

"This isn't a court of law, Damon," the Oracle said. "Ms. O'Connor is not on trial."

"Of course, of course, Lavinia. I understand that. However, the police are very concerned. Management is concerned." He twirled his platinum Mont Blanc between his fingers, managing to look gorgeous and troubled at the same time. "I must confess, I am concerned. As much as I would like to, I don't think it appropriate to keep Dal—"

"You don't have to keep me," I said in a rush. "Consider this my tendered notice."

"Ms. O'Connor!" the merchandising manager said.

I turned to him. "Yes?"

"Your work record is excellent, despite these demerits on clothing." He looked at Damon. "I really think we should give her a week's vacation. *Metamorphosis* has never looked better."

"Vacation!" Damon all but lost it.

"Agreed, Henry," the Oracle said. She looked at me. "Paid of course. At least until this unpleasant business is resolved."

"I—"

"What about the media? The reporters?" Damon said. "The Store is harboring a criminal element. Arson, murder, theft. What kind of PR is that?"

The PR liaison leaned forward. "Certainly better than dropping a loyal employee like a hot potato when they get into trouble. And most certainly better than the PR Ms. O'Connor could get if she took the story of this inquisition to any of the papers or TV stations. The Store has enough biases to overcome, simply by being upscale. We don't want any further alienation," she said. "Loyalty is one of the cornerstones of The Store, Mr. Whitside. Loyalty to both customers and our most important clients, our employees."

Damon was incredulous. Even I was a little stunned.

The Oracle spoke. "Ms. O'Connor is an intelligent young woman. If she were going to take someone's life, she would not display the body in a place where she was most likely to be the prime suspect. And according to what I heard on the news this morning, they aren't sure when this young woman was killed anyway. Dallas might not have even been in town."

Damon said nothing.

"Besides," the PR liaison said, "this will blow over in a week, just as soon as the stations get something new to sink their teeth into. My office will prepare a statement. Do you need an attorney?" she asked me.

If worse came to worst, I had my brother. I shook my head.

Damon was controlling his fury, but the few lines around his mouth were white he was so angry.

"What about *Metamorphosis*?" the merchandising manager asked me. "Isn't that due? Aren't you in charge?"

"Gary will handle it," Damon said. "I've already done the FPOs." He looked at the PR person. "What if this hasn't blown over in a few weeks?"

She shrugged, "We'll continue this discussion with attorneys, at that point." She looked at me with a smile. "I'm sure this will all be a bad memory by this time next week. You have nothing to worry about. Just stay out of the public eye."

Damon rose. "So we are agreed?"

Everyone murmured agreement.

"Do you understand?" Damon asked me.

Oh yes, I understood. Loyalty went only so far.

CHAPTER TWENTY

I was sitting in my Mustang, in shock. My dramatic exit had been sidetracked, but since it had been an example of temporary insanity, that was a good thing. Damon had stormed out of the room, not even saying good-bye. The PR liaison had wished me good luck, and the Oracle had said my work on *Metamorphosis* was "nicely done."

So here I was, just about noon on a Monday, with no job to go to, my house was swarming with reporters—thank God I'd parked my Mustang a few streets over—and . . . "And what, Dallas?" I said out loud. I needed to get to my truck, return Julie's Miata, go to the grocery store and . . . "Clear my name." Just saying it made me feel better. "Leo's too," I announced, and started my car.

How, was the real question.

* * *

The media had left my lawn, but the Starbucks' cups, the paper napkins and plates, along with water bottles, Coke cans, and candy wrappers, made it apparent they'd waited a while.

Raul and the Miata were gone. I made sure the door was locked, then slipped into my secret stash of croissants. Leo was always so thoughtful, so sweet. He couldn't have killed Ileana, it was impossible.

But had he been having an affair with her? I'd always assumed, I guess because of her work, that Ileana, though Greek, was blond. If she hadn't been, then their relationship might be more plausible than I thought. Obviously she had been keeping stuff at his house. Maybe she'd even been in New Orleans with him.

Did we have this backward? Could Ileana have killed Leo? Really, who was dead first? According to Raul, he'd photographed Ileana after she was—according to the police—dead.

But why would Ileana, who definitely had her flaws, but wasn't evil, kill her agent?

I spread Nutella on my croissant, a tip picked up from Zimona, a German model who'd stayed with me once, and took off my shoes, curling up in an armchair in the sunshine. If I had to think this through, I might as well be comfortable.

Gary called. "A week's vacation? Oh, I am jealous!"

I laughed. "Don't be. I have a month of laundry that needs doing, a dozen phone calls to return, and I'm behind on my bills. I'd rather be at work."

"Actually, not. Apparently April and the Demon had a falling-out. Over you, no less."

I sat up. "What are you talking about?"

"April was horrified to hear you were being punished, I

guess, for poor Ileana's demise. Or finding her, anyway. April almost lost it on Damon, I mean, really. She thought it was extremely unfair, and most of the people in the office heard why," he said with Gary-emphasis. "We'll definitely have to do martinis later, darling."

"I want to see the film."

"Your mermaids were a stroke of genius. How about sixish at the P? I'll sneak it out of here underneath Damon's disjointed nose."

I grinned. "You have a deal."

I hung up slowly. April. Blond. The second bottle of Joy. Why would she stick up for me?

The phone rang again, and I answered it. "I'm calling from the reporter," a man said. "I hear you want a Suburban."

"A specific one," I said.

"It's at the lot on Ross Avenue, just south of Fiesta." He hung up.

Carla had given my number out to strangers? I wasn't a paranoid type, but I had been shot at in recent days. I didn't appreciate this. However, if it was the Suburban . . . what, Dallas?

I changed clothes, then left voice mails. One to Carla, asking her to not give out information on me, but telling her I did appreciate the contact; one for Raul, asking him to call Jacob and get the name of the shoot they were doing the day Raul did the sixties shots of Ileana; and lastly, one for Diana— I had some information, weak as all get-out, that might be helpful. Call me.

One last stop: 7-Eleven.

* * *

Ross, south of Fiesta, went straight a long way. It was about three o'clock, so school zones were already in effect. I drove 20 mph, reminding myself to get my truck, craning to see all the vehicles in all the various lots. Used-car dealerships lined the road.

Then I saw it, parked on the back side of the street, between two apartment complexes. The Suburban, the same one that had chased me through Fossil Rim. I turned left, circled the block, wondering if this were some sort of setup.

Street work was in progress, the City of Dallas filling in a pothole—how often did you see that? The cross street bridged the way into a nice neighborhood, with duplexes and houses. A crew of Hispanics was sleeping underneath the trees, a half-finished driveway curving before a house.

No one looked dangerous. No one was close to the truck. There were plenty of people around, and it was the middle of the afternoon. I drove the block twice more, the Hispanics were going back to work, and I'd seen an au pair and child in a stroller.

I parked my Mustang across the street from the vehicle and locked my purse in the car, carrying my Big Gulp and disposable camera to the Suburban. It had been an hour since I'd called Carla, and she hadn't called back, so I assumed this was legit. After all, she was a cops reporter, who knew how she knew the people she knew, right? "I'm talking to myself," I muttered as I tried the door. It opened.

The inside stank of cigarette smoke and I opened all the doors and the back, letting in as much light as possible. I snapped a few shots of the front and back, wondering what I hoped to prove.

Then I pulled out my knife and got nose down in the carpet. Beige carpet. I removed the plastic shields that held the carpet in place and pulled some of it back. The glue was new, and it had been stapled into place by a homeowner's gun, not a professional's. My hands were shaking when I called Diana.

"Detective Mansfield," she answered.

"I think I found where Ileana was murdered," I said, staring at the carpet.

"Where? Where are you?" I heard the excitement in her voice.

"A Suburban," I said, and gave her the address. "Diana, what were the measurements of the rug y'all found in Leo's freezer?"

"Hmmm. Just about the dimensions of the back of a Suburban," she said. "I'll be there in fifteen minutes."

I called Carla again, but she was still out. "You're closer to your exclusive than you know," I said, and hung up.

The Big Gulp in my hand, I climbed out of the back and around the driver's side. A smoker, but beneath the heavy nicotine was something else, sweeter.

Expensive.

I opened the glove compartment; it was empty. I looked under the seats, clean. I ran my hand between the cushions in the back, nothing. I checked the passenger's seat, zippo. I got out of the driver's seat and slid my hand between the back and front.

And smelled gasoline.

"Fire!" someone shouted.

My fingertips brushed something plastic, narrow and engraved. I felt an arm around my waist, pulling me, heard the crackle of flame. I resisted, shoving more of my hand in the space. Smoke was filling the Suburban and I grabbed the thing from the seat, letting go suddenly.

I fell back, on top of my rescuer.

Sirens, shouting, black smoke against blue spring sky, and a firm, warm body that smelled of sweat and Herrera pour Homme.

"You idiot!" Diana Mansfield screamed at me hours later. "I can't believe you fell for such a simple, stupid, ploy!"

"It made sense," I said, still brushing soot off my shirt. "Carla knew I was trying to find the Suburban."

"Apparently so did the shooter," Diana said. She had a strong voice for being short.

"I tried to call and confirm," I said. I still hadn't heard back from Carla, but since the engine of the Suburban had spontaneously combusted, the police were guessing the whole thing was a setup.

Diana threw herself into a chair. We were back in downtown. Somewhere in this building the great-feeling, good-smelling man, who'd literally hauled me out of the burning vehicle, was also being questioned. I fingered the makeup brush, a delicate one, designed for lining eyes with cake eyeliner, and engraved with DC. "You say that is from Duchesse Cosmetics?" Diana asked, a little calmer.

"It's the logo," I said.

"Well, we impounded the Suburban, what was left of it," she said. "We'll know shortly if it was indeed where the carpet came from. You called me about something else though, before you went on your bird-brained attempt to kill yourself."

I leaned forward, I wasn't sure how to approach this. "I have a friend," I began.

"The same friend you claimed was in the studio?"

"Did you ever find trace of him?" I asked.

"Nothing. No fingerprints other than Jacob's and Leo's on the knife."

Maybe Raul had been wearing gloves already.

"This friend claims he saw Ileana after you think she was dead."

Diana sighed. "He's not alone. Neighbors of Leo's say the same thing. Some redhead was roaming in and out, long after Leo left. Even took his car."

Redhead again. "His Beemer is missing."

"Do you know anyone else who saw Ileana after, say, the fifteenth?"

A week before I found her. "I'll ask around, but I doubt it."

"The tenth?"

Raul had photographed her on the thirteenth. "I'll ask about that, too. I know she was here, in Dallas, on the third. And she flew to New York and back—"

"New Orleans and back, too," Diana said.

"When did she come back from New Orleans?"

Diana showed me the calendar, gave me the dates, and I realized that the driver for Duchesse had seen her get into Leo's car the day she'd returned. And she'd been in N'awlins the same time as Leo, only he'd come back first. The day I saw him.

"Is it possible the freezing confused the time of death?" I asked hesitantly.

Diana rose. "Don't worry about it, just let the police do our job. Call if you think of anything else, okay, Dallas?"

She bade me a chilly good-bye, and I hiked back up to street level. The hallway was empty again, except for one man. He turned around and I fought not to swoon.

Tall.

Dark.

Handsome.

Please don't be gay.

"And he asked you out?" Gary said, "Looking like that?"

"Some men like women who smell like a side of beef," I said, grinning, pushing grimy blond hair away from my face.

"That some men like women is astounding," Gary said. "I'm so glad you are safe. Whatever possessed you—"

"Don't start with me," I said, wagging a finger at him. "I have more than enough relatives who will sing that song to me."

"True, true. So y'all are going out?"

"Well, he said he'd call. You know what that means."

"I don't know Dallas. I think a tall, dark, handsome man named Alejandro might actually live up to his word." We clinked glasses while I hoped he was right.

"So let me see the film!" I said. It was the reason we were sitting at the Stoneleigh P's bar instead of a table. The light was better. I fished the loupe out of my purse and snatched the proffered transparencies.

The shots were drenched in color, they seemed to almost move through water. Thank God. The clothes looked great, and the models, too.

"This is freaky," Gary said, handing me another sheet. "Just brace yourself."

I finished my martini and nodded. "Omigod," I said.

"Isn't it just eerie?"

"It's like looking at a ghost," I said, staring at the film of April. It might as well have been Ileana Karagonis. Both were blond, perfect mesomorphs, and with the mesh over April's face, it was impossible to see any of the fine wrinkles she had, nor could you tell the extra half inch around her waist. "April could work as Ileana," I said.

April could work as Ileana.

That was it. The point of the film. "I have to make a quick call," I said, and ran to the ladies' room. The stalls were empty, and I dialed my house, hoping Raul might answer.

I hadn't given him a key, but that hadn't seemed to slow him. "Raul," I said to my own answering machine. "I bet money that Ileana was being photographed as April to prove she was as good, since April has been Duchesse's spokesmodel since before time began and Ileana was going for the job. Anyway, that's why she wanted you to do the test. Jacob's lights. It would look exactly the same."

And Jacob wouldn't be put in the uncomfortable position of betraying April's friendship. "That's why the makeup, the hair, the props. She was pretending to be April. Sneaky, huh?" I hung up. In her own way, Ileana was turning out to be as wily as April had been.

I was home, in bed, by eight. Not asleep, but pleasantly numb and drifting, watching the stars through my skylight. I picked up the phone on the second ring.

"I don't usually telephone women I pick up in the streets," he said. "I just think you should know that, up front."

Warmth that had nothing to do with vodka surged from my toes to my head. "I'll consider myself warned," I said, smiling, tucking another pillow under my head. "How are you, Alejandro?"

"Wondering how a certain, smoky blonde is feeling, though I guess from your voice that some doctor gave you painkiller."

"Dr. Absolut," I said.

He laughed. He had a wonderful laugh. And gorgeous dimples. I kicked the blankets off my legs. It was entirely too warm in here.

"Did you make it to your six o'clock appointment?"

"I did," I said.

"And would you make it to one, say, Wednesday night?"

"Oh, I don't know," I said. "I'm on vacation this week, so much to do, you know."

"And you're staying in Dallas?"

There was the little matter of the police, but I chose not to say anything. "It was kind of sudden," I said. "Unexpected."

"Would dinner at The Grape fit with your spontaneous scheduling, then?"

The Grape, allegedly the most romantic restaurant in Dallas. Of course, I'd never been. And I had time to shop for the perfect outfit. I could almost like Damon Whitside right now. "That sounds wonderful," I said. Could he hear my ear-to-ear smile? "What time?"

"Do you want to meet, or should I pick you up?"

I knew a model who lived upstairs from the restaurant.

She had amazing clothes and was very generous about loaning stuff. "I'll meet you there," I said.

"How will I recognize you without the Suburban?"

I laughed, and we agreed on seven-thirty. I dialed Ivy, the upstairs-dwelling model. "I've met the man of my dreams," I said to her voice mail. "And I don't have a thing to wear. Please rescue me."

The next time I answered the phone was almost dawn. A nonhuman, mechanical voice spoke to me: "What film is in Oak Cliff, Dallas?" It left an address. I raced downstairs, shaking, and looked at the caller ID. Unavailable.

I climbed back upstairs, but I couldn't resist checking over my shoulder. Again and again.

Alejandro would be downstairs at The Grape in twenty minutes. And I was still mostly naked. Well, I had on Fendi heels and silk underwear. I usually wear cotton, especially in the Texas heat, but this was a special occasion. Dinner with the constuction worker who'd saved my life. At Dallas's most romantic wine bar on a starry, starry night.

At least my hair looked great. I'd done a French twist and wore nice-sized diamond studs. A wedding present from Grandmama. But even though Ivy's walk-in closet doors were open, I didn't have a thing to wear.

My cell phone rang and I picked it up with a snarl. Fifteen minutes to create a miracle. Was he calling to cancel? I didn't even check the ID.

"Oh my God, Dallas, I just heard. I was out of town," Carla said. "Are you okay?"

"Delightful," I said, pulling out a Valentino suit. Too severe.

"Whew. Good. Sounds like you are burning off some steam," she said, "that's great. Well, I won't interrupt you for long, but I did get a name on that Suburban, the title."

"April Alexander," I snapped. The leather bustier was too eighties Madonna.

"No," she said. "I doubt this person is a model. The name is K.C. Wolchek."

"Wolchek?" I repeated.

"This guy is a serious loser, Dallas. Scary, even. He's spent the last decade in the big house. Arson is his favorite crime, I guess."

"Great," I said, sitting down. Suddenly I wasn't interested in clothes.

"All in all, Dallas, he's bad news. And I want you to know, I would never give out information on you, or your number to anyone, without checking first. I swear."

"Okay, Carla, okay," I said, a little dazed. "Just tell me, what is Wolchek doing now? Since his last attempt to incinerate me failed." Here was the shooter from Fossil Rim, I bet. The arsonist at JJS. I had started trembling.

"He doesn't live here, so I'm running a check on all the local hotels. I'll call you and the police once I know."

"I'll keep my phone on," I said, and hung up.

I was shaking all over—cold inside my skin. I wrapped Ivy's terry-cloth robe around me. Hot chocolate and a video were more my speed tonight. The phone rang again and I picked up.

"Good evening, Dallas," Alejandro said.

"Hi," I whispered.

"Are you all right?"

I swallowed. "Uh, sure."

"Well, I just wanted to let you know that I have your seat reserved and I'm waiting to open a bottle until I see your face. You are coming tonight?" He was downstairs. And he sounded a little . . . unsure of himself. "I'm really looking foward to seeing you," he said. "I'd noticed you, even before our, uh, explosive meeting."

I looked at my watch. "I'll be there in a few minutes. Go ahead and open the bottle."

I turned off my phone and threw off the robe. I had my priorities. Wolchek was just a hired gun, trying to kill me, but Alejandro was a straight, gorgeous, Dallas man.

Waiting downstairs. For me.

Honestly though, would Alejandro even want to stare at me across a tiny table? My skin looked like wax. I did fifteen pushups to get blood flowing to my face again. Coco always said "Corpuscles," when asked what the secret to great-looking skin was. Corpuscles and water. I finished my makeup, adding a dab of frosted lip gloss to my upper browbone, which made my eyes look brighter.

What I wore no longer mattered, so I grabbed the first dress—BCBG—and slipped it on, grabbed my Kate Spade bag with the essentials of lip gloss, cell phone, Altoids, and keys, and walked downstairs and into the bar.

It was tiny, intimate, with small checkerboard tables for two on a wine-colored floor. The aroma of scallops in butter wafted through, and the faint murmur of conversation mixed with the clink of crystal. It was the set of a romantic dinner. And I was here.

Thank you, Ivy, I breathed as I saw him.

He wore a navy, three-button suit with a monochrome shirt, open at the throat. It showed the breadth of his shoulders and narrowness of his waist. His shoes were dark, but I couldn't tell what kind. He was in profile, and I stood for a moment, admiring. His neck was strong, he had a square jaw, and the dimples I'd remembered . . . were just as perfect as I'd remembered.

He glanced at the door, then saw me and rose as I approached—Grandmama would love his manners, though she would abhor his occupation. "You look wonderful," he said, smiling with his eyes. "Do you feel better? It was a little rough for you."

He had been working, laying the driveway across the street, when the Suburban caught on fire.

"Thank you," I said, sitting down on the chair he held out for me. "In case I didn't thank you then."

The dimples appeared, along with a brilliant smile. "You did," he said. "And you are more than welcome." He gestured to the wine list. "Would you like a wine?"

"Yes, please," I said, still trying to catch my breath.

"Which do you prefer? The '95 Poppy Hill Cabernet? The '98 Merlot? Or the '97 Llano Passionelle?"

I pulled Ivy's pashmina over my shoulders. "The Llano Passionelle, I think." It sounded exactly right for this evening, though I didn't even know what color it was.

He ordered, then turned to me, taking my hand in his. His fingers were long and graceful, though his palms were callused.

I like that in a man.

"I'm very glad you came," he said. "You've been in my thoughts. A lot."

I nodded, mute. Could he feel my hand trembling?

Our wine appeared, warming at the first sip and perfectly wonderful. Alejandro held up his glass. "To a perfect evening, with a beautiful companion."

I blushed as we touched glasses. Beneath the table I spied his shoes: polished, black-leather oxfords.

You can tell everything about a man's self image by his shoes.

It really was going to be a perfect evening.

The telephone woke me before my alarm. I slapped my cheek to snap awake, then reached for the handset, wincing as I moved. "Hello?" I said, as clearly as I could.

"Good morning, Dallas," a man said. "How are you feeling today?"

I couldn't place the voice. "Fine," I said. "And you?"

"I'm good."

Uncomfortable silence.

"Can I help you?" I finally offered, rather than endure the awkwardness.

"Gary really needs some assistance," he said. Damon! "I'm not sure if you have seen the papers, but the hanging-model case has been resolved, and we need you back at The Store soon."

I rubbed my eyes and looked out the skylight, then at the clock. It was 8:30. "What do you mean by soon?"

"Perhaps, this afternoon?" Damon wheedled. "Tomorrow at the latest. We can't miss this deadline, Dallas." His voice was showing more steel: becoming more of the manipulative whip-cracker I knew.

My body's bruises were changing from black and purple to the more interesting shades of yellow, red, and green. I had a terrific headache from Monday's attempt at killing me, or more accurately, yesterday's three-bottle celebration that Wolchek had failed. "I'll see how I feel," I said. "Thanks for telling me, though."

"How do you feel?" Damon said, his tone completely familiar now.

"Lousy right now. Thanks for asking."

"But Dallas, what are we going to do? Gary has had to return to Georgia. Something about his mother," Damon said.

"I'm on a week's vacation," I said. "Enforced by you."

"Well, but that was before we knew—"

"I have to go now, Damon," I said, and hung up.

Then I bounded out of bed, ecstatic but delirious. I'd just blown off my boss! (My career?) Never, ever had I told him no.

"Dallas, can you work this holiday?" "Yes." "Dallas, can you stay late for this meeting?" "Yes." "Dallas, can you completely redo this concept in less time than it takes to brew a good cup of coffee?" "Yes."

Drunk on my feeble stab at liberty, I toddled downstairs and made café au lait, and reached into the freezer for my stash of croissants. Oh, Alejandro was so interesting! And smart, and sweet. He was tall, he was—

When I opened the croissant bag, instead of my fingers brushing frozen pastry, they touched plastic. I opened the bag wider and looked in. There, at the bottom, beneath a few more croissants, was a freezer container.

I put the pastries in the oven on warm, then looked at the container: clear serveware with a bright blue top. Obviously it was Leo's.

Turning it over, I saw it was full.

Of paper.

CHAPTER TWENTY-ONE

My hands suddenly trembling, I popped open the container. A paper-clipped note, in Leo's handwriting, fronted a double-folded sheaf of legal documents.

"Dallas—if you haven't heard from me in a while, the following might explain it all. Enclosed are some highly confidential, exclusive pieces of information. Show this to no one, unless I've been missing for a while. Love you—Leo."

I picked up the phone and dialed Gary's number, knowing he wouldn't be there yet, so I could leave a message. "I don't know what the story with Damon is, but I will be out of pocket today. If you need something, leave a message. I hope your mother is doing well. Love you."

Taking my croissants and coffee back to my bed, I read through Leo's packet of information: densely written notes and interminable legalese. A will; a contract; adoption papers; and a prenuptial agreement.

Clear motive, method, and opportunity for murder. The phone rang, and I raced downstairs to get it.

"Hey! How are you?" Raul's accent was immediately identifiable.

"Where the hell have you been?"

"I'll explain everything. Have you had lunch yet?" he said.

I looked at my watch. It was one-forty-five. I sighed, there was really no point in yelling at him, Raul was completely unflappable. "No, what did you have in mind?"

"Maybe just getting together, talking about this murder thing. Wow, K.C. Wolchek. It's hard to believe, I mean, that Leo killed Ileana, and then this guy killed Leo. I mean, I guess it's just not a safe world anymore, you know?"

"Wolchek?" I said stupidly. "Who, what are you talking about?"

"It is hard to believe," he said. "So where do you want to meet?"

A phone call beeped in, and I switched over to Alejandro. "Good afternoon," he said. "How do you feel after Monday's mishap?"

"Bruised," I said, still dazed by Raul's comment.

"Last night, you mentioned some guy named Wolchek, right?"

"Right."

"As a matter of fact, when we said good night, and I asked if there was anything I could do for you, you said to protect you from Wolchek."

I didn't remember that part—though the few minutes I'd

spent in his arms was clearly impressed on my brain. "Uh-huh," I murmured.

"Then can you tell me why he's dead?"

"Uh," I said, my mind racing. "Hang on." I switched callers. "Raul?"

"How about that noodle place?"

"Fine. An hour?"

We agreed and I returned to Alejandro. "I, um, actually don't know what you are talking about," I said. "I've been doing some work, I"—I clicked on the television as I spoke—"haven't seen the news today."

"I'll sum it up for you," he said, his tone extremely proper. "K.C. Wolchek was a guest at the Dallas Grand Hotel—"

"The submarine hotel," I said.

"What?"

"My nickname for the Dallas Grand," I said. I did a scuba gear ad there once, because the room doors looked like a submarine's interior. So I call it the submarine hotel."

"So you do work in the fashion industry," he said.

"Did you think I was lying?" I asked.

"No, well, no I didn't." He said it, but it sounded like he was trying to convince himself.

"Wolchek was staying there, when?"

"Before he was pushed from the twelfth floor this morning."

"He's dead?"

"He left a detailed suicide note, according to the morning news. Apparently it answers a lot of the questions about that model—"

"Ileana—"

"Who was murdered."

"What about Leo?"

He was silent a moment. "Did you know these people?"

Suddenly I realized how far apart our worlds were. "I have to run," I said slowly.

"Oh, certainly," he said. "We'll talk later." I doubted it, as I hung up. My first call was to Diana. Voice mail. Carla. Voice mail. I looked at the clock and realized I was supposed to meet Raul in twenty minutes.

I jumped in the shower, then into a pair of jeans, clogs, and a washed-silk shirt. Realizing that it would make me late, nevertheless, I ran all of Leo's documents through my fax machine, making copies. Then, lacking a better place to hide the originals, I put them back in the plastic, back inside the croissant bag. More and more I realized that the night Leo had returned from New Orleans was the night he was killed.

But he had been anticipating it.

I grabbed the keys to my Mustang and headed down Greenville Avenue.

"So you are telling me that this Wolchek didn't kill Leo?" Raul said.

"Well, no, I think maybe he did. I just think he did it for April Alexander. Why else would he?"

Raul looked over his noodles at me. "Why would she?"

I opened my mouth to respond, defend my newfound information, but Raul kept talking. "I don't know, Dallas. April was big-time. You know what I mean? That's like saying Christy Turlington would kill someone, and she's the nicest person in the business. Why? What would the Diva have to gain? Why would she hire some lame small-time crook? If she wanted someone killed, I bet she had plenty of connections, if you know what I mean. Under the table."

"You can take the boy out of Havana, but you can't take Havana out of the boy," I muttered.

"I mean, she could just hire a Mafia man." Raul forked another mouthful of meat-spiked noodles. "I'm sorry, but I don't buy it."

"Money makes people do strange things," I said slowly.

"She was already rich," Raul said. "She has big money, a big contract. Why more?"

"Why does anyone want more? But I think that's her reason why. I just want to figure out how." Leo deserved to have his reputation, his name, vindicated. I shut my eyes against the image of his face.

"Are you going to finish that?" Raul asked, looking at my bowl.

I'd picked the shrimp, crab, and vegetables off the noodles. My appetite was gone. "No. I always forget to order the glass noodles, I like them better. Do you want it?"

"Sure," Raul said, so I handed him my bowl. "Did he kill Leo and Ileana, or just one of them?"

"I haven't even seen the news, or heard from anyone officially," I said. "All I got were phone calls, telling me everything was resolved."

"So he killed Leo and Ileana for April?"

"Omigod!" I said, slamming my hand on the table. "That's it!"

"What?" Raul said, looking around. "What's it?"

"April thought Leo betrayed her! Maybe she found out he'd signed Ileana to take April's place with Duchesse. So April had Wolchek kill Leo. Then, I bet April killed Ileana, just so she couldn't do the work. April inherits Leo's estate, *and* she keeps her job." Except that I'd seen Leo's new will, and if April thought that she'd walk away with everything, she was wrong.

"Then Wolchek kills himself; why?"

"No, I think maybe April killed him, too."

"How?"

"He was on the twelfth floor, a room with a balcony. Maybe she just pushed him."

"I doubt it; she was a girl, a model."

"Don't be such a sexist," I said. "She has a body like a whipcord. But if she killed him, she destroyed the murder's last link to her. And it would give her a scapegoat."

Raul had finished both bowls of noodles. "Do you want some dessert?"

"You're an artist, you are supposed to be starving," I reminded him with a wink.

"So who was chasing us?" Raul asked, motioning for the waiter.

"Wolchek, I guess."

"And why was he shooting at us? Yes, we'd like a big piece of your most chocolatey stuff," he said to the waiter. "And two forks." The waiter left. "We didn't know anything."

He clinked his fork against the table. "Your theory, man, I know you like it, but it's wrong. Clever, but like that cheese that has holes in it, umm——"

"Swiss," I said. "Maybe he thought we knew something? Maybe——" I sighed. "Maybe you are right. But Wolchek didn't act alone, I'm sure of that. He was the kind of guy you hire, Carla told me that. And April hired him."

Raul gave me a dubious look as the waiter set down the

cake, three layers of dark chocolate, iced with raspberry and sprinkled with white chocolate. Raul handed me a fork. "April couldn't have done it."

I took a corner piece. "I wonder if anyone has told Ileana's family yet. They must have seen it on the news."

"Poor kid."

We finished the cake in silence, then split the bill. When we stepped outside it was raining, so we stood in the overhang until it lessened. "Then explain this," I said, in one last effort.

"Let's say Leo has an appointment to meet April. That is the night he brings over this bag of croissants to me, for times when I miss him, he says. No one hears from him again. Three weeks later, his body is found in the Trinity. Explain that."

As I drove out of the parking lot, he was still standing, thinking, in the rain.

Damon had called me, irate. I fast-forwarded through his message. Another two calls about renting. Jacob James left a message and a Montana phone number—he'd been hired to do a last-minute reshoot for a catalog company, and would be gone for a week or more. Call him. My mother, my sister Christi, and Alejandro.

Another Latino male. Dark eyes and Spanish-speaking. Would I never learn? Leo had always said women had "types," too, they just wouldn't admit it.

My ex-husband had been Mexican, from one of Mexico City's leading families. With *"muy amors"* and *"bonita señoritas"* and a body carved from teak, he'd wooed and won me from where I worked at the cosmetics counter at The Store in El Paso. After five years spent learning that once a trophy is acquired, it is rarely polished, I bailed out, divorced him, and moved in with my sister Ojeda. She was happily married and repopulating the earth with little O'Connors, from her home and florist shop in Nacogdoches.

Since then I'd avoided dark-eyed men completely. Blonds, brunets, redheads were easy to date; I was impervious. They were all safe for, and from, me. In fact, I'd begun to wonder if I'd become immune to men altogether. "You're like an alcoholic, Dallas," I said out loud. "Just erase the message and forget his face." I opened the refrigerator door. "But what a face." I closed the door, aware that I was losing this battle.

The telephone rang and I leaped at it, grateful for the interruption. "You know, that's a pretty convincing argument," Raul said. It took me a moment to realize he was referring to our lunchtime conversation. "But what about Ileana?"

"What do you mean, what about Ileana?"

"If April killed Leo, and you say she killed Ileana and the police, well, you know, they say she was dead a long time, how did I take pictures of her?"

"I don't know," I said flatly.

"And I called Jacob. The shoot I assisted on that Friday was for Talbot's. It's on the calendar. I shot Ileana that Sunday."

"Did you ask him about any leftover film?"

Raul sighed. "Yeah, he didn't have it." We were both silent a moment. "What do you do now?"

"Film!" I said. Was it another setup? But Wolchek was dead. "What are you doing now?"

"Right now?"

"Wanna take a drive?"

*   *   *

"You say this voice called and told you to come here?" Raul said, staring out the windshield. I was really glad to have a strapping, if short, man with me. "Nude Girls" flashed in neon on the front of the Oak Cliff building.

Nice and not-so-nice cars were parked in the lot and on the streets. I looked at the address again. "This is what I was told."

"Man, that don't look like no lab I've ever seen."

Me neither. "Well, let's go," I said, unlocking the door and stepping out of my recently freed Chevy.

"I'm gonna keep an eye on the truck," he said, looking up and down the street. "If you aren't back here in five minutes, man." He patted the Walther in his waistband.

For once that was comforting. I nodded and opened the door.

One smell was prominent inside, and I felt a little nauseated. Blinking, so my eyes would adjust to the near darkness, I saw a small office door to my left. I pushed it open a little and the middle-aged black man looked up. "You lost?" he asked.

"I'm looking for the lab," I said.

"Behind the theater."

"How do I get there?"

"Pay here, then walk through the theater and exit where the sign says exit."

"I have to pay to get to the lab?"

He smiled. "Lab's behind the theater. Gotta pay to get in the theater."

Outraged, I asked how much.

"Twelve dollars."

"For a porno movie!"

"It's a good one. A classic. *Debbie Does Dallas.*"

Like every lesbian I'd ever known hadn't said that to me. I threw down my ten. "It's what I have. I'm just walking through."

His eyes narrowed. "Cheap, ain't ya?"

"Yes," I snapped, and walked out of the office. The door to the so-called theater was shut and I hated to even touch it. There was nothing around, so I slipped the sleeve of my jacket down and grabbed the door's handle.

The exit sign looked a million miles away, and I walked as fast as I could, trying not to listen to the moans and groans coming from the film and the audience. As I opened the door, someone saw me and shouted, but I closed it behind me firmly.

"Hey, good-lookin', you here for an audition?" a greasy, mustached, dark-sunglassed man said to me.

My patience was about up. I crossed my arms. "No. I'm here to pick up film. I've already paid ten dollars for the dubious privilege of making it back here. I want my film now."

He was lounging on a sofa, pieces of a broken-down camera surrounding him. "Dubious. Big words, huh?" He didn't move.

"Today." I said, just in case I hadn't been firm enough.

"Your name, Miss Hotfoot?"

"The film is under the name Ileana Karagonis."

I had a feeling the eyes behind the seventies sunglasses were smarter than I expected. "And who are you?"

"A friend."

"The one she robbed, that friend?"

I sighed. "That was between the two of us."

He turned back to polishing his lens. "Not if you killed her, it ain't."

"Dammit, I did not kill her."

"It's right there," he said, pointing to an envelope on the edge of the table. With trembling hands I opened it up, holding the film to the light.

A woman in a picture hat, with sixties makeup. Same woman, same makeup, in a rhinestone dog collar. Also in a crocheted poncho. I pressed my lips together to keep from shouting. We had the murderer.

I fished the loupe out of my pants pocket and looked at the face of the blond woman in the picture hat. If my thoughts were correct, then this would prove April had killed Ileana. What had Jacob said about her eye, the freckle?

Her left eye. "Damn," I whispered. I looked at another exposure. Left eye was still clear. I scanned through the length of the film. It really was Ileana.

I stuffed the film in the envelope, muttered thanks, and walked out. "You were right," I said, shoving the envelope at Raul. "You did photograph Ileana. So much for my brilliance and insight.

"I told you," he said.

He had.

One call had come in while I was gone. The police. No one was claiming Leo's body, and it was ready to be released. Did I want it?

Leo's body, his faceless body. Now there was a funeral to arrange. I agreed, and called a cousin, who was a mortician, to pick it up, then hung up the phone, haunted by Leo's words.

"What can I do for you?" I whispered. He'd only wanted

one thing, an open casket. The one thing I couldn't give him. I glanced up. It was early enough, which meant the gay boys of Cedar Springs were taking naps before the parties began. The least I could do was book the entertainment. Debby Boone, aka Tommy, should be awake, assembling her feathered wig. I scanned through my caller IDs to find the number, then dialed.

The next morning found me appropriately attired in slacks and shirt, though my Fendi shoes were backless, poring over the many shots we'd taken for *Metamorphosis*. Gary was talking reshoots of everything that had been done in the studio, pre-murder; that was the word.

It was insane.

Clothes that were scattered across the country had to be found, a new concept created, new talent, everything different. The Store was distancing itself from the "unpleasantness" of the murder.

I had calls out to every single contact I knew, trying to find the merch, see when it would be available. When a designer sent out the next season's clothes, usually there were five or six copies—for the whole world. I knew one ensemble was at *Vogue*; it was scheduled as their cover shot.

Where to find the remaining merch, I didn't know. The network of stylists, stores, magazines, and models was actively searching on my behalf.

That was only the first request. Damon also wanted Jacob's lighting, which was a problem since Jacob was out of town. And his studio was in ashes.

Flipping through my notes, I got the list of crew members. We might not be able to get everyone, but we could get close.

"Coco, it's me. Are you free Monday?" I started explaining, then remembered I didn't even have any talent booked. I threw the sheets on my desk and scooted back, putting my feet up and sipping my latte while I looked through headbooks. I called Lindsay for some serious scheduling.

By three o'clock I had the CK merch coming in from San Francisco, from a private showing in Santa Fe, and from a shoot at *Elle*. DKNY was being shipped from New York and Seattle; Polo from Miami and LA; and lists of other designers and merch that seemed endless.

FedEx was going to be knocking on my door all night. I had the talent booked. Coco was on for makeup and hair, I had first and second assistants, with Francis as the photographer, at the studio he usually leased. Way out in Las Colinas, but he thought the new concept would work there.

Gary's new concept.

Since I would be there anyway, on a whim and a prayer, I put a call in to a special studio in Las Colinas. I wasn't sure if they could help, but it was worth a try.

CHAPTER TWENTY-TWO

"What did you set up yesterday?" Damon's voice was tight. I sprang awake instantly, noticing it was six-thirty. I needed to stop answering the phone this early.

"The reshoot," I said, sitting up in bed.

"With who? Who authorized this?"

"The same crew as before. Gary told me to."

Damon swore under his breath. "Francis Jourdan was the photographer?"

"Yes." My feet were on the floor.

"Call and cancel."

"What?"

"Mr. Evans"—he was The Store's wealthy, supervisory owner—"thinks to do anything other than change that entire section of the book would be profoundly distasteful. Different models, different clothes, a whole different look."

"That's what we're doing, well, the merch is the same," I said.

"In fact," Damon said, talking over me, "Mr. Evans said he'd like to use only young models—do something outside in clean, fresh air."

"With spring lambs cavorting in the fields?" I asked.

"Don't be snide, Dallas."

"By Friday, or is that another part to ignore?"

"By Friday."

"The merch is here," I said. "The last outfit will arrive at ten."

Damon sighed. "That's off, too."

I thought I would snap the receiver in two. "With new merch?" This was unheard of, the buyers, the board, the advertisers, the vendors—there were too many pieces to redo this. Was Mr. Evans completely unaware of his own business?

"I will let you know as soon as you get to the office. By ten I want some face choices. Young."

I lived in hell.

By five o'clock we had the faces, the clothes, the location, and a whole new crew. Francis hadn't been in, so I'd left the message for him. I was packing my purse when Damon came up to me.

His perfection was in an Italian suit today, his hair slicked back, and wearing Gucci wire frames. He placed a piece of paper on my desk. The pink of it stood out among the white. Two Store security guards flanked him.

I reached out—it felt like slow motion—and picked up the paper. "Terminated?" I read out loud, then looked up at Damon.

He nodded once. "Effective immediately. You have ten minutes to clear out your personal belongings."

Hence the guards, to make sure I didn't step over that time limit. Coworkers streamed silently toward the elevators, all eyes averted. "When was this decided?"

"Yesterday."

I looked at him. "You knew that I was getting fired, but you made me scramble to reschedule this shoot? And call back those people I'd booked, to cancel?" I felt my ears start to heat.

He shrugged. "You were the most effective way of getting the job done." His gaze held no animosity. "It was nothing personal, Dallas."

"It's always personal, Damon," I said, and began to toss things in my bag. One of the guards produced a legal file box. "Why are you firing me?" I hissed. "Three demerits on my clothing sent you over the edge?"

"Mr. Evans, if you must know. He wanted to clear the decks of anyone who was involved with this unfortunate event."

I glared at Damon. "How convenient for you."

"Not really. I need you and Gary right now."

I paused in the process of stripping my desk of photos. "Gary's fired, too?"

"He's taking an extended leave of absence. His mother, you know."

Poor Gary.

"He'll be telecommuting for a while." Damon stopped me from slipping a disk in the computer. "You can't take any files."

I shoved it in and heard it click. "These are personal files,

Mr. Whitside," I said. "I am not leaving an ounce of work here."

"Don't make me throw you out," he threatened.

"I dare you." I cleared off the desktop, ejected the disk and defiantly tucked it in my bra. Damon's expression was frozen in disapproval. "Talk to my attorney, if you have a problem," I said, hoisting my box.

"We need to look through that," he said.

"You watched me pack it!" He remained focused, so I handed it to him. The office was completely empty now, though I bet everyone was meeting for happy hour to discuss what had happened. Down the hall, into the elevators, out to my car. I slammed my door in Damon's face and peeled out of the parking garage.

To think I'd worn a suit today.

My Nokia rang as I was turning into the Fiesta grocery store's parking lot. I was going to stock up now on water, fruit, veggies, and queso fresca; who knew when I'd get another paycheck.

I picked up without looking at the ID.

"Go Stars!" Francis Jourdan shouted in my ear. I smiled. Francis was, had been, one of The Store's favorite photographers. He was also an avid ice hockey fan. I'd thought he was a lunatic, until he persuaded me to go to a game. Since then, I'd been hooked. Hopes of getting into the Stanley Cup playoffs were getting high. "How is my favorite felon?" he said.

"Free, at least for now."

"Free enough to make it to a game?"

I glanced at the clock on my dashboard. "I'm in a suit," I said. "I'm not going to a hockey game in a suit."

"You're a stylist! I know you have clothes in your trunk."

"My truck, and I'm in my Mustang."

"Whatever. Are you going to let clothing get in the way of a Stars game?"

"It's at six-thirty?"

"Reunion Arena. I'll be waiting for you at the Will Call."

"Sure." I started the engine—even if I left now, I would still be late.

"I'll buy you nachos," he said.

"Buy me Mike Modano's sweater," I said.

"Hey, what's this about Friday being canceled?"

"Remember *Mission: Impossible*?" I asked.

"Yes?"

"Remember the disclaimer that if anything went wrong, the Secretary would disavow any knowledge, et cetera, et cetera?"

"Yes?" His voice had lost some of its enthusiasm.

"Well," I said, pulling out of the parking lot, "we've both been disavowed."

Francis was quiet as I drove down Henderson toward Central. "Your ticket will be waiting under your name," he said. "Don't forget your ID."

"So we were all disavowed?" was Francis's first question. He was waiting for me just inside Reunion Arena, his ticket stub poking out of his shirt pocket. A Dallas Stars cap covered his red hair, but his untamed flaming red beard still made him look like a wild man.

"The whole crew," I said as I hugged him hello.

"You'd think they'd love the publicity," Francis said. "What could be more perfect? The girl is killed on the set, so everyone wants to see the set. People who would never, never have, picked up *Metamorphosis* would do so."

"I think marketing loved it," I said, as we stood in line. "But Mr. Evans thought it was in bad taste."

"Definitely bad taste, but when has that consideration ever stopped someone from selling something?"

He had a point.

"Do you think it will be just for this book, or are we all on some nefarious black list now?" Francis got about 45 percent of his income through The Store.

"I don't know. Damon and I didn't part on the best of terms. I think he was going to do *Metamorphosis*, since he'd shipped Gary off and fired me."

"He's got a good eye," Francis said. "Did they let Jacob go, too?"

"He's been in jail over this, so I imagine so. However, he's shooting in Montana, so I don't guess it hurts as bad."

We stood for the national anthem, shouting "Stars!" when they were mentioned in the song. For the next two hours, Francis and I were glued to the ice, cheering Eddie the Eagle, the goalie, and the rest of the transplanted Canadians and Yankees who made up Dallas's newest sports franchise. Buoyed by the Stars' win, 3–2 over the Islanders, we walked back to our cars.

"One thing you should know, Dallas," Francis said. "And I probably shouldn't tell you this, but whatever the big deal project that Leo was negotiating? Well, Jacob was going to be the photographer."

I knew that.

"But Ileana refused to sign if he was. Leo had to choose, the face or the photographer."

"No contest," I said.

"No. There wasn't."

"Dallas O'Connor?" I heard my name and turned. Alejandro stood ten feet away. He looked at Francis, then at me. "How are you?"

"Fine," I said.

"Enjoy the game?"

I nodded. He said good night before I could think to introduce him to Francis. "Damn!"

"Who was that?"

"A guy, who I think is adorable, but who thinks I'm a murderer or something. Because of Wolchek's suicide."

"That's bad. He looked straight. And he was really handsome."

"Rub in some more salt," I said wryly. "Now he probably thinks I came here with you."

Francis chuckled, "I will make sure and tell Patricia."

"Your wife is grateful I see these games with you," I said.

"So she doesn't have to miss TV."

You wanted Alejandro to stop calling. This should do it. "So Ileana was the one who screwed Jacob out of the job?"

"No, if he would have screwed her, he might have gotten it. But he refused to."

"Ah, rejection."

"It was going to be two years of work, probably at a day rate of 10K."

"That's a million dollars!"

As I drove home I wondered: Would a man who refused to sleep with an underage girl resort to killing her?

*   *   *

April had done it. I was convinced. How, was my only question. The media had decided the case was closed, based on Wolchek's suicide note. I still didn't know what it said, why everyone thought everything was taken care of.

Since my day was free, I filled it with errands. A stained silk shirt dropped off at the expensive but effective Lemmon Avenue dry cleaners; a run through the Farmer's Market; stopping by a few of the Snider Plaza boutiques to see what was on sale now that I had even less money than before; and the long drive out to Las Colinas to drop off some photographs.

I spent the evening flipping through magazines, seeing all the amazing things that stylists, probably freelancers, were doing. Finally, I scraped up my courage and dialed Lindsay.

"Okay," I said, taking a deep breath. "I'm ready."

"For?"

"Going freelance," I said. A call beeped in, disrupting my big, dramatic moment. I asked her to hang on and clicked over. I was grinning by the time I switched back to Lindsay.

"Freelance? What prompted this?"

"Well, Damon fired me, but he just called Gary telling Gary to hire me back, under the table."

"Gary is such a wuss."

"No, Gary told me to go freelance, charge The Store out the wazoo, and not have to put up with the Demon's moods."

"Well, I don't know about that," Lindsay said, "but you will definitely be a little more in the driver's seat. I'll need to see your book."

I didn't have one—I hadn't kept track of all the stuff I'd worked on. "I'll get it to you," once I find it all and assemble it, that is.

"Brilliant. And if Mr. Whitside calls you, send him my direction. You're going to finally be paid what you are worth."

"It's great to have friends like you."

"Well, if you like me as a friend, you're going to love me as your rep. Must run. Go have a good soak and buy a dress on the 'Net."

We hung up, and I decided to do just that.

I was in the bathtub enjoying the bubbles and the most recent issue of *W*, when the phone rang about 11 P.M. I cocked my head toward the door. There was a great deal of static, then a message in a voice that sent chills down my spine.

"What was Leo's and April's marriage like? Why did they have no children?"

The caller hung up.

I got out of the tub, tied my robe on, and went downstairs. My caller ID said Unavailable. Slowly, thoughtfully, I walked back to my bath.

I'd never thought about any couple's decisions to have or not have children. Coming from a large family it seemed normal to pattern rabbits. I thought my parents were insane and had gone overboard, but . . . why was April's decision not to have children important?

CHAPTER TWENTY-THREE

"That's what I know," I said to Diana as we sat at Breadwinner's drinking coffee and nibbling fresh banana bread in the unseasonably warm morning. I was in a sleeveless turtleneck, Capri pants and bamboo-soled thong sandals, and already sweating.

"Who do you think is calling you?"

"No clue."

She leaned forward, even more sprite-esque in a green polo with her navy cargo pants. "The department would like to let this be solved," she said. "Wolchek's note explains everything to their satisfaction."

"It doesn't make sense," I said.

"Neither does your claim that a supermodel did it," she said.

I pointed to the frozen letters in front of her. "Leo claimed it, not me. Besides, all that other stuff, his will, the prenup—"

"There is no proof that anyone other than his attorney and Leo ever saw those documents," she said.

"Ileana and April look so much alike," I said. "She could have pretended to be Ileana for weeks before anyone—"

"April has alibis for the murders," Diana said. "I understand you are angry and want some kind of closure because Leo was your friend, but April couldn't have done it. Being in two places at one time isn't possible, and her alibis are ironclad."

Diana's beeper went off. As we stood, she held out a hand. "I'm sorry, Dallas. It's a horrible thing when murder touches our lives. Sometimes there are no answers."

She shook my hand. "It's nice you chose to work with us instead of against us. Keep in touch. I'll let you know what happens."

Good thing she couldn't read my mind and guess what my next errand was.

By eleven, I was parking my truck, again, three streets away from Leo's house. I was donning gloves, again, only these were dishwashing gloves. Bright yellow.

If there were any big secret to them not having children, it would be in his files. Under what, was the great mystery. C for children? I for infertile, incompatible? V for vaginal delivery? B for blond?

This time the place was cordoned with police crime tape, and I had a little argument with myself over whether to enter or not. My curiosity won, and I slipped through the window again. Once inside Leo's office I saw his files had been searched, but nothing appeared to be missing. I sat down and began going through them, one folder at a time.

The room began to heat up considerably. Leo had intended to reinsulate this spring, before Dallas's traditional hundred-plus-degree months kicked in. I was in the lower desk file drawer when I saw the files were crammed together, as if something were jammed in between them. Suddenly nervous, I reached down and my fingers closed around a plastic case.

A Palm Pilot.

Ileana's missing Palm Pilot?

I inhaled deeply, trying to calm myself . . . and caught the faintest tinge of smoke. I sniffed again. Definitely smoke. I walked out to the landing, suddenly coughing. Smoke was coming up the stairs. There was a fire below.

Cursing, I ran to the Ralph Lauren room and tried to open the window. It wouldn't budge, so I picked up a chair and threw it through the glass, breaking it. Stepping gingerly I put one leg through, then kicked off, grabbing for the tree branch.

"Dallas!" Jacob called from the alleyway. "Jump, hurry!"

I scrambled up the branch, then down the other side, and dropped into the alleyway. "The Palm Pilot," I said, remembering, and looked over my shoulder at the house. Flames were starting to flicker behind the windows.

Jacob stood in the alley, the door to his SUV open. "Come on," he said.

"I thought you were in Montana," I gasped out.

He grabbed my arm and threw me in the car, peeling out down the alleyway. We had gone a few blocks before the strangeness of the situation began dawning on me. I wasn't sure how to form the questions, or even if it was safe to do so. He hadn't shaved in days, and his clothes were grubby. "Are you the pyromaniac?"

"No."

"But you know who it is." He didn't respond. "I'm getting really tired of attempted burnings," I said. "What is going on?"

"Why were you at Leo's house?" he asked.

"No, you answer first. How is it that you were supposed to be in Montana, yet you show up in the nick of time to keep me from getting barbecued?"

He glanced at me. "Montana was just a way to save face. I have no money, Dallas. I need to liquidate my assets. I'm finished here. Pretending that I have a job someplace else saves a little of my pride."

"So why were you at Leo's?"

He brushed his face with his hand. "That's a little harder, and more humiliating, to explain."

"Try me," I said. He turned onto Mockingbird Lane.

"I was going to rob him," he looked at me again. "Just a few things I knew he had, a few things that I could sell, make a little bit of cash. He'd offered to help me, before . . ."

"What about your house, your cars, this vehicle?"

"Mortgaged. I don't own anything."

We were almost to White Rock Lake. "You have a brand new Mercedes? How is that possible? You make—"

"We all have vices, Dallas," he snapped. "Mine are just expensive. And it's not my Mercedes, it's April's."

Of course, Duchesse yellow. Her bottle of Joy, her tape recording of Leo . . . omigod, it was Leo's tie.

Was Jacob her accomplice? "Do you know why April and Leo didn't have children? Actually, why she's never had children with any of her husbands?"

He sighed. "Don't ask me these questions, Dallas. I can't help you. Don't trust me." He stopped in the park off Lawther Road, facing the lake. It was a perfect day to sip iced tea on a patio and talk about spring hemlines and summer sandals.

Instead, I was talking about murder.

I turned to him. "You say don't trust you, but then you keep showing up like a damned knight on a white horse. What—"

He reached over, grabbed my face in both hands and kissed me. Hard, deep, passionately. All I could do was hold on. When he sat back, there were tears in his eyes. My toes were so tightly curled that I couldn't even think for a moment. I opened my mouth, but he spoke first.

"Shut up. Don't say anything, don't ask any of your Nancy Drew questions. I did that because I had to. I did it now because . . . all we ever have is this one damn moment in time. Nothing else is real."

He rubbed his mouth, looking out his side window. "Loyalty is a bitch, Dallas. Promises you make when you are young will break you when you're older." He turned to me. "Have you ever broken a promise?"

I stared at him, a little bewildered by the anger I saw.

"It's not a damned rhetorical question, Dallas. Answer me. Have you ever broken a promise?"

"The one that says, 'until death do us part,' " I said softly.

He looked away. "I never have. Never once have I broken a promise." Jacob grew very silent and still. "Now, now I think a promise is about to break me."

I reached out and touched his shoulder, but he jerked away. "Don't do that."

"You just kissed me," I said. "You are obviously in pain—"

"You know nothing about me, Dallas, just rumors you've heard." His blue eyes were cold and hateful. "You are such a naive thing, I could rape you and murder you and leave you in the lake, and no one would ever know."

"You aren't that kind of man," I said with some effort.

His glance was disdainful. "You say that, but you have no clue about me. About anyone. We never know another person. Haven't you learned that yet? The secrets your beloved Leo hid? The things Francis knows, but never says?" He reached out and touched my cheek, very softly. "The impulses that make me want to beat you and make love to you?"

"Did you do it, Jacob? Did you kill Ileana?"

He dropped his hand and looked away, his whole body seemed to shrink. "I might as well have," he said. "Just because I didn't use the knife doesn't mean I'm not responsible."

"Are you covering up for April?" I asked.

He started the Infiniti and screeched out of the parking lot. We drove in silence to my truck, still parked on the street. Black smoke filled the sky—Leo's house was probably almost gone. I was numb. Jacob slammed on the brakes, then unlocked the door. "You ask me that, and you don't even know why," he said. "Use your pretty head for something other than fashion, girl. Or your scarf-covered neck will be beyond even my protection."

He left me standing on the street, lost.

I made tracks to Ziziki's nouveau Greek restaurant. My cousin Suzette was the bartender. She was also a medical student. Unlike most graduate students, she didn't miss sleep because she'd never had it. Or needed it.

It was about four o'clock, and the place was almost closed.

Zetta, her nickname, was sitting at the bar, bent over a book, her face hidden by riotously curly red hair. The distressed walls were shaded in gold and orange, and autographed plates sat on shelves above the cloth-covered tables for two and four. Guitar music floated in from above, and the aromas of lemon, oregano, and olive oil made my mouth water.

"Can I get an order of dolmas to go?" I asked softly.

"Dallas!" she cried, hugging me. We exchanged news about our families—she was the middle child in a family of five, and I hadn't talked to mine—as she poured me a San Pellegrino. I asked how school was, and she started into a story about what she was researching, then stopped herself. "What's up with you? I saw all that stuff on the news. It's a wonder your parents aren't breaking down your door."

"It is," I said.

"What's up?"

"What are the causes of infertility?"

Her eyes bugged and her gaze checked my left hand before returning to my face. "Are you pregnant?"

"Are you insane?" I countered.

"Then why do you want to know?"

"This whole model thing," I said, sliding onto a barstool. "I think it might have something to do with infertility."

"I don't see the connection, but to answer your question, there are a million reasons."

"Like?"

"Well, some of the more obvious ones are low sperm count—"

"Maybe just the reasons on the woman's part," I clarified, sipping my water.

"Bad eggs, all kinds of genetic reasons—"

"Tell me about those."

"Genetic reasons?"

"Yeah, is there a genetic fault for a woman not being able to have children?"

"Fault is rather harsh, don't you think?"

"Whatever. My question stands."

Zetta twisted a finger in her hair as she thought. "I can do some research for you, if you want." Her brown eyes snapped back to mine. "When do you need this?"

"Yesterday," I said, "You can get me on my cell phone."

"When's the funeral?"

I stood up, straightening my shoulders. "Leo's?" I hadn't heard from my Las Colinas connection at all. It was discouraging.

She nodded. They'd met at a party or two. Gay men loved Zetta—she was tall, built, girly, and incorrigible. They wanted to *be* her. "I want to be there."

"I'll let you know." We hugged.

"Are you okay?" she asked.

I blinked, unable to look her in the eye. "I don't know." She patted me on the shoulder, and I moved away. "However, I think I may have met the woman of your dreams," I said, forcing myself to smile.

Zetta grinned back. "I'll get to work right away. My laptop is in the back, and it's an hour before dinner starts."

I waved and walked back to my car. I couldn't believe I'd left the Palm Pilot in the house. If I could only get proof, somehow get proof, that April had done it.

My Nokia rang as I was pulling onto McKinney, headed home. Raul greeted me like a long-lost lover. "I have it figured out," he said. "Have you eaten?"

"Raul, forget food. Tell me what you've figured out!"

"No, it's complicated. Meet me at Gloria's. This is celebration!"

Shaking my head, I crossed Central, headed for upper Greenville and Gloria's.

We walked in at the same time, and I noticed the looks my Rickyish friend drew. Immediately we had the best table, the fastest service and Raul was halfway through a Cuervo 1800 margarita. I sipped a Negro Modelo and waited while he ordered fried plantains and the seafood soup Gloria's was known for.

"No carne?" I said, after I ordered some nachos.

He smiled and reached into his pocket, then pulled out a strip of paper. "That's it!"

The white paper had a handwritten date on it and a scrawl that I could guess was initials. Across the top a series of printed numbers ran into a familiar logo. "Eckerd?" I said, looking up at him.

"That's it! I took the films to Eckerd."

I was confused. How many rolls of film were there? "I thought you left them at the studio," I said.

"I thought I did, but I found this in a pair of jeans, so I think it's the film." He was so proud of himself.

"If you shot color negative, you certainly could have," I said. The cooing waiter refilled our water glasses and assured us the food would be right out. "How do you know this is it?"

"Oh man, it's the date," he said, balancing his chair on the two back legs. "I must have taken it right after we shot it. Dropped it off, you know, to pick up the next day."

"What do you think that film is that we found in Oak Cliff?"

"It's not mine, you know why?"

"Why?"

" 'Cuz I shot before shots, and there weren't any on that roll."

"So," I said slowly, "that film of Ileana is not the roll you shot."

"No."

"You're positive."

"Yeah."

The waiter set down our food, asked if we needed anything else, and patted Raul on the shoulder at least three times. I didn't pick up my fork. "So you think Eckerd is where the real roll, the roll you shot of Ileana"—or April, I thought—"is?"

Raul was focused on his soup, and I reached over and grabbed his wrist, freezing his spoon in the air. "Hello?"

"Right, yeah."

I released his wrist and sat back, swigging my beer.

"You want one of these," Raul said, offering me a slice of plantain. I speared it and ate while he told me about Janice being picked up by Page Parkes Modeling Agency.

I fiddled with the slip of paper. The Eckerd photo receipt.

"So everything is perfect," Raul said. "We get the films, you go to the police, get us freed, and then we see about our relationship." He winked.

I turned the slip over, then looked at the front again. "That's great. Which Eckerd?"

Two days later, I was in the middle of laundry and making peanut butter cookies, which were good things to do in between calling every damn Eckerd Express Photo lab in the entire city of Dallas—there are forty-six—when Coco called. "I'm glad you're still speaking to me," I said. "I'm sorry about that last glitch with The Store."

She laughed. "When Damon is the AD, I always know it's going to be more of a pain than it's worth," she said. "How are you?"

"Better."

"You won't believe who just called me."

I popped a hot cookie in my mouth and immediately felt like a "Got Milk?" ad, it was so hot. Pulling the phone cord with me, I opened the 'fridge and drank from the carton. "Who?" I said, gurgling milk and cookie.

"Lindsay!"

I frowned. "She's your best friend. What's the surprise?"

"Oh, I don't mean her," she said, "but who the client is."

"Are you going to tell me or do I have to beg?" I asked, tipping the carton again. We teased Coco that she was incapable of linear thought, since her mother was Baptist and her father was Jewish. She'd been fried from the inside out.

"The Diva wants me to do her makeup! Isn't that amazing!"

I almost spit milk on the counter. "April called Lindsay?"

"That's what I just said! It's for a press conference she's giving at the Anatole!"

"Does she want an on-figure stylist?"

"I don't know," Coco said. "I'm so excited! What a face to work with!"

"You worked with her last week, and weren't excited. In fact, you felt doomed."

"In broad daylight? God, that was like photographing me in white spandex hip-huggers."

Coco was a big girl. Her point was made. "Congratulations," I said. "How come she isn't using Duchesse makeup and artist?"

"Ask Lindsay. Oh yeah, call her, too."

I called three more Eckerd Expresses, to no avail, pulled more cookies out of the oven, threw my whites in the dryer, then called Lindsay.

"Hallo?" She didn't sound extremely British today—the stress level must be down.

"I just heard from Coco."

"Oh yes. Do you want work?"

"Of course."

"This is far beneath you, Dallas, but I really need some help. I've gotten you a good rate, but, even then, you might not want to do it."

"Do what?"

"Pressing."

She was right. Pressing was the lowest job on the totem pole. I was one of the few stylists who hadn't started there. "Uh . . ."

"Just listen. It's because I'm in a bit of a jam. All of the pressers are otherwise engaged, and April simply insists on having one—"

"April wants a presser?"

"She's having a press conference, announcing her retirement from Duchesse, that sort of thing. Why she thinks anyone gives a bloody damn, I can't imagine, but you know how the locals love her."

"I'll do it."

"It's two hundred for a half day, which is outrageous for a presser. But working with April's standards, especially for her wardrobe—"

"I'll do it," I said, biting into another cookie. "Give me the details."

CHAPTER TWENTY-FOUR

The clothes the woman had! If murderers dressed this well habitually, I could see the appeal. I felt sick immediately for even thinking that. In the next room I overheard snatches of conversation while Coco was doing April's makeup.

She wanted all four outfits pressed, so she'd have options.

I'd borrowed a steamer from Lindsay, swearing that I wouldn't wreck anything. I'd put water in it, so I flipped the switch and checked out the composition of April's choices: Carolina Herrera's gray wool wide-legged pants and draped-back sleeveless top, which would steam well. Dana Buchman's white jacket and pants, which looked more like Miami, especially with floral Gucci slides. But they were linen, which likes steam. And the glitziest option, Armani pants and beaded top, with mohair, calf-length duster—not something I was anxious to mess with. Her final selection was a lemon yellow Versace suit, knee length and zip front. Probably the most "appropriate" choice for here, but, as I started working on it, a nightmare to steam.

As my face got hot and I burned my wrists from holding everything the wrong way, I wondered what I hoped to learn here. April wasn't going to confess. Jacob was right to call me Nancy Drew. I heard April's laughter from the other room, and wondered how she could do it.

She'd killed one, possibly two or three people. Was murder really like Sting claimed—easier the second time, a breeze the third.

An hour later, the clothes were done. I wheeled the hanger into the other room, setting the shoes and bags with each ensemble. Coco was laughing, but I caught her gaze; she had learned something. I heard a phone ring, and April waved at me. "Be a doll and get that for me, would you?" she said.

I picked up her Gucci alligator bag and opened the top, pulling out a sleek black Sprint PCS phone. As Coco brushed her hair, I eavesdropped. April said yes and no a few times, laughed, then hung up and handed it back to me. As I dropped the phone back inside, I saw a rug—that is, a cloth in which you keep a weapon.

April had a gun.

The next phone that rang was mine. I raced into the next room, snatched it. "It's Zetta, I'm between shifts, but I wanted to let you know. Have you heard of AIS?"

"AIS?" I repeated. "No. What does it have to do with fertility?"

In the background I heard her paged. "I'll tell you later, but suffice it to say, everything."

I hung up and stared at the phone. "AIS?" I whispered.

"Dallas," Coco said from the doorway. "She's ready."

I walked into the next room. April stood in her La Perla lingerie and sheer stockings. Her face was perfect, her hair beautiful. "I think I'm going to get a bite first," she said. "Order an egg-white omelet with a side of steamed asparagus. I'll be waiting in my suite."

Adjoining these two rooms was another, apparently her suite. She closed the door. Her handbag was on the floor beside her chair. Coco was cleaning up her makeup spread. As soon as I heard the TV go on in the next room, I dived toward April's bag, and opened the rug.

"Dallas!" Coco whispered. "What are you doing?"

I pulled out the revolver. "It could have been used on Leo," I said. "I gotta find out if it's the same weapon. And it's loaded," I announced. Looking sideways at the cylinder, I could see the rims of the cartridges projecting from the rear of the chambers.

Coco was backing up. "I'll order the food," she said, staring at the gun in my hand.

I looked around for a second, then grabbed Coco's staple gun and stuffed it into the rug, dropping April's purse on the ground.

The door opened and I hid the gun behind my back. "I'll wear the yellow," April intoned, staring at me with cold eyes. She shut the door.

Coco's eyes were bugged. "You replaced her gun with a stapler?" she said, her voice rising.

"Hush," I said. I handed her the yellow ensemble, then stuffed the revolver in my bag. Diana needed it—ballistics test could prove whether or not it was used on Leo.

April and Coco primped and posed for the next half hour.

I could almost feel the heat of the weapon in the other room, but tried to be calm. The gun that killed Leo. Stupid to keep it, but maybe April thought she'd never be caught.

I locked the door behind them and retrieved the gun. I dumped five rounds out of the .38 Special. Taking one bullet, I gripped the cartridge with my Leatherman tool, then rapped the tool on the edge of the bar, shielding my eyes as I did it.

The sharp motion dislodged the bullet and it fell harmlessly to the floor. I pressed the bullet into the forcing cone of the gun, until it was seated. Then I pushed it far enough into the barrel with the handle of my blush brush, so that the cylinder could swing closed. I put the other four bullets back and replaced the casing in the empty chamber, then swung it shut. It was a Smith & Wesson, so I rotated the cylinder counterclockwise until it lined up, one chamber short of top dead center.

I washed my hands, then cleaned up the gray powder with a dampened paper towel. Diana was out when I called, so I left a message to meet me at the Anatole.

Now I had nothing to do but wait. I cleaned up the room and paced. Finally, I checked my voice mail. Twenty messages.

"Dallas, honey why didn't you tell us you were in trouble with the law?" my father's voice boomed, heavy with a West Texas drawl. "Your mother is worrying herself sick about your whereabouts. You call us right away, young lady."

Oh God, I was busted.

"I tried to keep them from finding out," Houston said in his message. "It hit the Austin paper, then Mom called Dad, Dad called Uncle Byron in the U.S. Attorney's Office . . . you know how it goes."

Oh, I did indeed. The posse was coming.

This was a similar dance to the one when they'd tried to annul my marriage. Then they'd tried it again, when I ran away from my ex-husband and he'd told them I was on drugs and selling my body for cash. I pressed cancel and listened to the next call.

"It's Ojeda. Are you on the run again? You know you always have a home with me and Mike here in Nac, okay? Kids, say hello to Auntie Dallas," she encouraged her brood of five.

"I don't wanna say hello," my nephew Charles said. "I don't like the phone."

Sasha grabbed the phone. "Hi, Dallas! I'm five! Are you coming to see us—"

My sister took the phone back. "As you can see we're all—Eden, get down from there! Gotta run. Eden!" I was laughing despite myself.

Sound bites of the remaining calls showed that all my siblings had called in—and my mother had called three times, my grandmama twice, and my uncle Byron, who was as big as a house, once.

And the Eckerd on Ross Avenue had the film. It was about to be trashed, so I needed to pick it up immediately.

Down the hall, the journalists applauded. April's press conference. Diana should be waiting in the foyer by now. Instead, Jacob was standing there, his arms crossed over his chest, his expression as bleak as the weather. "Playing games again, Dallas?"

"It's not a game," I said walking by him, then I turned back. "Could you do me a favor? I know you told me not to trust you, but," I licked my lips, "I don't believe a kiss like that could lie."

"Then you are a fool," he said.

I handed him the revolver. "Give this to Diana Mansfield when she comes in, please. But be careful, it's loaded."

He turned gray, swallowing so hard I saw his Adam's apple move. "Don't ask this of me, Dallas."

I stepped closer to him. "You've never broken a promise, Jacob. That's what you said. But, it dawned on me, that promises aren't always good things. I'm not asking you to give your word, but I am asking you to be my hero. Give this to Diana." I placed my hand on the cold metal and pushed it gently toward him, staring in his bloodshot eyes.

He opened his mouth, blinking rapidly. "I am not . . . hero material."

"Heroes choose, Jacob. That's what makes them heroes." I turned and walked away before he could say another word. It was raining and cold outside, chilling weather.

Eckerd's was a tease. Oh, it was Raul's film all right, but cockeyed photos of bizarre art instead of retro photographs of a blonde. I bowed my head against the rain as I unlocked my Chevy in the Eckerd parking lot. It was almost dusk and cold. Chicken soup tonight, definitely. I opened the door, then heard a step behind me.

My head exploded in pain and darkness.

CHAPTER TWENTY-FIVE

When I opened my eyes again, I was still in pain and darkness, but I was lying on my side in a coffin. At least it felt like a coffin, only I was wedged in with bent legs and arms. A child's coffin. I stretched my arms out—a wide child.

I felt ghastly, like I was going to throw up. Running my fingertips over my head, I learned why in the form of a quail's-egg-sized bump on the back of my head, and bruising that covered my left ear and jaw.

What had I been hit with?

Determined now, I explored my darkness with my fingertips. Metal, carpeting. I pushed and banged, to no avail. Frustration made my head pound worse. Where was I?

Thinking this time, I ran my hands over the shape of the room. It was boxy, with a seam on the roof. I was in a trunk.

A damnably small one. Where was I parked, was the real

question. April was at a press conference. Who had whacked me? Jacob? I took a deep breath. I shouted and made noise, until my head hurt so badly I had to swallow back bile.

"I will not be a victim," I said out loud. "I will not be a victim. How the hell I will not be a victim, I don't know, but I will not be a victim." I couldn't move at all, and my body was cramping. "The times I wish I was five-two," I muttered.

"How dare you!" I heard outside the trunk. April, shouting. Where were we? But that answered my question: I was in the trunk of a new Duchesse yellow Mercedes roadster 230 SLK, I'd just bet.

"You can't go on like this, April. Leo, I understood, Ileana, God, I tried to help. But Wolchek was too much. You've got to turn yourself in."

"You said yourself that I'm not dangerous to society."

"I hoped you would take Leo's money and settle down," Jacob said. "But instead, you've turned into a monster!"

"I have not!" she shrieked. "I am everything either one of you said you wanted. Rich, beautiful, powerful! But you lie! You both lied. All you wanted was someone who could get fat for you, have litters like some animal. You promised you'd be loyal, Jacob, you promised."

"Dammit, I have been loyal. I've crucified my conscience for the sake of you!" Jacob's voice was gritty. "I've looked away when I should have told the police, I've washed warm blood off your hands, I've kept all your dirty secrets—"

"Then why are they closing in on me, Jacob?" April said. "Why did that little stylist bitch know AIS, Jacob? That was our secret. Why did you tell her? You are the only one who could have."

He was silent, and I knew who my creepy phone tipster had been.

"I was completely safe," April said. "No one knew I was meeting Leo that night. Leo didn't even know until I called him in New Orleans. It was a perfect plan."

"Ileana was dead and Leo to blame." Jacob's voice was flat.

"Your idea was brilliant, JJ. Your ideas always were. I should have married you, not Leo. You would have understood me, taken care of me."

My God, he hadn't just covered for her, he'd been her accomplice. Would he help me?

"So let me move back—" she started.

Move back? I knew it! She was the other bottle of Joy. She also was the one who called with Leo's message. April had done it all.

"No, April. This has to stop. It has to stop tonight."

"I'm free now, Jacob," she wheedled. "No one is left, I'm safe. I'll have Leo's money, and all the time in the world. Come with me. We can travel, do the things we've always both been too driven to do. We can enjoy life now. We can even adopt, if you want to."

There was silence.

April's tone changed. "Anything you say to the police will look as bad for you as it does for me. I can always claim temporary insanity. You knew what you were doing."

"Yes I knew. I was keeping my"—he fell quiet—"promises," he said, sounding strangled.

"So let's leave tonight. Right now. We can drive to the airport and put everything behind us."

"You forget, I have no money."

"I have money, plenty. I'll get Leo's, too."

"This isn't going to work, April. It's not right."

"Nothing can hurt us, Jacob. There's no film, no proof of anything. Not even a weapon. I'm very good at this," she said, and I could see the smile that went with that statement of pride.

"Only because you burned everything to the ground, including my studio."

"It was protection," April said. "I didn't know what Ileana might have done, but I've come to believe she did nothing. We're safe."

They must have moved closer to the car, I was hearing every breath clearly. Did she intend to just leave me in the trunk, let me die of . . . starvation?

"What's the other link, April?" he said. He was even clearer. "Or should I say, who?"

"I don't know what you are talking about."

"Dallas O'Connor. The stylist."

"Her," she spit. "Another little fecund blonde you'd like to take."

What?

"Yes." Jacob's voice was even. "And Raul?"

"The Dallas police were happy to get hold of him," she said. "People with criminal histories should be careful about snooping."

"What about Dallas?" Jacob said.

"She left before the press conference was even over, I think," April replied airily.

"I know you hired that weasel Wolchek to go after her. Taking potshots in Fossil Rim. The guy was an idiot."

"He was cheap," she said. "And ultimately, uncontrollable."

"Which is why you killed him too?"

"Jacob, honey, don't get all excited," April said soothingly. "Wolchek wasn't a good person. He got what was coming to him. Does it really matter how?"

"Where is Dallas?" he repeated.

If I banged on the trunk, would he be able to get me out? Did he think I might be in here? How did he know I was missing?

I tried to bang on the trunk, but April, standing closer to me, slapped the metal, shaking me and muffling the noise, then she started shouting again. "All the models you've had in your bed aren't enough to sate your need for youth and beauty? Now you are hitting on stylists? Jacob, how pathetic. Or is it because she is actually a woman, and I'm not much more than a mannequin?" April's voice cracked, then she laughed, and I recoiled at her words.

"It was so perfect, hanging that fertile little bitch, making *her* the mutilated one. She had it all, you know? Ileana had everything, and still she was taking what was mine. I couldn't let her do it, JJ. I couldn't let her do it." April started crying.

"He was going to marry her," Ileana said. "They were going to have a family together. My Leo. Mine!" She sniffled. "You said you understood, Jacob. You were on my side."

I started shaking. Jacob was right to warn me not to trust him. I felt betrayed, deceived. And more than a little scared. April was off her rocker, completely. And I was in the trunk of her car, with the only people who could rescue me either in jail or of suspect allegiance.

"Come with me," she said. "Please JJ, please. We always promised we'd stay together."

All I could hear was her crying, then finally, resignedly, Jacob said, "Okay. Okay, I'll go with you."

"Really?" April said with a sniff.

"Yeah, there's nothing here for me anyway except prison," he muttered.

"Will you meet me at the airport?" April asked, opening the car door.

"Sure. Let me get some cash," he said. "Get, uh, get us two tickets."

"Going where?" she asked brightly.

So Jacob had the gun, I guessed. Diana never got it, never knew that I'd gone chasing the film. I was on my own.

"Wherever you want."

"Don't be so sad, we can come back," April said. "Later, a year or two."

"You can, April. I'm jumping bail. I kiss my citizenship good-bye this way."

"Then we better go to South America," she said with a giggle. "We'll have such a good life, Jacob, you'll see. We're both ready for this now. We can appreciate each other."

A silence, then I realized they were kissing. I wanted to wipe my mouth where he'd kissed me, just a few days ago. "You aren't going to let your conscience get you, and go trotting off to the police are you?" she purred.

"No. Of course not," he answered.

"You promise."

"I promise," Jacob said.

Tears streaked from the edges of my eyes. Hanged by his own integrity, or was that a lie too? "I'll see you at American's international gate, Jacob. Remember your promise!" She hopped in the car and slammed the door. Music blasted me from all sides, and I covered my ears, cringing from the noise.

She drove like a bat out of hell, slamming me around as she took overpasses and turns at incredible speeds. This woman had obviously not transported delicate things—like groceries—often. We screeched to a halt, far too soon for it to be D/FW airport. She turned off the stereo and then the car. We were parked at an angle.

I heard her alight, then she slammed the door. The car moved forward a little. "Don't try anything," she said before she opened the trunk. "I have a gun on you."

She popped the trunk and I blinked. It was night, but I could see well, my eyes long adjusted to the darkness. April, dressed as Ileana, wore jeans and a Gaultier jacket. Her French-manicured hand was wrapped around a pistol. Aimed at me.

Jacob had given her the .38 Special, or was it someone else's?

"You heard everything, I presume."

I nodded.

"People should be happy with what they have, Dallas. They shouldn't want what others have. It's selfish."

So said the woman who was notorious for stealing jobs. I nodded.

"More than that, people should mind their own business."

This really was going to sound like Nancy Drew if she started in on my being "meddlesome" or something.

"I found the body. I was being held as a suspect. It was my business," I said.

She took off the safety. "You were going to be fine, until I heard you saying AIS on the telephone."

"Eavesdroppers never hear good things about themselves," I smarted off.

"Shut up," she said. "Never talk back to me. I'm April Alexander, and I can ruin you with one word."

Psycho killer . . . the song started in my head. *Pa pa pa pa pa papa.*

She looked at her diamond-studded Piaget. "Your Chevy is stripped now, on its way to South America, just ahead of me."

My Chevy Z71 with leather interior and CD player was gone? She was pissing me off. And damn it, my purse, my styling gear . . . I gritted my teeth. I was going to kick that pistol outta her hand, and enjoy doing it.

Just as soon as I could move.

"You do impressive makeup," I said. "The spitting image of Ileana."

"No," she snapped. "Ileana was the spitting image of me. I was first, she was nothing but a copy."

"So she *was* dead. You were the one Raul photographed."

"I don't owe you an explanation. This isn't the movies."

There was nowhere to run, no way to hide. "Get out," she said. "I stuffed you in there, but I'm not pulling you out. Hurry."

Wincing, I slipped one leg out from under me, and eased out. The things movies never do show. I creaked upright, holding on to the side of the car so the world stayed upright.

She jammed the gun against my jaw. "I don't know what to do with you," she said. "I can't believe Damon gave you more time to go prowling around, looking for information. Really, he's the one to blame for this. If you would have been working, you wouldn't have been a nuisance. It's very irritating," she said. "Drowning is out, since nothing is deep enough. I can't shoot you in my car. I was going to kill you in Oak Cliff, but"—she jabbed me with the barrel of the gun—"someone had replaced my gun with a stapler, so I had to go back to Jacob's and get his gun."

"He'll appreciate that," I said.

She smacked me with the nose of the gun, and I swayed. "It will be the final piece for the police."

"You aren't going to wait for him, are you?"

"Do you think I'm an idiot? Men betray, Dallas. Maybe you haven't learned it yet, but unless they can keep you pregnant, they betray."

I swallowed, fighting tears. Nothing in the trunk, nothing, not even a rock, on the ground. No cars around, no lights. Where the hell were we.

With Jacob's working, loaded, weapon.

"Now come on," April said, poking me again. "I need to get my stuff into Leo's car and get out of here."

Gun to my head, she made me carry her lipstick red Louis Vuitton to the trunk of Leo's Beemer. His car had new plates and paint. Even I wouldn't have recognized it. Every muscle ached, and I had to keep swallowing to keep from vomiting.

"What did you hit me with?" I asked, as I rested for a moment against the back of the trunk.

"Free weight," she said. "Still in my car from the club. Hurts, huh? Come on, hurry it up. I have a flight to catch."

With seven pieces of luggage, she wasn't going to D/FW, not even first-class. And she was traveling as Ileana, I guessed. She opened her train case and pulled out duct tape. With her gun aimed at my chest, she suggested I hold my wrists in front of me. She taped them together, then stuck a piece over my mouth. I held her gaze, her freckled stare. She turned around and I grabbed the Catwalk hairspray out of her case. I sprayed it in her face—her freckled eye—then threw myself to the ground.

She fired blindly as she screamed and I scrabbled beneath the car. I saw her feet as she fought to stay upright, and stuck my foot out. She fell hard, the breath going out of her for a minute.

I crawled out on the other side, looking for the gun. At least I still had the spray. She was lying on the ground, on her side, her face averted.

Faking me out.

I ran for her purse, spilling it to find her phone. I shoved it in my front pocket, then ran around the front of the car, ducking out of sight. She was breathing heavily, moaning. I looked over my shoulder. We were in a shed, the door opened to the road, to the Mercedes.

I had to get the gun.

Gingerly I moved forward. April was sitting up, her wig askew, rubbing at her face. Even in this faint light I could see the skin was red, splotchy. "I can hear you," she hissed and whipped the gun around. I threw myself behind the car as she fired.

She cocked the gun again. I crept around the other side. She was listening hard for me, her back to me, the gun in her outstretched hand, pointing away.

I jumped her, my bound wrists catching her at the throat, pressing her against my legs. She kicked out uselessly, and dropped the gun as she fought my arms, clawing at my forearms. I pressed the Catwalk spray again, as I turned my face into my shoulder. She screamed and fought harder.

I kneed her in the back of the head, then banged her with the spray can two or three times. She slumped and I jumped toward the gun, grabbing it in shaky hands.

She was clawing at her face, screaming with pain. I lowered the gun; she was in agony. I was going to ask her if she wanted some water, but I couldn't because my mouth was taped.

It was a good reminder: she had no mercy, Dallas. She was going to shoot you point-blank. She killed Ileana, then masqueraded as her. She killed Leo and fed him to the fish. I raised the gun again, in both hands, scooting back out of her range.

I ripped the tape off my mouth, taking the gun off her for a second, then reaimed. I got to my feet.

"You don't have the nerve," she said. "You women with maternal instinct never do." She looked up and I could tell that she couldn't see me clearly. She couldn't focus.

"I think history would prove you wrong," I said.

"This isn't history, Dallas. This is your chance to walk

away with a lot of money, freedom. Never having to kiss Damon's ass again."

"How much?"

She hesitated a moment. "Half a million."

"Yours or Leo's?"

"I made it for him," she said. "It's mine. He would have been nothing without me."

"Were you always this self-centered or did the industry somehow create you? Did modeling just convince you it was your right?" I asked, chambering the next round. I aimed for her thigh.

She laughed. "I created myself. Completely."

"You must be very proud," I said. I needed to hurt her again, or we'd be tussling all night long. "Where are we?" I scanned the sky for signs of Dallas, for the 747s we call fireflies, since they are always there, waiting to land. Nothing.

"The little town of Kaufman," she said. "Away from the madding crowd."

Southeast of Dallas. Of help. Cell phones might not work out here. I swore. It wouldn't even be dawn for hours. The gun trained on her, I got the tape and kicked it toward her. "Tape your ankles and knees," I said.

She didn't move.

"Do it!" I shouted, stepping closer.

She looked up and I saw her eyes were almost completely shut. Swollen closed. Mine watered in sympathy. "If you want me to do that, you'll have to make me," she said.

"Where are the keys?" I snapped.

"In my pocket," she said, then laughed. "We're stuck with each other, Dallas. Until one of us tires out."

I was exhausted already, achy before I even picked up the

revolver. Tiredness made for mistakes. All she had to do was watch for that minute I started to fall asleep, or slack off somehow.

My legs were shaking and I was light-headed. "Or I can just shoot you so you can't get away," I said. "Your upper arm, your thigh, something that wouldn't be really dangerous, but would get your attention."

She picked up the tape and wrapped her knees and ankles, then put her face in her hands, whimpering.

"Toss it back," I said. Three bullets left. Empty the gun and lose the threat? Or face the possibility that I would end up wounded. Maybe dead. April wouldn't feel guilty for a minute, that was apparent.

I walked to the other side of the car, and dumped the bullets in my hand, then stuffed them in my pocket. Armed with Catwalk, I approached April, wrapped her wrists in duct tape, then dragged her to the Beemer's bumper, and taped her to it, through her joined wrists, then around her legs, her waist. Her entire face was swollen and I thought fleetingly of how much some Preparation H could help the swelling.

"I'm sorry," I said, and kicked straight out, catching her in the chin. She slumped and I rummaged through her purse for keys, dialing the cell phone as I went.

Dawn streaked the sky as I drove toward the city; downtown was merely blocks of silver jutting up from the plain, reflecting the moving clouds. She couldn't have stripped my truck, it wasn't possible. Please God. My insurance company was never going to believe this story.

I squealed into the Eckerd parking lot, heaving a sigh of

relief as I saw my Z71, gleaming in the morning light, safe and sound. "She's just a liar and a murderer," I said to myself.

I parked Leo's Beemer beside my truck in the Eckerd parking lot, glad to be out of my dead friend's car. I climbed into my truck, locked the doors, and turned the engine over.

Nothing.

Was the battery dead?

I tried again, and it clicked.

I tried again, the smell of gasoline was strong.

On the fourth try . . . the engine combusted.

CHAPTER TWENTY-SIX

It was hard to say which terrified me more: waking up in a hospital with stark white walls and gown, tubes in my hands and immobile; or waking up with Damon on one side, brushing my hair back with his hand, and Carla on the other, her hand protectively on my knee.

Regardless, I screamed. Or squealed. It was intended as a full-fledged scream, but I just didn't have it in me.

"Are you okay?"

"Are you in pain?"

"Can we get you anything?"

"Do you need medicine?"

I wasn't sure who asked what, and as soon as they asked, I forgot the question. Was I on a set somewhere? This was too perfectly a hospital room to actually be one.

"Dallas?"

"Can you hear us?"

"Can you see us?"

I looked from one to the other, though I couldn't move my neck much.

"Why don't you get her something to drink?" Damon said.

"She has water right here," Carla protested.

"Maybe she wants some juice," Damon said, more forcefully.

"I—okay," Carla said, walking out.

Leaving me alone with the Demon. I felt terribly unsafe, off-balance, and felt myself pressing against the bed, as if it would make me disappear.

"Are you okay?" Damon asked gently. "It's really not a rhetorical question, despite your being in a hospital bed."

"How did you get here?" I croaked out.

"I was at McDonald's, when I heard the explosion. Well, of course I recognized that behemoth vehicle you drive. That was quite a fire." He swallowed loudly. "You were thrown pretty far." His hand touched my head again, gently. "Hurt?"

"Can't feel it," I said.

He smiled at me. My grandmama would marry me to him in a second, just for the genes. "It's been a rough week for you."

"I've been here a week?" I asked, horrified.

"No, no, it's just Thursday." He glanced at his Rolex, and I noticed that for once he wasn't perfect. His beard was dark, his shirt was wrinkled and unbuttoned, the tie askew. His jacket had a hole in the elbow, and dust and grease covered him everywhere, even his perfect square jaw. "Four P.M. Thursday, to be precise." His gaze fell to my throat, and I suddenly knew why I felt so vulnerable. It had nothing to do with the hospital and everything to do with a scarf.

I tried to turn my head, to hide the scar that ran from just under my jaw, across my jugular and almost to my clavicle, a jagged line made by a plate of shattered glass.

My personal prom-night party favor.

Damon pulled the silk pocket square from his jacket and folded it on the diagonal. "The police have been waiting for you to wake up, and so has your family," he said, reaching forward. "Not to mention that annoying little reporter and all her fourth-estate siblings." He slipped the fabric around my throat, pulling it wider to hide the scar, then tied it, twisting the knot to the side.

I blinked back tears of appreciation.

"Now that this nonsense with the model is completed," Damon continued, pulling my hair over my left shoulder to hide the last little bit of scarring. "Not officially, not yet, but I'll expect you back at work by Monday at the latest."

I just watched him. Dumbfounded. He'd fired me!

He sat back, observing his handiwork. "Pinch your cheeks a little," he said. "You're as pale as a ghost."

I did, and before I could say anything else, he opened the door. "The lady will receive," he announced, then turned back to me. "Don't forget, you are a representative of The Store."

My fifteen minutes of notoriety brought in hoards of O'Connors. The first to arrive was my hippie mother and my nearly Victorian grandmama.

"My poor angel! Look at your face!" my mother cried.

"My goodness, that gown is an ugly shade of green," Grandmama said. "And what are you doing wearing a man's pocket square over that unsightly scar?"

My mother kissed my forehead, the only part of me not sore. My grandmother pulled out a satin bed jacket in a becoming rose pink. "Since you will be having guests," she said. "A lady always feels better when her color is good." She handed me a lipstick.

"Mother," my mother said to her mother, "this child has just barely survived a terribly traumatic event—"

"Which is exactly why," my grandmother replied in a soft Southern drawl, "she should be made presentable."

My mother sighed and turned to face me, rolling her eyes. Their differences were as tangible as their dresses. My grandmother was proper in a navy suit with smart gold trim, matching Pappagallo pumps, navy stockings, gold jewelry, her hair fixed, makeup on, and a kelly green silk shell to bring out her eyes.

My mother, who had flown up here from Austin, where she taught Texas history, was in an Indian print skirt, sandals almost as ugly as Birkenstocks, a shapeless T-shirt, and her hair in a bun, speared with silver-tipped chopsticks.

Horror of horrors, she was letting herself go gray. My grandmother spent her time staring pointedly at my mother's hair.

The door burst open again, and three more O'Connors joined the mix. My brother Beaumont, a flight attendant for American, resplendent in his uniform and pearly white smile; Christi, in shorts and T-shirt, her hair short and makeup dark; and Houston, his tie loose and shirt unbuttoned.

My room wasn't big enough. And there were still more coming. My head was starting to ache, as everyone exchanged greetings, then the rituals that had long been in place began.

Grandmother thoroughly approved of Houston. He made her glow. Sherman, though the eldest, displeased her greatly. He'd dared to drop out of medical school. Augustina and Mineola came in together. Mineola was in grad school in New Mexico, and Augustina was considering the Church as a vocation.

My mother, Camille Smyth, of the East Texas Smyths, had married a Catholic. My grandmother had vowed at their wedding to drop dead on the spot, should any of her grandchildren be named any form of "Mary." I wasn't sure she was speaking to Augustina. The children shouting in the corridor warned us of the impending arrival of Ojeda and crew.

The kids ran in and jumped on me, stopping short of kissing me when they saw my "owies."

"What happened, Dallas?" Sasha asked. "You have big owies."

The room quieted. "What did happen?" Houston asked. "Since you never called on your family to help."

There was a firm knock, and the door opened. My father, all hulking six feet five inches of him, stood on the threshold. The room seemed to shrink. "Look who I brought," he said, stepping to the side.

My grandfather walked in. "You're a mighty pretty girl for having a purple face," he said. The clan parted before him, the patriarch of the O'Connors. He tipped his hat to my maternal grandmother, then bent down to kiss me gently on the forehead. "You tired?" he whispered.

"Yes."

"I'll shoo these folks outta here, let you get some rest. We'll talk more when we get to the house."

"Thanks, Grandpa."

He turned around, leaving one callused hand on my shoulder. They were still strong hands, now veined and sunburned to the color of mahogany. They worked horses, cattle, and anything else with two legs or four. "I'm hungry. I made reservations at The Palm," he announced to them all.

Any word of dissent was quelled as he told my father to open the door and began dismissing people. A chorus of "bye Dallases" and then it was quiet. I fell back with a long sigh, my eyes almost closed.

A tap on the door. Who had forgotten what. "Yes?"

Diana Mansfield poked her head around the door. "I hate to say this, but you were right."

"Your murderess is in Kaufman," I said.

"I know. Apparently you were pushing the speedometer of Leo's Beemer, so you had a tail. Williams heard the description of Leo's vehicle on the radio, then sent the Kaufman police to see where it had come from." She shook her head, with a pixie smile. "What a sight for those officers. Did you write that book, *101 Uses for Duct Tape?*"

I would have shaken my head, but I was too dizzy. "What made you believe me?"

"We looked more carefully at April's alibis. The night before she hung the body—do you mind if I sit down—" she asked, then put a box of Godiva on my bedstand.

"Please," I said. "Truffles."

"Yeah, they're my favorites." She grinned, and I smiled back. Zetta was gonna love me forever. "Anyway, no one had actually seen April past eight o'clock that evening, after the shoot."

"That's not unusual for models," I explained.

"No, but she had a lot more miles on a new car than she could account for."

"You asked her?"

"Some questions, nothing out of the ordinary. I didn't want to spook her. We did some other kind of checking around."

"Where is she—"

"Custody right now, along with your friend Jacob."

I jerked upright. "The gun! It's dangerous! I pulled the pin."

Diana stared at me a minute. "Didn't quite trust him, did you?"

I dropped my gaze. "He was in a bad position, for what he believed."

"He's still in a bad position," she said. "Accessory after the fact."

"Did, did he know?"

"I haven't talked to him yet," she said.

We sat silent for a moment, I was drifting off to sleep, then she got to her feet. "I better be going. Umm, Dallas?"

I forced myself to focus on her and grunted.

"The Morning News is, well, they're doing a story on me," she said.

My eyes did open. "That's great."

She blushed. "It's the High Profile section."

"Congratulations."

"Well, that reporter Carla wants to ask you some questions, about this whole thing."

"I'll give you all the credit," I mumbled.

"Oh no, that's not it. Just, would you mind talking to her."

Already I owed Carla an exclusive. "Only if you will meet someone," I said. "If you aren't involved. I have a cousin." Diana's expression had frozen. "She," I said, "is a med student."

"I like medicine," Diana said, suddenly relaxing and smiling. "We'll talk when you're out of here. But you have a deal." The pixie winked at me. . . .

I heard another tap on the door. " 'Lo?" I croaked.

"May I come in?"

Ah damn, it was Alejandro. Clean-shaven, in flat front khakis and a pressed white shirt. I looked at his shoes—work boots, but camel-colored and polished 'til they gleamed. "Sure."

He stepped into the room with a bouquet of flowers—wildflowers. Indian paintbrush, bluebonnets, and a dozen others I was too speechless to recall. "That's illegal," I said.

He grinned, looking for a place to set them down. They were already in a vase. "From my own yard. I plant a backyard of wildflowers, because I rarely have time to mow the lawn." Alejandro put the vase on my bedside table. "They really got you good, didn't they?"

" 'They' was a solitary 'she,' I'm chagrined to say." April had gotten the last laugh by rigging my truck. I touched my face, which looked even worse now than before. Fortunately, they'd been able to clean my head without shaving my scalp.

"I—" he said, then we both looked up as the door swung open.

"Dallas!" Raul cried. "I'm free!"

CHAPTER TWENTY-SEVEN

Five days had passed since I'd been blown up by April; almost four weeks since Leo had been killed; two since I'd found Ileana hanging and my life had turned upside down.

The funeral was this afternoon.

The waitress came, and predictably Raul got meat, Jacob ordered pie à la mode, Francis requested *pommes frites*, and I ordered an omelet. She set down four cups of coffee, cream and rolled-up silverware sets, then stomped off.

"Have you gotten any styling calls yet?" Jacob asked. He was being remarkably calm for a man out on bail. Confessing everything seemed to have done him some good.

"Not since my last job ended in an explosion and arrest," I said.

Everyone laughed. Outside, sun was peeking through the

clouds, evaporating the threat of rain. I wondered if the lilies had been delivered yet.

"So what's up?" Raul asked.

"April's pleading temporary insanity," Francis, who had just returned from seeing her, said.

"Normally I might not believe that, you know," Raul said. "But in her case, man that chick was crazy to kill all those people." He turned green eyes to me. "Leo, Ileana, Wolchek, and then thinking about taking you out, man, that's crazy."

We all stirred our coffees, avoiding each other's gazes.

"We might as well get this out of the way," Jacob said, reaching into his portfolio. He brought out film with the Talbot's logo on it. "I think this is the film you took, Raul."

"You look," Raul told me. Jacob handed me a loupe and I held the film up to the light. The same lighting, the same blonde with hat, then rhinestone collar, then crocheted poncho. But there were five shots before: a modern redhead becoming a retro blonde, in stages. I looked closely.

The freckle was there, in the corner of April's left eye, a speck so small it looked like dust. But it was there, in every shot. "You shot photos of April," I told Raul, "and she made herself look exactly like Ileana, looking like April, looking like Ileana."

"Didn't Julie Andrews do a movie like that?" Francis asked.

Laughter was strained.

"I need to get the details worked out in my head," Jacob said. "I've got to connect the dots, I'm trying to understand."

Francis agreed. "I'll tell you what I know."

"First of all," I said to him, "why are you the one talking to April? I thought y'all had a falling-out?"

"We did." He was noticeably silent. The waitress came back, threw our food down before us, grudgingly asked if we needed anything else, then left.

"She's not happy," Jacob said. "So anyway, let's figure this out from the beginning," Jacob said. "The last time I saw Ileana was at the headbook party."

We all nodded, except Raul. "I guess I never saw Ileana," he said, a little ruefully. "Maybe that's why April picked me, huh?"

"Actually," Jacob said, "Ileana had Kevin do that same test, the whole sixties thing."

"That's the roll of film in Oak Cliff!" I shouted. "It's been driving me crazy, trying to figure that out."

"Okay," Jacob said. "When was the last time anyone saw Leo?"

"The Monday after the party," I said. "He came in from New Orleans and stopped at my house. He left about eleven, said he was going to be late."

Jacob looked at the table. "The night April killed him, I think." He looked up, meeting each of our gazes in turn. "I didn't know anything about it until after she'd killed Ileana."

"That's why you were late that morning, right?"

"Right. She came in and told me about her marriage to Leo. About AIS."

"So when Ileana got in Leo's car at the airport," Raul said, "she was getting in with April?"

Francis nodded. "April drugged Ileana, then moved her into the Suburban. That's where she . . . killed her."

We fell silent, but I was grateful that Ileana had been

drugged. Maybe the pain had been less . . . though the fear—
stop it Dallas, you can't do anything. Just forget about it.

Francis coughed. "When April killed Leo, she realized
she would have to kill Ileana, just because she knew too much.
Ileana flew in, April picked her up, killed her, and left her at
Leo's."

"In the freezer?" I asked.

Francis nodded. "She didn't know what to do. Then somehow she found out that Ileana had been doing tests to show
Duchesse how much she could look like April."

"Man, that was incredible," Raul said. "Twins, man.
Twins."

"Exactly. And April realized that if Ileana could look like
her, then April could look like Ileana looking like April. Ileana
had used Kevin when Jacob turned her down, because she
needed his lighting, his studio. April did the same thing, finding
an assistant who would have access—"

"Man, she used me!" Raul wailed.

"She was a manipulator," Jacob said. "Don't feel stupid."

"How did the body," it was easier to say that than Ileana,
"get on the set? My set?" I asked.

"April needed an alibi. So she set up the shoot with Raul,
she made sure she was seen by the neighbors on the dates
when the police were probably going to place the death, due
to the freezing confusing that time."

"And all the while the body was in the freezer?" I felt
sick.

Francis nodded. "She's not sane," he said.

"Man, you got that right," Raul said.

"April had Ileana's Palm Pilot, so she knew that she was
scheduled to work *Metamorphosis*. That gave her a deadline

to present the body. She knew she couldn't pretend to be Ileana with me and JJ on the set. This is where Wolchek comes in."

"That guy was an idiot," Raul said. I nodded agreement.

"April and Wolchek hung the body, but you and Raul showed up early. She was trapped in the studio and heard Raul tell you that he could prove everything, or something like that, with the film."

"The test film that she'd done," I said.

"Right. So she and Wolchek torched JJ's studio, thinking that the film, maybe even Polaroids, would go up in flames."

"But if she knew the film was going to go against her—" I started.

"She didn't think of that until Raul said he could prove everything. Then she panicked."

"She remembered the freckle," Jacob said. "She became obsessed with getting the film."

"Where was the film?" I asked, gesturing to the envelope.

"It probably sat, undeveloped, on the table in the studio for a week," Jacob said. "I thought it was Raul's, then began to wonder if it was mine. So I sent it out with a bunch of Talbot's film that went directly from the lab to the client."

"It's been sitting at their office in Arlington all this time?" I asked.

Jacob nodded slowly.

"*Jesus*," Raul said. "So April chased us?" The waitress refilled our coffees, staring at our plates. No one had eaten a thing. She harrumphed and walked away.

"Wolchek did. First to get the film, then he went a little crazy and April couldn't call him off," Jacob said. "So she pushed him off the balcony after getting him stoned."

"Wow."

"She hasn't said much more," Francis said. He looked at Jacob.

"She told me some of the details after she'd hung Ileana." Jacob said. "She came home at seven that morning, covered in slime and soot, just as I was leaving, and I could see she was an emotional wreck. I got the whole story of her life with Leo, his emotional abuse, the AIS."

"What is AIS?" Raul said. "I mean, I heard of AIDS, but—"

"Nothing alike," Jacob said. "AIS, Androgen Insensitivity Syndrome, is a genetic fluke. The women who have AIS are missing vital female parts."

"She was infertile," I said. "And that's why?"

"Yeah. She didn't have a uterus." He shook his head as he played with the handle of his coffee cup. "The best I understand it, she was genetically male, just in a female shape."

"But man, she was so beautiful!" Raul's expression was stricken. "But you're saying she had, no—" He glanced at me and leaned forward, whispering a crude, Spanish word into Jacob's ear.

"She didn't," Jacob said. "One of the symptoms, if you want to call it that, is these women are usually beautiful, unbelievably so. Very tall, lean bodies, gorgeous complexions." He looked at me. "But they can't have children. They don't even have menstrual cycles." The waitress had been approaching the table, but she turned when she heard that word.

"So she was not only losing her position at Duchesse to Ileana, she was also losing Leo to her."

"More than that," Francis said. "And on this topic, April

goes ballistic." He leaned back and focused blue eyes on me. "Ileana was beautiful, successful, and young. But that was no big deal. April had seen a thousand like her come and go. The difference was that Ileana had had a child, and she had everything else too. Now she was going to give Leo the child that he had wanted from April."

"I didn't know Leo wanted children," I said.

"It was really why they divorced," Jacob said. "April couldn't give him children."

"April just went crazy then?" Raul asked.

"She would have gone crazier if she knew Leo was also adopting Kalista," I said. "And that he'd written his will so Ileana was the sole inheritor."

"If he knew she was gonna kill him," Raul asked, "why did he go, you know? Why put himself in that danger?"

Francis and Jacob exchanged looks—two decades of secrets and experiences passed between them. But I understood, too. "Leo wanted a fresh start," I said. "He was trying to make everything right, tell the people he loved that he loved them, get everyone else's forgiveness."

"He hadn't been good to April," Jacob said. "Not that that's justification, but he realized it as he grew older." Jacob's blue gaze was on the table again. "You get to a point in life and realize you have been hard on the people around you."

"He felt he owed it to April to meet her," Francis said. "If he was going to be killed, he had everything in place to take care of Ileana. If he managed to make an ally of April, then everything would be perfect in his new life."

"But Leo wouldn't be free to embrace his new life until he'd dealt with old business," I said.

"April shot him instead?" Raul said.

"They were walking along the Trinity," Jacob said. "She did it in anger, not really intending to kill him."

I could imagine her fury, her panic. Then she shoved rocks into his suit pockets and pushed him in, hoping no one would find out.

"I bet he never imagined she'd go after Ileana," I said.

"Probably not," Francis said.

"What about Ileana's Palm Pilot," I asked after a moment.

"I had that," Jacob said. "I found Ileana's stuff, then when Leo was found, I began, slowly, to come to terms with April having killed them both. As I deciphered Ileana's notes, I left you tips."

"Then you planted the Palm Pilot in Leo's house, the day of the fire," I guessed.

"Right."

"The fire that April set," I said. "She learned how to do that from Wolchek?"

Francis shrugged. "Makes sense, but April isn't really saying much of anything for an explanation."

"What's going to happen to her, man?" Raul asked. "I mean, she is crazy, but is she going to go to prison?"

Again, Francis and Jacob exchanged looks. "She'll get off," Francis said. "She has the best attorneys, minimal circumstantial evidence against her—"

"What about the gun, ballistics tests?" I asked.

"There was nothing left from Leo's . . . head, no bullet fragments to match," Jacob said. He reached over and squeezed my hand. "I'm sorry, Dallas."

"She'll end up in a psych ward for the rest of her life," Francis said. "For April, that will be punishment enough."

I picked at my omelet, suddenly overcome with the urge

to cry. They were really gone; and we had to move on without them. Outside, thunder rumbled. Please don't rain on Leo's funeral, I thought.

At home I put on a Tahari black voile dress, with hat and gloves, because I knew Leo would love it, then floored it—in my Mustang since my Chevy was another fatality of these past weeks—to the funeral home. It was a smallish place, and the parking lot was already filled. Inside the vestibule, the average height was six-one and the average heel was three inches. Black picture hats fought for space, and the sound of sniffling was underscored by deep voices.

Leo's world. At least part of it. I slipped toward the front, where the only Baptist minister I'd been able to cajole here awaited me. "How are you doing?" he asked me softly.

"I'm glad to finally lay him to rest," I said.

He patted my hand. "Your friend had a lot of very tall girlfriends," he said.

"Uh, he did indeed."

"Are you ready to step into the sanctuary?"

Lilies—in baskets, planters, on hearts, crosses and triangles, with ribbons of pink, lavender, blue, black, and white—adorned the room. A stained-glass window cast pastel shadows on Leo's white coffin. I swallowed as I blinked back tears. Fingers linked into mine—Jacob held my hand for a moment, then bussed my cheek. I introduced him to the pastor, who looked a little relieved to see a man, an identifiable man, in a dark suit.

"Are you one of the pallbearers?"

"No."

The pastor was going to faint when he saw the pallbearers. "Are you about ready to begin?"

I nodded and he led me and Jacob to the family waiting room. "Could you get hold of his parents?" Jacob asked.

"They are having a memorial service out there," I said. "Mississippi."

Jacob looked much better. His hand was still holding mine. "You did everything right," he said. "Leo would be so proud."

I nodded, praying that was true.

It was standing room only by the time we were seated, as family. Raul was already sitting down, his black suit and bleached hair drawing a lot of attention from the "tall girl-friends." In the third row, Officer Williams sat next to Diana, also in black. I saw Zetta in the back, standing. I had to introduce those two.

Acres of black, white gloves, and net-draped hats filled the room. I sat down as the choir in the back—one of Leo's Oak Cliff choices—started to hum quietly. The pastor got up and gave a brief, mostly colorless, recounting of Leo's life.

Then it was my turn. I walked up to the front, past the coffin, and mounted the stairs. "Leo's death was a mistake," I said. "A mistake born of fear, anger, bitterness, and jealousy. His life, however, was filled with beauty. Good things. You, his friends whom he loved, his home with its dozens of projects, his orchids." I didn't dare say, "his fiancée," so instead I motioned for Tommy, as Debby Boone, to stand and start singing.

As she began the chorus, the pastor opened the coffin. I waited for the shrieks, the snorts of disbelief, anything. All I heard was renewed crying. I peeked over the podium and saw

Leo lying there, perfectly handsome. The FX guys in Las Colinas had done a fantastic plastic reproduction of his face and head, using the photographs I'd gathered from our years as friends.

As the mourners filed by, leaving mementos and trinkets, kissing his face, all I heard was how beautiful he was, how handsome, how perfect. I love you Leo, I thought. I hope you can see this. The gospel choir began to sing as the coffin was closed and carried out by six Valkyries with Dragon Lady fingernails, to the waiting hearse.

Beneath April sunshine we interred Leo. Then the party continued at my house: banana splits for everyone. I was standing on the porch when Jacob came up to me, slipping his arm around my shoulder. "How did you do it?"

"Special effects," I said.

"That didn't come cheap, Dallas."

"It was a promise I made," I said.

He sighed deeply. "It was a good promise to keep."

By the time my house had emptied, ice cream had melted into wine and the stories of Leo's life had grown absolutely raucous. The clock said it was two-thirty, certainly the longest, and wettest, Baptist funeral I'd ever attended.

Raul walked in from the kitchen and handed me the fortieth glass of wine.

"You never told me," I said. "What did you go to jail for?"

"You never told me, how much did Ileana really steal from you?"

I took a gulp of wine. "If I tell you, will you tell me?"

"You mean tell you what April told the police about me, why they arrested me?"

I took a sip of wine. "Yeah. What's your deep, dark secret."

He sat down, right there on the floor, then patted the space before him. "C'mon, Dallas O'Connor, sit with me."

I plunked down.

"You go first," he said, and smiled his Ricky smile. "Since you are a woman. One *caliente* lady."

"Okay. Four years ago Ileana was in bad shape. Gary had gotten her off a plane from Paris and had no place to take her. He was living in a one-bedroom apartment. So, I volunteered for her to stay here. No big deal, I thought. I have three sisters, I've been around sick girls before." I took another sip of wine. "Well, Ileana wasn't just strung-out, she was going through withdrawals."

"Coke?"

I shrugged. "Something. Gary I don't think, knew. One night I was sleeping and heard a noise downstairs, so I went to look." Fortunately, I had not taken my pistol. "She was going through my silver. When I asked her what she was doing, she freaked out and attacked me."

"*Jesus.*"

"She took the silver, and my truck, it was a Dodge, and ran away."

"Did you get hurt?"

I lifted my arm to show him the scar that ran down my forearm and over my elbow. "This is what a good-quality silver tray will do, if it's wielded correctly," I said.

"Oh man," he said, touching my arm. "Did you get it back?"

"The silver? Yeah, I use it for Thanksgiving every year.

She wrecked my Dodge though, totaled it." I shook my head. "My insurance company can't believe how fast I go through trucks. Anyway, I got a check in the mail for $16,000 from her, but Ileana was too ashamed ever to face me again. She refused to work with me. It wasn't until last year, on Kalista's birthday, that she called and asked me to forgive her."

"And the money?"

I laughed. "If I ever had twenty thousand, or fifty thousand, or a million dollars, I certainly wouldn't leave it where it could be stolen!"

"But the news said—"

"The news repeated what Leo had told me the rumors were. When I heard those, I figured Leo was still alive." I finished my glass of wine, suddenly sad.

"Why didn't you say anything, you know? Like defend yourself?"

"Because the more I thought about it, the more that being physically beaten by her, and her wrecking my truck, were good motives, maybe better motives."

"You got a point," he said. We sat in comfortable silence.

"Your turn," I said around a yawn, refilling both of our glasses.

"I violated parole," he said.

I choked on my wine. He slapped my back as I coughed and snorted my way back to air. "For what."

"Manslaughter."

"What?" I was sobering rapidly now.

"I ran over an old man in Miami. He was a drunk, it was a dark rainy night."

Was no one what he seemed?

"Since I was drinking, too, though, they took away my

license and sent me to reform school. That was where I learned to pick locks." His green eyes glittered. "But I didn't want you to know. If you knew that, you would have never trusted me. You would have turned me over to the police, oh man, so fast."

"Is there anything else I should know?" I asked, finishing my wine in one gulp.

"I would very much like to make love to you," he said solemnly.

"I'd like to have a career as a freelance stylist, but it ain't happening."

He dropped the seducer demeanor and sat upright. "I'm so sorry! Oh man, I forgot to tell you!"

"What?"

"You had a message. From Lindsay."

"Lindsay? My new agent?"

"Yeah, that's it. She called about six, you know. It was something, well, she said to pack your bags if you were interested in more adventures in styling." He smiled. "Something about freelance. She said, if you are interested."

Freelance? I was interested.